I Survived A Stalker

By

Sharon Velisek

ISBN: 1-4107-3085-9 (e-book)
ISBN: 1-4107-3086-7 (Paperback)

This book is printed on acid free paper.

1stBooks – rev. 06/17/03

Author's Note

This is a true story…a personal account of a most extraordinary event in my life. I am revealing my personal experience in the hopes that others will come to recognise their own mistakes when they read about mine. In my opinion, the most effective way to prevent yourself from being stalked is to be able to identify and avoid questionable relationships to begin with. For those who are already being stalked, I hope this book offers you support, help and hope.

To protect the privacy of the people I write about, most names have been changed.

I have dedicated this book to Rajwar Gakhal and everyone else who never got a chance to tell their story.

"Who then can so softly bind up the wound of another as he who has felt the same wound himself?"

Thomas Jefferson

Table of Contents

Part I

Sharon Velisek

Prologue

"Larry, don't do this," was all I could say. I backed up as he came towards me. Head cocked, one eye shut to gain an accurate sighting with his gun. I turned and ran quickly to the other side of my small blue Nissan. He ran after me. My heart pounded in my chest. No time for logic - just pressing fear and panic. I was circling the car when he stopped. I saw him resting the gun on top of the car, aiming and waiting for my head to come into range, but I saw it too late. I had to keep running - running as fast as I could to get out of the gun's range. "Please, please," I prayed. "Don't let me hear the sound of that gun go off." I knew I was going to die, but I didn't want it to be from having my head blown off.

Luckily, I'd moved fast enough. He was chasing after me again. On our third trip around, he tried to aim at me again from the roof of my car. "Not the head...not the head," I whispered as I ran. My prayers were answered and once more he turned to chase me. Every time I reached the front of my carport, I yelled for help as loud as I could hoping the neighbours or someone - anyone, would hear me. Seconds became eternity as we went around and around my car.

I came around one more time, absolutely frantic. I'd failed to notice that Larry had stopped running. When I turned the corner, I came face to face with the barrel of his gun. He was standing stock still, bracing himself to finally pull the trigger. I knew this was it. He had me.

I turned and ran and managed to get a few feet out of my carport onto my driveway when I heard the blast. It hit my left arm with such a force that I thought half of my arm had been blown away. I collapsed onto my cold

3

concrete driveway. Larry walked up to me, put the sawed - off, 12 gauge, double barrelled shotgun on my back, and shot me again.

This shot should have been more than enough to kill me, but he'd shot too far to the right. Amazingly, I was still alive! I rolled over and pretended to be dead, letting out a groan and shutting my eyes. I lay there, completely motionless and completely at Larry's mercy.

Then I heard another shot and something go 'thunk' beside me. I opened my eyes and was shocked to see Larry lying beside me. He'd shot himself in the heart! He groaned and his eyes closed as his head fell to the side. He was so still now…a lifeless body next to mine on the quiet, frosty evening of November 22, 1995.

Finally! Finally, I thought. It was over - truly over. He was dead and I was alive. And I was glad he was dead. His death brought me relief beyond words.

But…breathing was becoming very difficult.

The Beginning and Ending of our Relationship

Eighteen months before, I'd met Larry Scott through an ad in the singles column of the local paper. I'd been looking for a man to have some fun with. Someone who shared my interest in doing things that were sporty and exhilarating. Someone easy to talk to - someone who could be a friend. I wanted this for me, not for my kids. I wasn't looking for a father figure. I was quite content to keep raising my kids on my own, but I knew I needed time away from the constant pressures and responsibilities of raising five kids, especially since my three boys had all turned into teenagers. The man I was looking for was to be *my* fun, *my* time out, *my* escape.

My girlfriends had tried to help by fixing me up with a few blind dates, but they turned into disasters and I decided there would be no more blind dates for me. Consequently, how one goes about meeting a "nice" guy became a constant topic in our conversations and we spent many an hour over coffee trying to figure that mystery out. Certainly, the bar scene was out...we all knew what the guys there were looking for. One could join various clubs or take a course in something, but that took time and money, both of which I was very short on. One night Sandy said to me, "Why don't you try the singles ads? I've heard it's a great way to meet a nice guy. Some men feel just as frustrated as women do, thinking it's next to impossible to meet a "good" woman, especially at a bar, so what do they do? Where do they go to look? They put an ad in the paper and go from there. It's worth a try anyway, don't you think? You can always say no, if you don't like the sounds of the guy."

I just couldn't see myself answering a singles ad. It simply wasn't like me to do something like that. I was a mother, for heaven's sakes - not an experienced single woman, free to shop through a newspaper for a man. And then there was the fact that seventeen years of marriage to the same man had left me completely inexperienced, vulnerable and lacking confidence when it came to other men. I had no idea what to look for or what to watch out for. It was just too crazy. Still…there was a part of me that was intrigued. As silly as it all sounded, I took the newspaper home with me anyway. And in the privacy of my own bedroom, I sat up till midnight studying the singles column. I went over every one of them, circled a few, but for some reason, I kept coming back to one particular ad:

> *"SWM looking for fun loving 40 - 50 year old female with sense of humour. 5'11", blond, blue eyes, athletic. No head games. Great with animals. Kids are okay. Send letter to Box…"*

What was it about this particular ad that caught my attention? The man sounded decent, just looking for fun and laughter with a partner - the same thing I was looking for. There was no boasting, no feather fluffing - just simple statements of fact. "Athletic" attracted me. I wasn't about to just sit around with someone. No head games made me curious. I wasn't sure what it meant, but it sounded like something I wouldn't want to be involved in either. Being great with animals was a bonus. I had a dog, a cat, and a bird. Kids being okay was a must since all five of my children were living with me, three teenage sons and two daughters. No matter how many ads I looked at, I was always pulled back to his. It just felt right - sort of wholesome.

Oh, what the heck, I thought. I need to break away from my insecurities and try something daring. How else was I ever going to get any experience? I sat down at my computer and composed a letter about myself that was open and honest, including the fact that I had five children and was *not* looking for a father figure. I even included my picture. It was late when I finally finished. I decided to sleep on it and if I still felt like mailing the letter in the morning, I'd go through with it, otherwise I'd just throw it away.

When I woke in the morning, my first thought was to forget about the letter and the guy. Get a grip, I told myself, you're a mother and duty calls twenty four hours a day, as it always will for years and years to come. You've no time for anything else. I stepped past the mess in the bathroom, into the shower. It was a crazy idea, I knew it, but as the hot water slowly transported my mind from sleep to the full reality of the day, my curiosity started getting the better of me. By the time I stepped out of the shower I was asking myself: But why not? What's the worst that could possibly happen? Maybe he'll call...maybe he won't...maybe I'll say no...and maybe I'll say yes. Why not see what happens? Surely, a little adventure in my life isn't going to hurt. That's it - don't think about it anymore - just do it, Sharon. I quickly dressed and went straight to the mailbox half a block away, and dropped the letter in. I closed the lid and immediately felt the butterflies in my stomach. I walked home slowly. A cool April breeze gave me the shivers. What on earth had I just done?

I was expecting at least a week to go by before I'd hear back, that is if this fellow would even bother to call at all. Much to my surprise, two days later, while I was in the middle of cooking supper, my most hectic time of the day with pots boiling, T.V. blasting and kids running around bugging each other because they're hungry, the phone rang and it was for me.

"Hi, this is Larry Scott. I'm the fellow who placed the singles ad you answered." He had a nice sounding voice. I tried to keep my wits together despite the commotion going on around me so that I would sound somewhat calm and intelligent. Fun loving was not how I was feeling at that moment; more like irritated and aggravated. We managed to talk for a little while - enough for me to find out that he was a professional tennis coach and what's more, that he lived on a resort! This was all sounding pretty good to me - better than I'd expected, that's for sure. We discovered that we'd both grown up in Saskatchewan on a farm and that we liked similar sports and weren't afraid to try something new.

"If you're interested, maybe you could come to the resort this Sunday and we could play some tennis and even some golf. There's a nine hole golf course right outside my door and this time of the year the resort is usually fairly quiet, so we'd have the whole place to ourselves," he offered.

Here was the part where I was supposed to say we should just meet for coffee first in an impartial place, just to play it safe. But I liked the idea of getting to play tennis much better than going for coffee. I loved the game, but hadn't had time to play since my university days twenty years before. And to be at a resort - well, that conjured up all sorts of impressive images in my mind - all more tempting than a coffee shop.

"That sounds wonderful," I heard myself say. "You'll have to give me directions to the resort though. I've never even heard of it before."

"Why don't you meet me in Kelowna at the park and then you can follow me out to the resort? That'll be the easiest thing to do."

"But how will I know what you look like?" I asked.

"I'm close to six feet tall, fairly slim, I've got blond hair, blue eyes, and I'll be wearing a blue track suit. I'll meet you by the sails sculpture in the park at 10:00 on Sunday morning."

I felt a twinge of hesitation. It was all happening pretty fast. But I'd come this far already, and riding the wave of that inertia, I agreed. I told myself it would be okay. After all, it sounded like fun, not to mention the fact that he sounded gorgeous.

After we hung up, I continued to stir the bubbling pot of spaghetti, but my mind was elsewhere. A tennis pro! Imagine, a blond - haired, blue - eyed tennis pro being interested in *me*! Imagine, a tennis pro who lived on a resort being interested in *me*!

"Who was that, mommy?" Daisy, my five - year old asked. Her question quickly brought me back to reality.

"Oh," I said. "Just a friend I met. We're going to play some tennis on Sunday."

"Can I come? Can I come?"

"No, not this time. I'm going to see if you can go over and play with a friend for the day."

Sunday came very quickly. Between friends and neighbours, my kids had been taken care of for the day and I managed to arrive early at the sail sculpture. My stomach had been too nervous to eat breakfast and since I had some time before 10 o'clock, I found a hot dog vendor close by and bought a hot dog. I went back to the sculpture and started to eat, although my appetite dwindled while my nervousness increased as 10 o'clock drew near.

I had a fairly clear picture of this "tennis pro" in my mind. He would be *very* handsome with soft, tousled hair, a smile brimming with self - confidence, a beautiful golden tan, a body that is strong and agile but not too muscular and he'd walk as though he owned the world, but not in a boastful way - just calm and self - assured.

I was still eating my hot dog, looking around to see if anyone around could match the glorious vision in my mind, when I saw a man in the distance in a blue track suit walking towards the sails sculpture. Could this be Larry? No, it couldn't possibly be. He didn't walk like a tennis pro. He walked like he was stiff, with small, choppy steps. And as he got closer, I could see his hair. It was blond, alright - very blond. Obviously a dye job, but worse than that, it was gooped up with some sort of shiny gel in a slicked back fifties style. By now, he was only ten feet away and he was looking right at me with a well - practised smile pasted on his face.

"Hi, you must be Sharon...I'm Larry Scott."

I swallowed hard. My mouth was still full of hot dog. This was not what my tennis pro was supposed to look like! A voice inside me said, "Turn around, run, get away from this fellow, don't start anything up with him. It's not right, he's not your type." But instead of listening, I told this voice to be quiet as one should never judge a book by its cover. I cleared the rest of the hot dog from my mouth.

"Yes," I said. "I'm Sharon. Nice to meet you. Sorry about the hot dog. I was hungry and thought I had enough time to eat before you came." I had a hard time coming up with anything else to say. I was too busy trying to deal with the discrepancies in my mind. Was I really going to follow this man, whose manner seemed almost offensive to me, out to the resort and spend the day with him? Of course he was nervous, as was I, but even so, I felt repulsed instead of attracted to him. All of a sudden the coffee shop type meeting was looking like a great idea. Standing there face to face, I couldn't exactly say, "Now that I've seen you, I've changed my mind," and turn and go home, so I decided to settle my anxieties by going to the resort with him as planned and make my judgement after spending more time with him, rather than going on my first impression. Maybe he wasn't my picture of a tennis pro, but that didn't mean he wasn't a nice person and I thought I owed it to him to find out what he was like.

"So where is this resort anyway?"

"Well if you follow me, I'll show you. It's about a half - hour drive from here. We go back over the bridge and onto the back road. You can go back home to Vernon on that road, rather than coming back into Kelowna. It's shorter that way once you know where you're going. Where's your car?" he said, looking around.

"It's the white Subaru right over there," I said as I nodded towards my car. "The one with the stripes."

"Just pull around to the grey Nissan over there. That's my car. I'll wait for you and then you can follow me."

It was a strange feeling - to just follow another car, not knowing where it's leading you or what type of person you're following or what you're going to find when you arrive. I could have lagged behind, turned around and gone home to safety and security, but I found the thought of doing something risqué rather exhilarating. My life up to that point had been anything but exhilarating - problematic perhaps, with the divorce and everything, tiring at times, with kids and work and work and kids, but definitely not exhilarating. So I kept following Larry's car and as we drove mile after mile, I felt the desire for adventure growing in a part of me that I had long ago thought was dead.

We were soon on the back road, which became increasingly narrow and windy the farther along we went. The forest seemed to close in around us with trees that were the largest I'd seen since leaving the hobby farm my ex - husband and I had, three years before. Larry drove rather recklessly, I thought. He'd go awfully fast on tight corners and wandered out of his lane a lot. He seemed to be looking at the scenery rather than the road. There was steep mountainside on one side of the road and a steep drop - off to the lake on the other side for most of the way. I was trying to figure out where there could possibly be room for a 400 acre resort in this sort of terrain when I noticed Larry's signal lights flashing. Then I saw the sign as well - *Blue Water Resort.*

As I drove in I couldn't believe what I was seeing. Surely, this was none other than Fantasy Island itself. There were flowers and brilliant colours everywhere I looked. The trees were all in bloom with their smells floating on warm, soft breezes and I could actually hear birds singing as traffic noise was non - existent. And the buildings! There were so many buildings, all on different levels of the hillside. Upper town houses, lower town houses, private homes, the club house, swimming pools, hot tubs, several tennis courts, and a golf course! I felt like I had stepped right into a vacation magazine, only this was for real. Suddenly, I didn't care what Larry looked like. I was going to have some well - deserved fun in this fantasy land without hearing the word "mom" every few minutes.

Larry drove slowly through the resort, with me behind trying to take it all in, until we came to the last building. He parked his car and I pulled in alongside him.

"I can't believe this place," I said as we got out of our cars. "I figured a resort would have to look nice, but never in my wildest dreams did I imagine it could be as beautiful and as large as this. Where's all the people?" I asked. There was virtually no one around except the two of us.

"It's still early in the spring," Larry answered. "People don't usually start coming until the May long weekend. So we've got the run of the place today. Do you want me to show you around?"

I looked at him. How much can I trust him, I wondered? There were a lot of bushes around and no people. But I saw in his face a look that did indeed look trustworthy. In fact, he looked much more comfortable and natural in this setting than he did in the city when we met.

"Alright," I said. "Where do we go first?"

"The riding stables are just a bit further down this road, so we may as well go there first since they're the closest. This is my apartment right over here," he said, pointing to one of the units in a building just off the parking lot.

Yes, well...there's no way I want to take a look at your apartment, I thought. I'll pretend I didn't hear him... "You mean there's riding stables as well? Let's take a look at them."

There were a couple of horses in the corral. We spent some time petting them and exchanging our most terrifying horse experiences. It was obvious neither of us were equestrians, but being around horses again reminded me of the hobby farm I'd lived on for seventeen years, and that felt good. Leading off the corral were all sorts of hiking trails winding through tall trees. They looked inviting, but tennis and golf were what we had come to play, so Larry and I decided to finish the tour later, time permitting.

I went to my car to get the tennis racquet my sister had given to me and Larry went to his apartment and got his. Together, we walked to the tennis courts back along the road we'd driven in on. The resort's privately owned houses were along this road and as we walked by Larry told me about the people who owned them. There was one that was very different from all the rest. It was owned by Larry's best friend, Connie and her husband, Cliff. They were very wealthy people, he explained, wealthy enough to own houses in other cities and other resorts, but Connie would be spending her summer here, and Cliff too, except he spent most of his time travelling all over the world taking care of his business. I was impressed…what would it be like to be best friends with millionaires?

We came to two fenced tennis courts, back to back. Larry unlocked one for us and went into a small building and came out with hundreds of tennis balls. I wasn't sure what we were going to do with all those tennis balls, but I soon found out as I had my very first tennis lesson. Larry stood in one spot and hit them to me, while I had to run all over the place trying to hit them back. He became so serious about giving me a lesson that I thought I'd better ask if I was going to have to pay for the lessons.

"No," he laughed. "This is the only way I know how to teach."

He was *very* patient, even though I rarely hit the ball properly and kept sending them off in all directions. There was no sarcasm or criticism, just continual reinforcement that I would get it if I kept on trying. That explained the need for hundreds of balls. And when he had no more left, we both went around and picked them up, mostly on my side of the net.

A short water break was needed, so we went into the Club House to get water and sit for awhile. It was very high class inside - beautiful paintings and sculptures. Larry showed me the indoor viewing area for the lighted tennis courts, as well as where the expensive and normal restaurants were and the bar, where we sat and sipped our water. He didn't waste any time on small talk. Instead, he started talking about his two children and the relationship he had with them. It sounded like they were very important to him. He emphasised many times how good his relationship was with his kids and how devastated he was when his ex - wife left him in Vancouver and took the kids with her to Penticton, especially since he didn't even know why she'd left. He had no choice but to drive three weekends out of four all the way from Vancouver to Penticton, just to spend time with them. He'd work till four on Friday, hop in the car and make the six - hour drive, grab a hotel and then spend all day Saturday and Sunday morning with them. Then he'd head back to Vancouver just to do it all over again the next weekend. He finally got tired of all the driving and decided to move to Kelowna to be closer to them. And that was how he ended up in Kelowna. Whew…the whole story in less than five minutes! I told him I found his desire to spend time with his kids very admirable, but I couldn't help wondering why he was so intent on having me believe his relationship with his kids had been and was, great, and why he was telling me such personal stories when we'd only just met an hour ago.

I spoke a little about myself and was pleasantly surprised to find that Larry was very interested in what I had to say. He would nod and ask me questions as though he understood and agreed with my feelings completely. He was very empathetic, and I liked the attention, especially since being understood and sympathised with was not something I was used to. I soaked it up like a sponge.

After the water break, we went back for more tennis. Larry put the baskets of balls away and we volleyed instead, which was a lot of fun. We played for hours, until I was utterly exhausted. But, I felt great at having all that wonderful exercise and fresh air in such a beautiful outdoor setting. Not to mention that I hadn't heard anyone calling out "mom" all day long.

"So, do you think you can handle some golf yet, or are you too tired?" Larry asked after we put the tennis gear away.

I didn't want to go home. Not yet, anyway. I was enjoying myself too much to want it to end so soon. It was only mid - afternoon and I knew my kids would be okay for the whole day.

"I think I can play for a bit anyway. Although, I know next to nothing about golf. First, I'm going to need to take a break, though."

We went to sit down on one of the benches under a tree that overlooked the resort. The combination of tired, but happy muscles and resting in a spectacular outdoor setting had a euphoric effect on me. I felt great and I loved being right where I was. The sun was shining on us keeping us warm, but we could see some dark clouds starting to form in the distance. We weren't sure if it was going to start to rain or not, so we decided to get the golf clubs and get going in case we'd miss our chance.

It was a good thing we were the only ones on the golf course as my balls were going everywhere. Larry was better than I was, but not much. He definitely was a tennis pro and not a golf pro. He became less serious, now that he wasn't teaching tennis. He'd do goofy things while he was trying to hit the ball, and laugh and joke around, which he hadn't done at all playing tennis. I started to become more relaxed too and found I was enjoying his company quite a bit.

We were on the third or fourth hole, when the rain started to come down. A little at first, and then a gradual increase until it was really pouring. We were going to have to go for cover.

"My place is right over there. Why don't we go there and wait until the rain is over?"

Are you kidding? I thought to myself. There was no way I was going to follow him into his apartment - just the two of us. But Larry read my mind.

"Don't worry. I'm not going to try anything. I'm not that kind of guy," he assured me.

Just how much could I trust him, I wondered? He did indeed seem genuine so once again, I believed him.

We ran across the golf course to his apartment, getting wetter every second. He left the door wide open, I suppose to make me feel safer. Once we were inside, neither of us were sure what to do. His apartment only had one room, and that included the kitchen. Right smack dab in the middle of the room was a queen size bed, which I was bent on ignoring as well as I could. But being that it was the most prominent piece of furniture in the room that was hard to do. He seemed to feel as awkward as I did. He went over to his desk and got his photo album and showed me some pictures of his kids. They were nice looking kids, and I told him so. He seemed pleased at that. I continued to flip the pages of his album. There were quite a few photographs of different women in the album, some taken with him and some just on their own.

"Who are all these women?" I asked.

"They're women that I dated in Vancouver after I broke up with my wife. None of them ever seemed to work out, though. Some of them broke up with me and some of them I broke up with."

Neither of us was comfortable going any further with this conversation. We looked outside. It was still pouring. Larry walked over to the wall where he had some framed and unframed works of art. He brought them out to show me. They were mostly expensive prints that were quite good, in my opinion.

"Why haven't you hung these up?" I asked him.

"This place is too temporary to hang up paintings. It's just a motel room and certainly not what I call home. I'll put them up when I get my own place."

Finally, it quit raining. We went outside to look at the sky. It had rained a great deal and the grass seemed far too wet to continue to play golf. However, I still did not want to go home, even though it was getting close to supper time. The kids will have to fend for themselves, I thought to myself. This is my first time out in three years and I'm simply not ready to leave.

"Well, I'd still like to have the rest of the tour, if that's okay with you. I would especially like to see what it looks like by the waterfront," I said.

"Sure, that's fine with me, but we'll be cold down there. I'll get my leather jacket for you so you won't be cold."

Ooh, a leather jacket! I'd never worn a leather jacket before, plus I was touched with the chivalrous way he cared about how cold I was going to get.

It was a long walk down to the lake. The path zigzagged back and forth across the steep rocky bluff the resort was built on. The lake was calm, now that the storm was over. The air was fresh and cool. Larry took me to the dock first and showed me where he'd caught fish with his son. Then he took me a little further down a narrow path to a more secluded spot where the fire pit and picnic table was. When the resort was in full swing, this is where they had their bonfires for the guests.

We sat down on an old brown picnic table and looked out over the quiet lake. There were no other people around to spoil the solitude and the only sound that could be heard was the gentle lapping of the water on the shore...over and over and over again, as dusk slipped into dark and the stars came out. We talked and talked about everything and anything - just sharing with each other what life had handed us. And then, ever so slowly, the full, golden moon slid itself up from behind the mountain, it's reflection dancing on the lake. It was magical. Very carefully, Larry put his arm around me, as though he thought I would push it away. But I had no intentions of telling him to take his arm away. It fit the mood perfectly. And when he kissed me, I melted.

We stayed at the lake until the cold drove us away. Holding hands, we walked very slowly back up the zig zag path towards my car. I was finally ready to go home. It had been a beautiful day and an even more beautiful evening. My mind was whirling from the presence of a new man in my life. So many new emotions had been unleashed inside me. I wanted to go home and think.

We leaned against my car, looking up at the millions of stars and the giant trees whispering back and forth in the breeze.

"You know, Sharon, I've had a lot of responses to the ad I placed, twelve to be precise," Larry said, "but after tonight, I'm not going to answer any more of them. I don't want to jeopardise the relationship we've started tonight." And then he added, "Why don't you stay the night?"

"No, I can't," I said. "I have to go home. It's very late and my kids will be wondering what happened to me." Kids! Oh my God, I'd even forgot I had them for awhile.

"Please stay," he persisted. "If not for the night, then just for a little while."

"No, Larry. I can't. Besides, we've only just met. There will be other times."

He put his arms around me and held me close. "I don't want to let go of you yet. Come inside, just for a little while. Please."

Why do I always have to do the 'proper' thing, I wondered? Why can't I act like a 'wild woman' for once? My friends do, and I could just see them shaking their heads saying "You should have stayed, Sharon...you should have stayed."

I heard myself saying, "Okay Larry, I'll stay. But not for long."

I'd started the whole relationship wanting to be daring and adventurous. I certainly succeeded our first night together.

As I drove home from the resort, much later that night, reality came back to me. I hardly recognised myself. I had indeed been a wild woman...a wild woman with five kids, a dog, and a cat to take care of. I felt a little guilty, a little crazy, and very excited. What, I wondered, was I going to tell my kids?

Everyone was fast asleep when I got home, but as for me, falling asleep was impossible. Every nerve ending in my body was firing. Thoughts of Larry filled my head - and I could think of nothing else. I worried too. Would he really call me the next day as he said? Or would I be disappointed by the end of the day? Maybe he'd already had everything he wanted from me. No, it couldn't be - he seemed far too genuine. But then, more experienced women than I have been fooled before. In the end I fell into a fitful sleep.

In the morning Jake, my oldest son, at sixteen years of age, was ready with an interrogation. He wanted to know where I'd been and what I'd been up to and why I hadn't called. Talk about role reversal. All the kids had been worried when I didn't come home by supper with no phone call to explain where I even was. Didn't I realise how worried they all were, they asked? I apologised profusely. They were right, it was not responsible of me at all. Boy, if they only knew, I thought.

I told them about my whole day at the resort with Larry and how much fun it had been and how nice Larry was and how beautiful the resort was, everything except how the evening ended. I promised them that I would call next time if I was going to be late. They looked at me as though they weren't sure if they liked what was going on or not. But I didn't pay any attention to their concerns. Overnight I'd grown a second identity, separate from the mother raising her children, and I wasn't about to squelch that new identity. Rather, I wanted to explore and discover the new me.

For the rest of the day I couldn't eat, I couldn't work, and I couldn't stop thinking about Larry. I wasn't sure how I'd manage to wait the whole day for his phone call in the evening. But finally, evening came, the phone rang and it was Larry. I felt a surge of gratitude. I thought perhaps I'd been dreaming as it all seemed just too good to be true.

I took the phone onto my deck for privacy and Larry and I talked for a long time. He told me how crazy he was about me and that he couldn't quit thinking about me all day, which was a sign to him that we were meant for each other. I told him I'd been feeling exactly the same way and that I was also sure our relationship was "meant to be". How else could we explain the quickness and intensities of our feelings for each other? Obviously, we agreed, it was meant to happen.

Talking with him seemed so easy. We were both so interested in what the other had to say. We could have talked all night, but it was a long distance call. We ended by arranging to meet the next day during lunch hour, when Larry would drive the 45 minute distance from Kelowna to Vernon just so we could spend our lunch hour together. His willingness to do this, just to be together for an hour, made me feel very wanted.

"Sharon, I've never met anyone like you before. I think I'm falling in love with you," he said as we said good - bye. "I can hardly wait to see you tomorrow."

I hung up the phone smiling inside and out. Surely, I thought, this must be a dream - or a movie - or a fairy tale - to meet someone and fall so quickly in love. Could this really be happening to me? Yet, I heard him myself - I heard him say he was falling in love with me.

We met the next day at lunch and for many lunches thereafter over the next few weeks. We did this as often as Larry could get away between tennis lessons. Once, when I commented on the heroic efforts he was making just to see me during the day, he said, "Believe me Sharon, if I wasn't crazy about you, I would never be doing this." He made me feel so desirable - so loved.

During our first few weeks together, we seemed to be able to talk and talk. It was all so effortless. I felt we were developing an open and honest relationship with each other. Which was why I couldn't understand why Larry was making such a game of telling me his age. I'd asked him several times, but he'd always laughingly make a comment like, "Oh, you don't need to know everything about me all at once, you know," or "That's for me to know and you to find out." Maybe I was being too nosy, but the fact that he wouldn't tell me made me want to know all the more. When the right moment came along, I'd ask again, but always he would evade the question.

During most weekends, I would drive to the resort at least once. If I'd speed, I could get there in an hour and ten minutes, and I'd always speed. The road reminded me of the windy Italian roads you see in movies. Rocky cliffs, lots of sharp corners, steep drop - offs, lakes and mountains. The speed limit was 60 m.p.h., but I'd often go 100 just to get there sooner. It was invigorating - speeding around corners, rushing to see Larry. Ten minutes before I'd get to the resort, my heart would beat faster and I'd start to physically shake, just from the thought that I would see him in a few minutes. As odd as that reaction was, it was equally odd that whenever I'd catch first sight of him, I'd hear that small voice inside me saying, "What on earth are you doing? This guy's not your type." Then Larry would walk up to me, give me a hug and a kiss and the little voice would be gone again until next time.

There was a lot of sex during my trips to the resort. Sex before tennis, sex after tennis and occasionally in - between. Neither of us could seem to get enough of it. Larry would often give me massages from head to toe, as well. No one had ever taken the time or interest in giving me a massage before. That was something I was sure only happened to other people. Yet here I was getting massage after massage. He never seemed to tire of it, and neither did I. Pampering, I discovered, was a delicacy I welcomed eagerly. Once I had a taste of it, I found I desired it again and again.

"I'm not used to being treated like this Larry," I'd say, feeling soooo relaxed, while he was gently massaging away.

"Well you just better get used to it, because that's how you're going to be treated from now on," he'd always say. And I believed him. I thought I'd finally found someone who cared for me, who loved me and would do things for me for no other reason than to make me happy. That's when I knew that I loved this man.

As the weeks progressed, I started to feel guilty about leaving my kids alone so much of the time. My neighbours had been very kind up to this point, keeping an eye out for them while I was off at the resort, but I knew it couldn't continue. The only solution I could see was to take them to the resort with me - not all five at once - just a couple at a time. Larry was quite agreeable to this. He wanted to meet them finally. He told me they would be welcome to use the pool, just like the paying guests and they could even use the tennis courts and golf course as long as they weren't already booked.

I took my two daughters first: Billie, who was 11 years old and Daisy, who was 5. The long windy drive had left Billie feeling car sick, but Daisy was excited when we finally turned into the bustling resort. I hoped a jump in the pool would fix Billie's stomach. We parked the car in front of Larry's place and walked with our swimming gear to the tennis courts, where we thought we'd find Larry, teaching tennis. He was just finishing a lesson so we watched him for a bit. When he saw us, he came straight over with a big smile on his face. I did the introductions and everyone said 'Hello' as politely as they could. There was some awkward small talk and some equally awkward silence. I could feel Billie and Daisy staring at him while we made plans to all meet at the pool after his next lesson. After we turned to go, Billie asked me, "What's the matter with his teeth? Why are they so crooked?"

"That's not very nice of you Billie," I said. "Not everyone is born with straight teeth. Besides, teeth don't make a person who they are." I was a little put out that she'd noticed his crooked teeth instead of how wonderful he was. Couldn't she see how gorgeous he was or how worldly he looked? Couldn't she feel the same warmth I felt in his presence? Daisy didn't notice anything other than the fact that she was getting hotter and hotter standing in the sun. "Let's go to the pool," she said. "I'm hot."

The three of us had a good time in the pool, after we got over our guilt of playing in a pool reserved for people with much larger incomes than mine. An hour later, when Larry came to join us, I went to join him sitting on the edge of the pool, while the girls kept playing. I could see them sneaking glances at Larry when they thought we weren't looking. It certainly added a new dimension to our relationship. Suddenly, it wasn't just me and Larry having fun - it was me and Larry and the kids sizing each other up. I found it very nerve wrecking. Were they going to like him? Was he going to like them? What could I do, what could I say to make sure everybody liked everybody? It wasn't nearly as much fun as coming to the resort by myself.

After awhile, we all walked back to Larry's place to pick up the food for a wiener roast at the beach. I knew the kids were curious to see his place. They thought because he was a tennis pro and lived on a resort, he probably was rich and had a ritzy place and even though I'd told him his place was just small, they still hoped their mom had struck it rich with this guy, which in turn would mean more opportunities for them. When they walked into his small motel room, they were most disappointed. It certainly wasn't what they'd pictured.

Larry tried to be friendly to them, but Billie kept her distance. Daisy warmed up to him quickly, though. Mostly because he bought her an ice cream at the pro shop on our way back from the pool, and for a five year old who likes treats, that is sometimes all that is required. We had an enjoyable wiener roast by the lake, which reminded us all of the camping days we'd left behind after the divorce. By the time we left the resort that night both girls seemed okay with the resort and with Larry. Daisy was glad I'd taken her as now she knew where mommy was going all the time and this made it easier for her to let me go. Billie was more reserved in her enthusiasm, but she could see how happy I was, so she kept her true feelings to herself, and told me he seemed alright.

Back at home, Billie and Daisy told the others about the resort and Larry. I felt it was a good time to have him over for supper so he could meet the rest of my crew: Jake - 16, Matt - 14, and Tom - 13, all big rambunctious boys. I knew this would be harder for Larry. A man meeting two young girls on his own turf was one thing, but to meet 'the boys' in their own home, was another.

He was very nervous when he came in. I could tell he really wanted to make a good impression. After the intro's and initial awkwardness, we went into our backyard and played some badminton to loosen everybody up. That went pretty well. The boys seemed impressed with Larry's skill and agility in the game. Being a tennis pro, they expected that of him and they certainly tried to test him. But he stood up to their onslaught quite easily. After badminton, Larry sat at our kitchen table with the kids all gathered around him and showed them some neat card tricks that dazzled them, while I watched from the kitchen putting supper together. They couldn't figure out how he was doing the tricks and they bugged him and bugged him to tell them. After quite some time, he did indeed let them in on the secret and taught them how to do the tricks themselves so they could try them on their friends. The boys were the perfect age to be very pleased with this new knowledge. There was a lot of laughter and fun over supper.

Later that evening, both Larry and I let out a sigh of relief as we agreed that the evening had gone pretty well. The kids certainly seemed to like him well enough and he liked the kids. The green light from them was reaffirming for me, and just made it that much easier to continue on with our relationship.

When it came time for me to meet Larry's two children, I found I was the nervous one. His son Joey, was 8 years old and had come to the resort for the weekend to visit Larry. His daughter hadn't come this time because she was doing something with a friend. I took Daisy with me to the resort hoping Joey and her would get to know each other and hopefully hit it off. We met Larry and Joey just before Larry was to give a tennis lesson. He asked me if Joey could go to the pool with us, and then he'd join us after his lesson. That was fine with everyone and we parted. Joey asked me if we could play catch for awhile first. I think he wanted to impress Daisy and I with what a good catcher and thrower he was. So Joey, Daisy and I played catch in the parking lot below the tennis courts. I was very impressed with how patient he was with Daisy, especially since she couldn't really catch or throw the ball yet. He always threw the ball very gently to her and never seemed to mind running to catch her helter skelter throws. I was also impressed with how well he could catch. His level of skill did not require easy throws from me and I found his aim to be excellent. We had a nice game of threesome for awhile, and then we went to the pool.

My first impressions of Joey quickly changed, however, as Daisy and I got into the pool. As soon as Joey saw me, he came over to me and attacked me, trying to wrestle my head under the water with a great deal of wily determination. His actions took me by surprise. My own sons had never done anything like it. I took it as horseplay for awhile and wrestled with him, but he wouldn't let up and after trying to ward him off and watch Daisy at the same time, I had to tell him to stop it. I was glad that he listened and stopped. Shortly after that, Larry came to join us in the pool. I stood there wide - eyed and mouth agape when Larry headed straight over to Joey and started to wrestle with him and push his head under the water. Joey would no sooner get his head up, than Larry would push it under again, giving him no chance to get some air. I was sure the little guffer was going to drown. Daisy and I stayed at the other end of the pool, watching with concern and curiosity. After awhile, their water wrestling subsided and they came over to join Daisy and I. Joey didn't want to sit though, he wanted to race with me. So Larry stayed with Daisy in the shallow end and Joey and I raced many times from one end of the pool to the other. He was a good swimmer and I was hard pressed to keep up and occasionally beat him. We asked Larry to race with us, but he didn't want to. I didn't find out till later that he couldn't swim.

After swimming, Larry bought us all an ice cream treat on the way back to his place. Larry and I walked hand in hand, licking ice cream cones, our kids playing together running circles around us, the sun shining...it all seemed so good. We got back to Larry's place and everyone changed out of their wet stuff. I can't remember how it started, but somehow a tickling session began. Many times Larry and I had tickling bouts, but this time the kids became involved and everyone was tickling everyone. Joey and Daisy seemed to love it, but after awhile it got a little rough for both Daisy and I and we backed off and watched as Larry tickled Joey relentlessly. I was impressed with how resilient Joey was. He would rarely say 'give' and when he did, he'd wait till Larry would stop for a few seconds and then he'd fly at Larry again which brought about more tickling and even wrestling holds. Daisy and I watched in amazement, not wanting to get close enough to get drawn back into the fray. We'd had our share, and it looked awfully rough.

When all had finally calmed down, we went outside to play catch by the playground. I'm not sure if Joey was trying to impress me again, or his Dad this time, with his throwing and catching abilities, but he certainly was trying to impress somebody. He did not want to be thrown the soft, easy balls Larry was tossing to him in the air.

"Throw them to me like you throw them to Sharon," he'd say over and over to his Dad. Larry and I had played catch many, many times since we'd met and I can attest to how fast his throw was - extremely fast. I was a good catcher, but I still had to concentrate and be on my toes to catch the balls Larry threw. They were fast enough to cause serious bodily injury if I missed. I didn't expect Larry to throw that kind of ball to Joey, but I knew he could have easily taken his speed up a few notches to make Joey feel good about himself. But he didn't, and eventually Joey ended up frustrated and quit playing with us altogether and went off sulking to play with Daisy at the playground. 'Twas a pity, I thought. I found myself liking Joey and I got the feeling he liked me, and Daisy too. It was plain to see he was trying very hard to get his Dad's approval, without much luck. I hoped in time this would change and that maybe I could help somehow.

I had very little time for my friends ever since I'd met Larry. Whatever spare time I had was spent either with Larry, or talking to Larry on the phone. But when my friends did call, I would tell them all about Larry; that he was caring, patient, very attentive, an excellent tennis coach, well travelled, educated (he was an x - ray technician in England), that my kids liked him, he was fun to be with and on and on.

"How old is he?" they'd ask.

I didn't want to be asked that question. I still didn't know. "He hasn't told me yet." And with that, I became determined to find out one way or the other. I knew who his family doctor was and since I also worked for a doctor, I knew it would be easy to obtain his date of birth from his doctor's secretary. I knew I was being dishonest and sneaky, but I dialed the number anyway.

"Hi, it's Sharon calling from Dr. so and so's office. We need to know the DOB of one of your patients. I wonder if you could get that for me?" was all I needed to say.

"Certainly, just a minute." I waited, feeling terrible, knowing that not only was I lying, which I detested in myself, but that I'd stooped to being unethical as well, and for what - why was his age so important and why the heck didn't he just tell me anyway? I was just about to hang up when the secretary came back on the line and said, "Hi, sorry it took so long. It's October 17, 1944."

"Excuse me, I don't think I heard you right," I said. "Did you say 1944?"

"Yes, that's what it says in his file. Is there a problem?" she asked.

"No, no…I'm just surprised. I thought he was much younger, that's all. Thanks for your help." I slowly hung up the phone. If he was born in 1944 and I was born in 1954, that made him 10 years older than me! That made him 50! This came as quite a shock to me as he looked like he was no more than a couple of years older than me, if that. Suddenly I understood why he didn't want me to find out. He probably thought I would think he was too old for me and end the relationship. However, nothing could have been further from the truth. His age didn't bother me, once I got over my shock, but trying to hide it from me did.

When he came to Vernon that evening, we went to a local pub for an evening out. I found I was nervous about telling him that I knew his age. Partially because I thought he'd be upset at my knowing and partially because I had found out in such a sneaky way. After the waitress brought us our beer, I told him that I knew how old he was and waited to see his reaction. Surprisingly, he acted as though it was no big deal! He just laughed about it. This didn't make sense to me at all. If it was no big deal, then why didn't he tell me his age to begin with? What I'd practised to say over and over during the day, trying to cover all the angles of the conversation I thought we'd probably have, was useless. All I could manage to say in my confusion was, "I just want you to know Larry, that if it doesn't bother you, it doesn't bother me."

"No Sharon, it doesn't bother me." Then he changed the subject and we continued to talk awhile longer at the pub. All the time I felt inside like I was being spun around with my eyes closed, but I kept myself together enough on the outside to be able to carry on our conversation. Later on that night, when I was alone I had to ask myself if perhaps I had made the whole "secret age" bit up, or if I'd made a mountain out of a mole hill. After some soul searching, I came to the conclusion that the past didn't really matter anymore. His age was out in the open now and we were both comfortable with it. Or were we? He certainly seemed to be and I tried to be. It just took me a few more days to win over that nagging voice inside of me that I truly was too.

A few weeks later, we went to the pub again to meet with my friend, Sandy. The same Sandy who had given me the singles column to begin with. She was curious to meet "Mr. Wonderful," "Prince Charming," and "the man of my dreams." Sandy and Larry got along very well, very quickly. Both of them had travelled extensively so they had a lot in common to talk about. Having very little travel under my belt, I sat and listened. I felt left out as well as rather jealous. After Sandy left, Larry said to me, "I bet she has no trouble getting boyfriends with those long legs of hers." I looked at him, feeling even more jealous. Being a woman, the benefit of long legs was something that had never occurred to me before and I was surprised it had occurred to him.

"Is that what men think of when they're talking to women?" I asked curiously.

"Sure, we're always sizing women up," he said. "Don't women do the same thing to men?"

I had to think about that for awhile. "I can't say for sure," I told him. Obviously I'd been married too long and had lost whatever "sizing - up" abilities I may have once had.

The next day I called Sandy. "So, what do you think of Larry?"

"He seems very nice," she said. "He's easy to talk to and quite interesting. He doesn't look the way I had him pictured though. But still, I think he's very nice."

Very nice - that's all? Not…wow, Sharon! He's really something…I can see why you think he's so great. She's just jealous, I thought.

One day at the resort, I was attempting to help Larry run a tennis tournament. However, never having been involved in one before, I found I wasn't much help, and more often than not, I was in the way. So, I spent a lot of the day by myself, wandering onto the deck of the clubhouse, watching the matches below, while Larry was running the entire show from inside and outside the clubhouse. Occasionally, some of his tennis acquaintances would come and stand beside me on the deck and talk to me. I found it quite endearing that Larry would always come out onto the deck when this would happen, just to join the conversation and put his arm around me. I could tell he was jealous. I was his, and he was letting everyone know that. I closed my eyes and sent thanks to whomever. I felt so special being wanted and protected by him.

That day, when the tournament was finally over and we were alone in the clubhouse, Larry sauntered up to me smiling and told me that he wanted me to pick something out from the Pro Shop - whatever I wanted, and that he'd pay for it. Money was no object. "I love you," he said, "and I just feel like buying you something. All you have to do is pick it out."

I liked the sounds of this, but at the same time it frightened me for some reason. I'd never had such an offer before. "I don't feel right about this Larry. I'm just not comfortable with the whole idea, or maybe I'm just not used to someone "buying" me something. I don't honestly know what it is, but it just doesn't feel right," I said. "Let me think about it, okay?"

"I'm not going to push you to do something you don't want to do," he said, "but just think about it and maybe you'll change your mind. The offer's always open."

I did think about it. A lot, actually. I knew men bought nice things for women all the time, and I was often envious of this, so why did Larry's offer to buy me whatever I wanted make me feel hesitant? Maybe that was it - it was an offer, a carrot dangling on a string. If he would have just bought me something and given it to me, I wouldn't have been feeling the way I was. Having to make a decision about his offer, however, was like asking me to declare which fork on the road of our relationship I was willing to take. On which side of the fence was I going to jump? Was I going to allow *him* to pay for something *I* wanted? Or would I take care of myself? Would I feel I was "less" of a person if I accepted his offer? Would it set up the order of command in our relationship? Larry, the provider…Sharon, the recipient? Would it be the start of inequality among us? Would I feel like a "bought" woman? And what if I said "No"? Would that hurt his feelings?

I tossed my feelings back and forth for a few weeks, finally coming to the conclusion that once again I was making a mountain out of a molehill. After all, it was just a little token of Larry's affection we were talking about. It was a sincere and sweet offer and I had no desire to hurt his feelings, so I decided to go with it and see how it felt to be treated to a gift.

He was beaming with delight as we walked, holding hands, from his place to the Pro Shop.

"Why does it have to be the Pro Shop, Larry?" I asked.

"Well, it doesn't 'have' to be there, but they give me a good discount, so it's better for me if we buy something there."

There was a lot of nice clothes to choose from. I had a hard time deciding between practical and elegant - a sweatshirt versus a sexy short dress. Whatever money I had, I'd put into my kids, which left my clothes closet pretty bare. A new sweatshirt would have been very useful, but maybe I should grab this opportunity to get something a little more elegant, I thought, something I would have felt too guilty to buy for myself. While I was looking and trying to choose, Larry was doing goofy things. He'd try on different hats and then act out the personality to go with it and he did it so well, I'd laugh and laugh. Especially when he put on a woman's sun hat. Or he'd hide behind a clothing rack and grab me when I'd walk by and I'd jump. Finally, I managed to choose enough clothes to try on so I took them into the dressing room. I'd be in the middle of changing only to have Larry fling back the curtain and poke his head in asking how it fit, to which I'd go flat against the wall and tell him he had to let me get it on first so I could show him. This was a side of Larry I didn't see often, which was a pity, because it was a part of him I really liked. He was carefree and funny and spontaneous and it just felt good to be around him.

I finally settled on a white tennis outfit, complete with short shorts and a sleeveless top to match. Both practical and elegant, as tennis at the resort was usually played wearing white, and since I was playing more and more tennis, and even getting a little bit better at it, I decided I needed a white outfit as well. It was much more skimpy and fancy than anything I'd ever owned, and I felt quite grand when I had it on.

I saw Larry writing out the cheque and noticed a pang of guilt in my stomach, but only a small one. I looked away as he finished paying. This was something I knew I could get to like.

For the first few months of our relationship, Larry came to my house two to three times a week. We'd cook supper together and then go into my backyard to play badminton. Sometimes the kids would play as well. We were all competitive, especially Larry. If it looked like he was going to lose, he'd start to play at a much higher level than the kids, spiking hard to far corners or pretending to drive the birdie and then just plop it over the net. When there was a question about the rules or whether the birdie was in or out, he never gave my kids the benefit of doubt and always insisted he was right. It became impossible for the kids to ever win against him and after awhile they lost interest in playing with him. I, on the other hand, became more and more driven to beat him in badminton, partially because I am very competitive, but also because it's a challenge to beat someone who's always winning. We had many serious games of badminton in my backyard, often with my neighbours cheering us on from their deck. I wasn't sure if the grass in my backyard would ever grow back. Once in awhile, I would come very close to winning, which triggered Larry to really play hard, and in the end, he always beat me, which would frustrate me to no end and I'd want to play another game and another, until I'd finally give up for that day.

One day, while we were making supper, I asked Larry: "How do you think your ex - wife would describe you? What do you think she'd say about you?" I'd read somewhere that this was a question you should always be sure to ask.

"Stubborn," he said with no hesitation whatsoever. "She'd say I was far too stubborn. And my Mom would agree with her. I remember my Mom always saying to me as a kid 'Larry, you've got to quit being so stubborn'. I think I must have given her a hard time when I was young."

"Stubborn!" I said. "I haven't seen a single sign of stubbornness in you once in the four months we've been going out together. I just find it really hard to believe that anyone would call you stubborn."

"Well, they did. It's the main complaint of everyone I've had a relationship with in the past. Maybe you just haven't picked it out yet, or maybe you bring out the best in me."

I thought back over the past four months to see if there was even a hint of something I could call stubborn. He was certainly competitive and didn't like to lose, but I wouldn't have called that being stubborn. He was always very easy going and accommodating with me. Maybe he's right, I thought, maybe I do bring out a better side of him. After all, he keeps telling me he's never met anyone like me before. I didn't see where his so - called "stubborn nature" was anything I needed to be too concerned about so I filed it away in the back of my head.

When the summer holidays came, Larry was no longer able to drive to my place. He was just too busy giving tennis lessons to guests at the resort. It was his busiest time of the year. It was also the time that provided the bulk of his yearly income. So, it was fine with me when he told me I'd have to be the one doing the driving throughout the summer. The drive always relaxed me and I found being at the resort very comfortable, sort of an affordable vacation getaway for me. Actually, it was my only getaway and source of fun in my otherwise hectic life of two part time jobs and five kids. Everyone at the resort knew about Larry and I, and welcomed me. I had free range, as though I was a guest. I often brought a few of my kids or my kids and their friends. We'd play golf, or swim, maybe even the odd game of pool and of course, tennis, when Larry wasn't busy teaching and a court was available. Sometimes, we'd take part in their karioke night or whatever else they had going on. And then in the late evening, we'd drive back. Unless, of course, I was by myself, in which case I'd usually stay the night and drive back the next day very early in the morning.

Larry had many acquaintances that lived at the resort, but only one couple he'd call his friends. Actually, it was really only the wife of the couple, Connie, that he considered a true friend. He'd known both Connie and Cliff ever since he'd moved to the resort, which was a few years before I met him. Cliff spent most of his time away managing his company, so Connie had a lot of free time, which she filled with her passion - tennis. Before Larry met me, he also had time to fill when he wasn't teaching tennis. Keeping himself exposed playing tennis drummed up more business as well, so Larry and Connie spent a lot of time together playing tennis at the resort. And when they weren't playing tennis, they'd talk over coffee, over beer, over dinner, and at her parties. They became very close friends.

I remember one of Connie's parties…it was an impromptu party, but a lot of people had been invited and Connie wanted Larry and I to come as well. Both of us really wanted to go, but I had Daisy with me and she was too young to come and too young to be left alone at Larry's place for the night and I didn't know of anyone at the resort who could babysit. So, I drove all the way back to Vernon and arranged with the neighbours for Daisy to sleep over and then rushed back to the resort to meet Larry for the party. Three hours of rushing! When I got back to the resort, I went to meet Larry at his apartment, and was surprised to find that he wasn't there. No note or anything. I walked to the tennis courts, but he wasn't there either. I went to the Pro Shop to see if they knew where he was, but they hadn't seen him either. So, I walked back to his place thinking that he may have returned and would be waiting for me. But no, he still wasn't there. I felt abandoned. Where could he be? We were supposed to meet at his place over half an hour ago. I decided to walk to the restaurant and pool area to see if he was there. On the way, I met Connie and I asked her if she'd seen Larry.

"Yeah, I did actually. He was heading down to the restaurant about half an hour ago."

"You're kidding," I said. "I was supposed to meet him at his place half an hour ago."

"That's strange," Connie said. "You'd think he could have waited for you and you guys could have gone out together to eat."

That's what I thought too. I knew the resort gave him, and him only, meals for free. I figured he went for his free meal before I showed up, just to avoid a situation where he might feel he had to pay for my supper. I was ticked off because I'd been rushing around like crazy and driving way too fast just to get back to the resort on time, and there he was eating, obviously not caring about being on time to meet me. I turned to go to the restaurant. I was going to tell him a thing or two. I walked in and saw him look up at me, a dessert spoon stuck in his mouth. Did he look guilty? Not in the slightest.

"Hi Sharon, you're back already? What time is it anyway? I don't have my watch on. I thought I'd grab a quick bite to eat before we went to the party. Come and join me, you can share what's left of my dessert," he said so innocently. He took the wind right out of my sails. I had myself all worked up for nothing and I felt bad for letting my anger surface so quickly. We finished the dessert, went back to his place so he could get changed for the party and then slowly walked over to Connie and Cliff's. Why, I asked myself, did I rush like a mad woman? No one else is in a rush?

There were very few people at the party that I knew. The guests either played tennis religiously or were rich, or both. I was neither and felt as out of place as a wilted flower in a fresh bouquet. Everyone was dressed in the latest sporty look, except Larry and I. I had an excuse. I bought clothes for my kids - not myself. But what Larry chose to wear really surprised me. He'd slicked his hair down even more than usual in a sort of wet, wavy Elvis Presley look. Instead of sneakers and white tennis gear, which was pretty much the only thing I'd ever seen him in, he wore cowboy boots, tight, and I mean tight, bluejeans and a black leather jacket. He stuck out like a sore thumb. I even overheard one of the guests saying, "What's up with that guy? He looks like he stepped out of a 1950's Brylcreem commercial!"

I glanced at Larry to see if he'd heard. It didn't look like he had, but then I looked at him from this other fellow's perspective. He was right. He did look like he belonged in a Brylcreem commercial or on a western movie set. If I hadn't known him at all and just met him at the party I would have thought he was too weird to talk to for sure, but instead I'd somehow managed to fall in love with this man! How could this be? What had I done?

"Sharon, come over here. I want you to meet Danny," Larry called out to me. I jumped back to reality. Best to put these thoughts aside for now.

I was glad to finally meet the infamous Danny Fisher. Larry had told me all about him and how they were partners teaching tennis to the Junior Tennis Team at Hedley's Gym in the wee hours of the morning through the winter and how Danny was always late for that because he'd spend most nights partying, which meant Larry would have to the responsible one and make sure he was at the gym on time. But, Larry was always quick to add that Danny was one heck of a good tennis player and an equally good coach, and a friend, so he always forgave him for being so irresponsible. Plus, he liked Danny's sense of humour, which always seemed to be present in any situation.

We shook hands. "Larry's told me everything about you" I said. He was sort of short and dumpy with the beginnings of a pot belly. For some reason he reminded me of Humpty Dumpty. His pale blond hair was thinning on the top. His complexion was very fair and his face was kind of oval and puffy with small black eyes that sparkled behind short white eyelashes.

He just laughed his choppy chipmunk laugh that I was to become very familiar with over the next year, and made a naughty wise crack back, along with a smile and raised eyebrows. He seemed so jolly - certainly a personality that liked to live for the moment and enjoy whatever he was offered. I doubt there was ever a cruel or vengeful bone in his body. He was harmless and happy and I enjoyed talking to him because it always ended in laughter. But he certainly didn't look like a tennis player, especially with his limp.

Why do these great tennis players look like anything but tennis players, I wondered? First Larry and now Danny. Connie, however, was a different story. She did indeed look every bit like a tennis player from a magazine. She was tall and slim, with bouncy blond hair and a body that was tanned every month of the year. From what I could see, she spent all her time playing tennis, or training, or buying just the right things for her house, or giving parties. She was very open and friendly though, and liked to talk, but mostly she liked to play tennis. We got along quite well, but I always felt like I was less than her somehow, not that she ever tried to make me feel like that, just my own perception of myself. I remember being very surprised to find out we were the same age. She seemed much more mature and sophisticated than I felt myself being.

I enjoyed meeting new people through Larry, so when he told me that Steve, a good friend and tennis player from Vancouver had called and was planning to come to the resort in a few weeks, I was excited at the prospect of meeting yet another one of Larry's wealthy friends. Steve, according to Larry, was an artist of sorts and travelled the world with his job, which he was in high demand for. He was coming to the resort for two reasons: to see his buddy Larry and to have some fun and relaxation, which meant playing tennis. He knew about Larry and I, and asked Larry if I had any girlfriends that might want to join us for a foursome. At first I couldn't think of anyone. I didn't have too many friends of my own. But then I remembered Shelley, who'd just been through a nasty divorce. I figured she would probably appreciate the offer to have some fun just to tone down the stress she'd been going through.

I told her what I knew about Steve from Larry, which wasn't much: he was wealthy, he was lonely, he was a nice guy, he was honest, he was good looking, he was single and he played tennis quite well. So did Shelley. She agreed to meet with Steve. Plus, she was looking forward to finally meet Larry after all I'd told her about him.

Our first meeting was to be a supper at a special waterfront heritage restaurant. Shelley and I drove together from Vernon and Larry and Steve drove together from the resort. I was looking forward to showing Larry off to Shelley, plus I was curious to see what Steve was like.

We arrived a little early, so we waited for them by the front door of the hotel. We waited and waited, watching all the other people going in, wondering why Larry and Steve were late. Then I saw them walking towards us. Oh no! Larry was wearing his skin tight jeans and cowboy boots again, and his hair was all slicked down. Fortunately, Steve was dressed normally. Looking at them walking side by side, it was hard to picture them as friends. They looked so different.

"Hi. Sorry we're late. Have you been waiting a long time?" Larry asked as he walked up and gave me a kiss.

"A little while," I said. Actually, I was annoyed that we had to wait at all, but said nothing.

After introductions all around, we went inside to find a table. The room was crowded and noisy, but I could feel a hush when we walked in - all eyes on Larry. Some of the guys at the bar looked a little tipsy and I worried one of them would say something derogatory to Larry and then he'd feel he had to defend his honour in front of his girl and friends, which would not be a good way to start the evening. Please, please, please, I prayed. Just let us get to that one available table on the far side of the room. We slowly worked our way there, attracting lots of stares, but nothing verbal. After we were seated, I silently declared that I would find the Brylcreem and tight jeans and somehow get rid of them when Larry wasn't around. They were just too much.

It turned out to be an enjoyable evening, otherwise. We all got to know each other and I found the conversation stimulating. After a few drinks, Steve nodded to me and said that he's never known Larry to go out with anyone for more than a month or two, so I must be a very special person indeed.

"Yeah," Larry added as he looked straight at me. "I never realised still waters could run so deep." I was beaming. A special person? Me? Still waters? I must have more depth than I thought I had. "Once," Larry continued, "I even drove away from a gas station without paying because I was thinking about Sharon. And that's just not like me."

I loved the feeling of being so special to another person. To be so desired, what more could I ask? Yes, I loved my Larry, slicked down hair, tight jeans, and all.

When we drove home later, Shelley was quite excited about meeting Steve and thanked me profusely for introducing them. They'd really hit it off and had made plans for tennis, supper and hot tubing the next day at the resort. I promised to come to the resort after supper and meet them all for the hot tub. "But Shelley," I asked, "what did you think of Larry?"

"Well, he doesn't look like I'd pictured him, but he seems very nice. I guess I wasn't expecting the tight jeans and slick hair from a tennis pro. But you two certainly get along well together." Funny, I thought. That's the second person who's said they pictured him looking differently than he did.

"Yes, well…the tight jeans aren't my favourite either. Normally, he wears tennis gear, which he looks much better in. You'll see tomorrow. But I do love him, and I know he loves me, at least he tells me he does, over and over."

The next day Shelley, Steve and Larry played a lot of tennis while I worked at home. There was only so much time I could spend away without everything falling into absolute ruin at my house. I joined everyone for the hot tub in the evening though, which turned out to be so enjoyable, with the dark sky and bright stars twinkling overhead, that we stayed well past closing time. It was nice to see Steve and Shelley getting along so well. In fact, they ended up continuing their relationship even after Steve left to go back to Vancouver, which made Larry and I feel even more established as a couple ourselves, since as a team, we'd brought them together.

Life was going along full blast for both of us. Larry was busy teaching tennis and I was busy with my part - time jobs and kids. I spent all my spare time on the weekends at the resort. Usually, my older kids were off playing with their friends in town so Daisy would come with me and we'd jump in the pool on the hot afternoons. Larry seemed too busy to keep his place clean so sometimes I would clean it up for him while he was teaching. I'd always bring food for us to eat as well, as more often than not, he would have forgotten, or not had time to shop for groceries in Kelowna and there would be nothing there for us to eat. Sometimes his kids would be visiting and we'd all do things together. It was a nice summer and seemed to pass quickly.

With the arrival of September, Larry's schedule changed. There were fewer people staying at the resort since school had started again and therefore less people signed up for tennis lessons, so he could start coming to Vernon again during the week and on some of the weekends. My birthday was soon and because Larry had said he wanted my birthday to be special, he planned to come and spend the entire weekend with me in Vernon and we would do whatever I wanted to do on my birthday.

Hmm...what do I want to do? I wonder just what he means by 'special'? I wonder how he's used to treating girlfriends on their birthdays? Does he give expensive gifts, or standard gifts, or thoughtful gifts, or does he bother to give a gift at all? Wouldn't it be nice, I thought, if he was the kind of guy that took the time and interest to arrange a surprise party or a special gift just for me? After all, he had bought me that expensive tennis outfit in the early summer, so surely he would at least buy some sort of a special gift. I had a great yearning to be treated special, especially on my birthday and not knowing what to expect allowed me to have high hopes.

Finally, the weekend of my birthday came and I was excited. Larry had come as he'd said he would.

"So what do you want to do on your birthday tomorrow?" Larry asked.

"Well," I began slowly. "I've thought about it a great deal and I've decided I want to do something we've never taken the time to do. I want to go hiking in Hillside Park. I love going out there and spending the day hiking around and it will be even nicer to do it with you. The only thing is, I've promised to drive Tom out to the fair in Armstrong before we go. It'll only take an hour to go there and back and then we can go hiking."

"You mean we've got to take Tom all the way out to Armstrong and back? Can't he get a ride with someone else or just stay home?" I detected no enthusiasm in his voice whatsoever, which was unusual for Larry.

"It'll be okay. I've already promised that I would do it. He's going to get a ride back with a friend so at least we won't have to go and pick him up." I was not about to let Larry's unexpected resentment dampen my spirits on my birthday.

The next morning, we left for Armstrong. A friend at work had given me a cassette tape of an African band that she knew I really liked for my birthday. I decided to play it on the way to Armstrong, thinking that way Larry would be able to enjoy it too. We were driving along with Tom in the back seat, Larry in the passenger seat and me tapping my fingers on the steering wheel to the strong beat of the music when Larry said, "How can you listen to that stuff? Don't you find it irritating?"

"I can listen to it because I don't find it irritating. In fact, I even like it." I said. I'd never seen him tired and grumpy before. I figured he just needed to recuperate from the hectic summer schedule he'd just finished. I turned my music off so he could sleep the rest of the way and hopefully wake up in a better mood, as he was certainly not acting like his normal self.

We had planned to head straight out to the park when we got back to Vernon, but Larry said, "You know, I'd sure like to go to the fruit packing plant here to pick up some cheap apples before we go hiking. Why don't we make a quick stop there first, since it's on the way?"

That was fine with me. We had all day, even though by now it was already lunchtime. I drove to the packing house and we walked around looking at what they had. Their apples and pears looked nice and the prices were good. You could pick out your own fruit from big bins for the cheapest price possible. But, there were pesky flies everywhere, absolutely everywhere. Buzzing all around you, crawling over the fruit and getting in your face. Coming from the farm, this didn't bother me too much, but Larry was really disconcerted by it. He'd wave his hands all over in the air and grumble while he attempted to pick out some fruit between his flailing. Finally, he just walked away telling me he couldn't handle it anymore so I'd have to pick out the fruit for him. I was not impressed. This was supposed to be my special day - a day where we'd be together, enjoying each other's company and there I was picking out the fruit that Larry wanted amongst a million buzzing flies while he watched from a safe and sanitary distance. The good mood I woke up with was starting to slip away.

We paid for the fruit and left. We drove in silence. This was not the Larry I'd been having so much fun with at the resort for the last five months. Instead, beside me sat a moody, self - centered man, whose fear of germs surprised me greatly as his own kitchen and bathroom were never clean and neither was his car. It seems Prince Charming did indeed have a flaw. I pushed and pulled my thoughts around in my mind until I came out with a conclusion I could accept: no one's perfect, I thought, so why should I expect Larry to be? He's still got the same positives he had before so why let one little negative ruin your birthday hike? It was still a beautiful autumn day and we were going hiking, never mind anything else.

By the time we reached the parking lot, my excitement was back to full strength. I was sure the beauty of the park would bring him out of whatever mood it was that had grabbed him. I hoped it wouldn't take long because I really wanted to share this beauty with him. Being September the breeze was warm, but not overbearing like in the hot summer. The high yellow grass on either side of the path swayed back and forth as we walked, still in silence. I reached for Larry's hand since we always held hands whenever we walked, but it was like grabbing a limp fish. I tried talking to him - no response. I tried asking him questions, but he wouldn't answer with anything other than the odd grunt. Try as I might, I couldn't get him back to the Larry I knew. My heart sank. This was supposed to be a romantic walk between two people in love, sharing and enjoying their time together, and instead a wall had gone up between us. We continued walking in silence for two unbearable hours and by the end I was barely managing to hold back my tears.

We drove back to my house, still in silence. When we got there, my kids had a birthday cake and presents waiting for me. I swallowed the tears that wanted to fall, and put on the happiest face I could muster for them. Larry seemed to do the same and for awhile, we were back to normal. We had supper, and the cake Billie had made with the help of a neighbour. And there were presents too! All my kids had either made or bought me something. It was all very touching. Larry handed me his present as well. It was an envelope. We all wondered what it could be. Maybe a trip for two to some exotic place? No, he's not that wealthy - still…maybe reservations in a fancy restaurant for a romantic dinner for two complete with candlelight and violins? I had my doubts about that after the afternoon we just had. I opened it slowly, wondering…would Larry come through for me after all? I looked inside…what's this? A $50.00 bill. No card or anything else - just a $50.00 bill! I looked up at him, not sure what to say.

"I thought you could go and buy yourself something that you liked. I had no idea what to get you," he explained.

No idea what to get me!! If he only knew how insignificant that statement made me feel. We'd done nothing but talk about ourselves over the past five months. Hadn't he been listening or did he just not care, I wondered? But then I remembered some of the nice things he had said and done in the past and I could see that he did indeed care, so probably he just didn't know how to be romantic on birthdays, I figured.

The kids were all looking at me. To them, fifty bucks was a great gift which any of them would have been more than happy with, but they were waiting for confirmation from me. "Thank you Larry. I'll go shopping soon and find something very special to buy with this." And I gave him a hug and a quick kiss.

The weekend was over, my birthday was over, and my euphoric relationship with Larry was over. The magical bubble had burst. Once that happens, it's gone forever. I found myself faced with the stark realisation that Larry wasn't my Mr. Perfect after all, and I wondered why I'd put him on such a high pedestal to begin with. Obviously, I wanted to love and be loved...so did he...doesn't everyone, for that matter? But why had I wanted it *so* much that I was willing to close my eyes to anything other than what I wanted to see? As much as I didn't want to admit it, it had to be from need. I'd been desperate for love and attention, and hadn't even realised it! I wondered if it was the same for him.

I found it difficult to grasp just what my new realisations meant in the way of our relationship. What do we do now? Or to be more precise, what do I do now, I wondered? I knew I could never continue on in a relationship with anyone who was capable of grumpy, sullen moods as it reminded me far too much of the marriage I'd walked away from, and I couldn't put my blinders back on, carrying on as if nothing had happened. There was nothing left to do but go forward, but what was forward? It was confusing for me. My emotions were all a - jumble and I couldn't seem to discern what was important and what wasn't, having had so little experience in relationships. But then I remembered a saying I'd heard so often: "A good relationship doesn't just happen - it has to be worked on. Relationships are work."

Right! There was my answer. Up until the past weekend, there had been no work - just fun as we went from day to day taking whatever it gave. We both showed nothing but our best sides for each other, keeping whatever bothered us to ourselves. But not anymore. Now there would be purpose and direction in our relationship to replace the simple need I'd felt before. I was eager to get started. I went to the bookstore and discovered book after book about 'working on relationships'. So many, in fact, that it was obvious that everyone was affected by relationship problems at one time or another in their life.

I read and read, as often as I could, as much as I could. What I discovered, according to the experts, was that I needed to give Larry his space and try to understand him and where he was coming from. Most of all, I needed to learn how to communicate with him - how to talk about my feelings and his feelings and work towards the common goal of "us," once we decided what "us" meant. So far, we'd just been having fun together and maybe that was the problem. There was obviously some "feelings" going on for Larry that were causing him trouble, which we needed to talk about, and after the birthday weekend, I had "feelings" of my own that needed to be discussed. I felt confident that we could handle that. We could make it work. I called him up.

"We need to talk Larry. I know something was really bothering you last weekend. I've never known you to use the 'silent treatment' or be so grumpy before, and I'm just wondering if you know what it is that's bugging you?" I asked.

"Yeah, you're right," he sighed. "I've been feeling a little down the last while. I'm not sure exactly what it is, but I know I feel badly that I haven't been spending very much time with my kids ever since we started going out together. We seem to spend all our time with each other instead and I guess I'm missing my kids."

"Well Larry, if that's all that's bugging you, that's easy to fix. Why don't we see less of each other and you can spend more time with your kids and I can spend more time with mine. I've been feeling the same way about my kids for awhile now too. Plus, I haven't taken the time to do anything around my house for several months, and I'm missing that too."

"You know, Sharon," he said, "we don't always have to go out and 'do' something. I'd enjoy helping you fix up your house, so don't be afraid to say, 'Larry, let's just stay home and fix this or that'. I'd be fine with that. And I'll get my kids down to my place this weekend and spend some time with them."

"We should have talked about this long ago. I had no idea you would be happy staying at home working on my place. I'd like that very much." I said. Now I could relax and not feel like my whole life was being devoted to Larry and only Larry. It surprised me to find out that he was feeling the same way. The books were right. It does help to talk about your feelings and get everything out. What a difference. All the tension I had in my shoulders just melted away and I was sure it was the same for Larry.

Everything went well for a few weeks. Before, we'd both made the effort to be with each other as often as three or four times a week. We cut that back to once a week and it was wonderful. I had lots of time to catch up. I went for coffee with old friends and did yard work around my house and was home a lot more for the kids, which they really appreciated. But I found myself thinking about Larry a great deal of the time. Sometimes several days would go by before he would call me and the less I heard from him the more I thought about him. Sometimes

I would panic, thinking he wasn't going to call at all. And that's when I realised how much I truly wanted this relationship. I wanted him and I missed him. Especially his love, his attention, his caring, his touch. I wanted us to be a couple and I found it very comforting to feel such strong feelings for him.

A man by the name of Dieter Heizmann and his wife had come to Kelowna from Germany that summer. He'd just retired and wanted to spend time he'd never had before, learning the game of tennis. He was given Larry's name as one of the best instructors in Kelowna. They seemed to hit it off from the very first lesson. Dieter could not say enough good about Larry - how patient he was, how good his instructions were, how kind and caring he was. After teaching Dieter for a few weeks, Larry told me about him and how wonderful it was to have a regular student who had no qualms about paying for the lessons. He pulled out his wallet and took out a piece of paper saying, "Look at this! Just come and look at this Sharon."

It was a cheque made out by Dieter to Larry to the tune of a few thousand dollars - future lessons paid in advance, plus three hundred dollars with which Larry was to buy cartfuls of brand new tennis balls. Dieter was used to, and wanted nothing less than, the best. Larry bent over backwards for Dieter, answering his every call no matter what time of the day, and over the ensuing weeks, they became more than player and coach - they became friends, often going for coffee after Dieter's lessons.

When Dieter's birthday drew near, he invited Larry to his birthday celebration, saying that he would be happy to have Larry bring me as well so that he could finally meet me. Dieter upheld a German tradition where the person who has the birthday invites his friends to a restaurant of his choice, makes an eloquent toast to each and every one of them, and ends the evening by paying for the entire meal. This tradition, I assumed, was one for wealthy Germans, which Dieter most definitely was.

The meal was exquisite, with no less than fourteen people seated around a heavy wooden table in a quaint German restaurant overlooking the lake. Wine was poured as soon as we sat down and I couldn't help notice how quickly our half empty wine glasses were topped up. When the wine's effect was felt and before the meal arrived, Dieter stood up to make his toasts. He started at one end of the table, introducing every guest and telling always an interesting and warm story about them in his rich, eloquent manner. I was seated before Larry and when Dieter came to me he said only that he did not know me yet, but that I was here with Larry and, feeling the way he did about Larry, he was most assured that I had to be an absolutely wonderful woman. Amazing, I thought, what this man could do with words. He had every guest at the table spell bound with his speech.

Dieter then turned to Larry, and said that in all his years, he has never met anyone with the amount of patience he has found in Larry. And, with a little laugh, patience was definitely required as his stiff old body learned to move again, but through all the missed balls and huffing and puffing, Larry stayed supportive and gave nothing but encouragement. Not only did he exhibit fine characteristics on the tennis court, but as a friend as well, and he held his glass up to Larry and offered his friendship for a long time to come.

It was a beautiful speech, spoken with such emotion, that I had tears in my eyes and when I glanced over, I saw Larry's eyes glistening too. Apparently I was not the only one who felt lucky to have met Larry.

Throughout early fall, Larry would spend most weekends at my place. Sometimes he would bring Joey and on those weekends we'd try and organise something fun to do with Joey and Daisy. We'd go to the movies, or swimming, or skating, or whatever else we could think of. Usually Joey and Daisy got along well together, but there were times when I could see Joey getting a little jealous when Larry gave his attention to Daisy. And Daisy was good at getting all the attention she could get. She liked having a male in her life and even went so far as to call Larry, Daddy No. 2, which Joey winced at when he first heard it. I could see trouble brewing between Joey and Daisy and Larry.

On weekends when Joey couldn't come, Larry would come by himself. Being around every weekend meant my kids saw a lot more of him, which turned out to be detrimental. Larry tried to take on the role of "man of the household," thinking it would be helpful for my kids to have a good male influence in their lives. But, whenever my kids would talk about something they did or someone they knew, Larry would jump in with a chuckle and tell them about one of his own experiences which was always more exciting or unbelievable than what they had just said. He was not able to simply show interest in what the kids were saying or ask them questions about it. Instead, he would try to one up them, which did not go over well at all with my kids. After awhile, they lost interest in even sharing their stories because they knew Larry would just try to show he was better. The same thing happened with games. It was impossible for them to win against Larry in badminton or crocinole or any other game. They complained to me about him being such a "know it all" and they would make sarcastic jokes about Larry when he wasn't around, mimicking him. Their jokes bothered me, but I could see the truth in them. He did act just the way they were portraying him.

The tension started to grow in our household. I knew my older kids would rather not be around Larry and I knew Larry thought his manly presence in our household was doing them good. I couldn't bring myself to tell him that Billie and all three boys thought he was a farce instead of a hero, and that he thought too highly of himself. He would be shattered if I did. Talking about feelings, as the books suggested, was one thing, but shattering someone's image of themselves was another. But I could see trouble ahead for us. I felt like I was being torn in half, leading two different lives, one with Larry as a couple and one with my kids as a mother and as hard as I tried to mix the two together, I had no more success than with oil and water. Was I eventually going to be forced to make a choice between my kids and Larry, I wondered? I could have talked to Larry about it, but I chose to avoid such a confrontation and instead, decided to let the problem ride for awhile and see what would come of it. Maybe things would sort themselves out in time, I thought, or at least I sure hoped they would. Fortunately, Daisy still enjoyed having Larry around and they would often end up in tickling sessions that would send her screeching all over the house with Larry in pursuit. The rest of my kids, however, would go to their friend's place if they knew Larry was coming, which always left me feeling like I was betraying them.

It was mid October and Larry's birthday was just around the corner. I'd been trying for weeks to think of something special to do for him on his birthday. In the end, I decided to take him out for a picnic to one of the fishing spots above the resort that he'd been talking about, but never had time to go to. An afternoon of fishing for just the two of us, a bottle of wine, good food spread out on a rock, and one of my famous homemade birthday cakes to follow back at his place. And for a present, I'd bought a brand new fishing tackle box, as his old one was falling apart.

I drove out to the resort by myself as this was to be a special day for just the two of us. I showed him the multi - layered birthday cake I'd made for him, covered in strawberries and whipped cream and candles. He was, after all, turning 50 and needed a gorgeous cake to commemorate the day, even if it was just us two celebrating. We put the cake in the fridge and headed up to the fishing spot. The fall colours were everywhere and the sun was out, making it warm and pleasant to be standing beside the creek fishing. I did not have a rod, so I just watched from the rocks as Larry happily fished. I think he liked that I was watching him, rather than competing with him. After awhile, I spread the tablecloth on the flattest rock I could find and put all the food out. We sat down to potatoe salad, cheese and wine. Larry was surprised that I'd prepared something more than just sandwiches. It was a wonderful meal. We were both very relaxed and content.

"No one's ever done anything like this for me before, Sharon," he said.

"You're kidding! You mean your wife or all those girlfriends you had never made a special effort to do something nice for you on your birthday?"

"No, they didn't. I mean, we did lots of things together, but I don't recall someone doing something special, just for me."

"That's a real pity, don't you think? That's what people who love each other are supposed to do." I hoped he'd remember this concept for my birthday.

"Yeah, it is a pity. But then again, I never knew anyone quite like you before. I didn't tell you this before, but Steve told me he didn't think we'd last a whole year. I told him he was dead wrong."

"Steve didn't think we'd last a year!" I said, rather surprised. Steve's comment sparked in me a determination to show him he was wrong...sort of like accepting a challenge. "We'll have to show him then, won't we?" Larry heartily agreed.

It started to get dark, so we packed up and went back for the cake that was waiting for us in Larry's fridge. I made some coffee and then we lit all 50 candles. Larry closed his eyes and made a wish. He blew them all out, with a few tries. When I looked up at him, I saw tears in his eyes.

"What's the matter?"

"No one's ever made me a homemade birthday cake before! It's beautiful."

Poor guy, I thought. I wondered just what kind of a marriage he'd had.

"Sharon, how long do I have you for?" he asked.

"I have to be home by 10 o'clock."

"No, I mean, how long do I have *you* for?" and before I could figure out what he was talking about he continued, "One day you'll be Mrs. Scott!"

Dead silence. Did he just say *Mrs.* Scott? That would involve marriage, right? Was he proposing to me? Pretty lousy proposal if it was. What was I supposed to say? What did I want to say? He must have seen the stunned look on my face. He came up to me and put his arms around me and hugged me for a long time. Then he looked at me and said, "Let's eat the cake."

All the time we were eating we were talking about this and that, but my mind kept thinking about the mention of marriage. The subject had come and gone so quickly that I wasn't sure if I'd even heard him right. We'd never talked about marriage before, and actually, we weren't even talking about it now, but what else could he have meant by *Mrs. Scott?* This was certainly a turn I wasn't expecting. But marriage… "Do I want to get married?" I asked myself. "Do I want to marry Larry?" The answer came quick - no, not really. The idea of marriage was too permanent for me. On the other hand, raising five kids by myself was proving to be very demanding and tiring at times. To have a partner's help was extremely appealing. But no, what was I thinking? It would never work. Most of my kids made fun of Larry. Marriage would only bring problems instead of solutions and the last thing I wanted was more problems.

But…the thought kept creeping back. Larry actually wants to *marry* me! I couldn't deny how good the feeling of being wanted in this way by someone else made me feel. Just the sheer fact that someone wanted to actually marry me made me feel good about myself - like I'd been given a stamp of approval as a woman. And that feeling made it too hard to just toss the possibility of marriage aside. After all, I wondered, how many guys am I going to meet that would be willing to marry someone with five kids? In the past, most guys I'd met had turned and walked away as soon as I mentioned the word "kids". Here was an opportunity I knew I should at least consider.

Back and forth I went. Yes, it will work…No, it's not what I want. The idea of marriage changed everything for me. It meant our relationship was serious now, which meant there were lots of areas to explore that we'd never even touched upon before. Things like our religious beliefs, our philosophy of life, our attitudes towards commitment, raising kids, extended family and on and on. No more surface chit chat. I needed to get to know the real deep down Larry if there was going to be any consideration of marriage. Our relationship had certainly been progressing and I was looking forward to taking it one more step and seeing what would happen.

"Good news, Sharon." Larry called on the phone a few days later. "My Aunt and Uncle are visiting from Saskatchewan and they want to take the both of us out to supper tonight in Vernon. Can you make it?"

"Yeah, I think I'll be able to arrange something for the kids. Where do they want to go?"

"Meet us at the Village restaurant at 5:30. I've told them all about you and they're anxious to meet you."

"And just what did you tell them about me?"

"Oh, just how nice you are and how lucky I am."

Nice! Sometimes I wondered if I really was a nice person. I could think of a few people who would not have described me that way, my ex being number one on the list. But if Larry felt that way, I was willing to go with it.

When I walked in to meet them, they were already seated around a table. Larry stood up and gave me a kiss and did the introductions. I could see approval in their eyes immediately, which put me at ease. We ordered, and then Larry started to tell me about his Aunt and Uncle.

"We did so many things together when I was little," he said, "and I always remember Uncle Joe being there for me to answer questions and show me things. In fact, I used to think he was my Dad because he was always around."

I thought this was a nice tribute to his Uncle, who seemed like a genuinely caring man with eyes that never stopped smiling. He would have been a wonderful man to have in a child's' life. His wife seemed equally nice and from what I could see, they got along very well together, teasing each other and laughing a lot. We spent a very enjoyable evening eating excellent food and talking about Saskatchewan and each other's experiences. It was a nice treat for both Larry and I. We said good night and parted. I went back to my place and Larry went back to his place with his Aunt and Uncle.

That went very well, I thought. I hoped his parents were as nice as his Aunt and Uncle. Later that night, after Larry's Aunt and Uncle went to their hotel, he called me to talk. "They really liked you," he said. "They thought you were every bit as nice as I had described you."

"They seem very nice too," I said. "Are your parents as nice as they are?"

There was a slight hesitation. "Not really. No one else in my family is like my Aunt and Uncle. My parents, especially my Dad, is very different. My Dad and I didn't get along very well when I was a kid. That's why I spent so much time with Uncle Joe and that's also why I think of him as my Dad. We had a lot of fun together and I knew he liked me. I never got the feeling that my Dad thought too highly of me, though. I wasn't what he wanted in a son. He never seemed to have any time for me because he had such an important job at the brick factory. He was a mechanical wizard and could figure out any problem and then fix it, so he was always busy fixing the problems that came up at the plant. Unfortunately for him, I was never interested in anything mechanical, so we sort of went our different ways. He was disappointed that I didn't follow his interests and I was disappointed that he never had time for me. We never felt about each other the way Uncle Joe and I feel about each other."

There was no sound of happiness in his voice at all until he spoke of his Uncle. "How do you feel about your Dad now?" I asked.

"He's my Dad, so of course I respect him, but we're not close. We never were, so how could we be now? He never trusted me and I still don't understand why. I don't think I was that bad of a kid."

"Weren't there other kids living close by that you could play with?" I asked.

"Yeah, there were some, but it was the same thing. I wasn't interested in doing the things they were interested in and vice versa. So, I'd spend most of my time wondering around the hills behind our house with my gun, hunting gophers and birds. I knew every inch of those hills like the back of my hand."

"What about your Mom? Were you close to her?"

"No, I never got to see much of her. She was always sick. When I was really little, she was so sick that she couldn't take care of me, so I was sent to my Grandma's to live. I lived with her for a long time. My mom is a very nice person, but she's been sick an awful lot in her life, so I never got very close to her."

"What was she sick from?" I asked.

"You know, I'm not really sure anymore. It was always one thing or another. I was always told to be easy on her because she's weak and fragile, mentally as well as physically."

"That sounds so sad, not being able to live with your Mom and Dad when you were little."

"No, it was okay. My Grandma was great and so were my Aunt and Uncle. I know they loved me."

"Now I know why you are so attached to them. It was pretty obvious in the restaurant - you were so enthusiastic about everything." I said. "Are your Mom and Dad still travelling? Do you think they're going to come for a visit as well?"

"They've been talking about coming and after my Aunt and Uncle get back, they might decide to come."

After all Larry had said, I was curious to finally meet his parents. His childhood did not sound happy to me at all, but he didn't seem too choked up about it. He just talked about it in a matter of fact way, as though he'd accepted what life had dished out to him. To me, he sounded more disappointed than hurt by the distance there was between him and his Dad. I couldn't imagine what it must have been like to be sent from your own home to live with your grandparents when you're just a little tyke. Times must have been tough.

A few weeks later Larry called to say his parents were coming to the Okanagan and were going to Penticton to visit his children for a few days and then they were coming back to stay at the resort with him for a few days and wanted to spend one of those days in Vernon to meet me after hearing so much about me from Larry's Aunt and Uncle. We were to meet at the Junction Ranch for lunch, Larry's Dad's treat, and then we would take in the festival at the Cozy Farm Theatre, which was fine with me.

I wasn't sure what to expect as I drove into the parking lot. I saw Larry's car and went to park beside it. They'd just arrived themselves and were getting out of the car and I did likewise. Once again, Larry did the introductions. "Sharon, this is my Mom and Dad and Mom and Dad, this is Sharon."

I felt the tension between them immediately. It was as though years and years of family problems had been swept under the carpet - and here that family was, carefully walking on that carpet, making every attempt not to disturb what they'd covered up. I knew I was in for a very long afternoon.

"Why don't we go inside and see if we can find a table?" Larry said. With that, we all made our way into the restaurant, men in front, women behind.

"It's certainly a beautiful day today, isn't it?" I said to Larry's Mom.

"Yes, it is." Nothing more. Just 'yes, it is', with her eyes looking down in front of her.

I figured she probably wasn't feeling well and hoped she'd feel better inside.

We made ourselves comfortable and placed our order. As we waited for the food to arrive, we all did our best to make conversation, but nothing flowed easily like it did with Larry's Aunt and Uncle. As time passed, it became really difficult to find something to talk about. Larry's Mom spoke only when spoken to and then answered with as few words as possible. I was curious as to why she was so quiet, but then I remembered Larry's Dad telling me she was not feeling very well that day.

The lack of conversation was starting to get a little embarrassing, but then, quite by accident we came upon a subject that was of interest to everybody: blepharospasm and Botox®. Blepharospasm is a medical condition where the eyelid muscles quit acting as they should and consequently the eyelids won't stay open. This can be quite a problem as it makes walking, reading, cooking, driving and most anything next to impossible and unsafe as the only way the eyelids will stay open is if they are held open. One of the treatments for blepharospasm is to inject a substance called Botox® into the muscles of the eyelids, which makes them work for a period of time, after which, they have to be re - injected again. It just so happened that Larry's Mom had blepharospasm and that the doctor I work for is one of the few doctors who specialises in the injections for it. Finally, some conversation that flowed with interest and excitement. According to Larry's Dad, his Mom had this condition for many, many years, even before the special injections had been discovered. Before they became available in Canada, they had to make the two day trip all the way from Saskatchewan to Seattle, three to four times a year, just to have the injections. Larry's Mom nodded in agreement. And then, they found someone in BC who did the injections at the coast which cut down on the travelling time a bit, but now they were able to get them done right in Saskatchewan, so it had become much easier to treat the problem.

I told them of some of my experiences with Botox® patients at the office and because Larry's Mom was the one with the condition, I tried to speak to her, but it was rarely her that answered. Her husband spoke for her and sometimes, Larry did as well. I found this so strange. I knew she could speak.

When our meal was over, we all got into Larry's car for the drive to the Cozy Farm Theatre. Larry drove and his Dad sat in front with him. Larry's Mom and I sat in the back. Larry was driving slowly through the windy country roads. The scenery was beautiful. We all commented about it throughout the drive. Countryside and weather - two standard topics for anyone from Saskatchewan.

As soon as we drove into the Farm, I realised it was a mistake to go there.

"It's full of hippies!" Larry said as we got out of the car. I could tell from the look on his face, that his Dad was thinking the same thing. His Mom had the same smile she'd had for the last two hours so I wasn't sure what she was thinking.

"They're not hippies," I said. "They're people who live in the country and grow their own food - like farmers from the prairies. They just dress differently."

He looked at me. "You like these kind of people, don't you? You'd fit in with them, wouldn't you?" I wasn't sure if he was being curious or condemning.

"I've never thought of myself as a hippie," I answered, "but I used to grow my own food and probably did dress like this when I lived in the country. I feel comfortable here, but you obviously don't." He was wearing his tennis whites and stuck out like a blinding fluorescent sign.

"No, I'm okay. I was just surprised and I feel out of place the way I'm dressed, but I'll be okay. I'm not sure how my parents feel about it, though…it's pretty hot and dusty." Larry went over to where they were sitting in the shade and asked them if they wanted to stay. It turned out that they did, so we started to wander around from booth to booth and spent over an hour there. I got the feeling they were actually enjoying themselves. At the very least, I thought, it would give them something to talk about back in Saskatchewan.

It was getting close to dinnertime when Larry's Dad suggested we all go to Vernon to eat. We drove back to Junction Ranch so I could pick up my car.

"Why don't you ride into Vernon with me?" I asked Larry's Mom.

She looked at her husband and Larry. "Yes, that would be nice," she said after they nodded their agreement.

I thought it would be a very quiet ride, with me trying to make conversation the whole way. But as soon as we got on the highway, she started to ask me questions about

Botox®. She seemed to come alive. She was excited and interested and *very* talkative, not to mention intelligent. I only managed to get a few sentences in edgewise. What a surprise - she was a different woman!

We pulled into the restaurant's parking lot and parked beside Larry. As soon as she saw her husband she became quiet again and I was sad to see the same suffering smile she'd had on her face all day long, as she turned to join us after closing her car door. And for the rest of the night she hardly spoke. Poor woman, I thought. What on earth has happened to her?

When his parents had left for Saskatchewan, Larry came to my place and we sat on my deck and talked. "What was wrong with your mother?" I asked. I told Larry how she'd talked up a storm when we were alone in the car, but then became quiet again. "Why doesn't she talk when she's around your Dad?"

"I guess they're both used to Dad doing everything, with her being sick for so much of her life. He does all the cooking and cleaning and shopping and driving and pretty much anything that needs to be done. And I guess he does her talking and thinking for her too. She tries to help him with whatever she can, but she doesn't do much and he doesn't require much. I remember how it used to bug Theresa, my ex - wife when we'd go to Saskatchewan to visit them. My Mom had to ask my Dad for everything - money, a ride, or anything. She was completely dependent on him and that really bothered Theresa."

"Do you think she needs to be so dependent? She doesn't seem that sick to me."

"No, she could probably do a lot more than anybody lets her do. I don't know…it's a strange relationship. My Dad certainly has the control." Larry looked despondent and said he didn't want to discuss it anymore, but I certainly spent the next while thinking about it. I thought of how difficult his childhood had probably been on him and I knew he was going to need love and support and understanding from me, which I was more than willing to give.

My parents came from Saskatchewan to visit as well that summer. One evening, I took them to a bar in Kelowna to listen to my neighbour's band play. Larry came from the resort to meet us. I marvelled at how good he was when it came to impressing my parents - saying and doing all the right things. And they agreed that he seemed very nice. The next day I took my parents to the resort where Larry lived, so they could see how beautiful it was, and yes, this impressed them as well. I also took my sister Jennette there as well that summer, when she visited from Victoria. She also thought it was a beautiful place and that Larry seemed like a nice fellow, even though he looked quite different from how she'd pictured him. When my brother and his family came to visit, Larry even gave them all tennis lessons and I remember how impressed he was with my nephew's tennis abilities and how impressed everyone else was with Larry's teaching abilities. Everyone seemed to think he was a nice enough fellow, or at least that's what they said to me, or perhaps I should say that that's what I wanted to hear them say.

Larry wanted to start looking at property. He said it was because he wanted to get to know the surrounding areas of Vernon and to see what was between Vernon and Kelowna in case we started living together and wanted a place of our own. I wasn't so sure I wanted to live with Larry and I was definitely not sure about selling my place and moving. I liked my place and so did my kids. Their friends were close by and so was the school and most of the activities they were involved with were within walking distance.

"It won't hurt to look, Sharon. I'm not saying something is going to come of it. It's just to get a feel for things," he said.

The last thing I wanted to do was squelch his dreams and initiative, so I went along with it, thinking it certainly can't hurt to just look. I was also okay with it because I had a secret plan of my own. I thought the time spent driving offered the perfect opportunity to discuss our lives on a deeper level. It would be time spent together discovering and sharing the beliefs that make us what we are.

We spent several weekends driving around to different areas - just looking. I tried to find out more about his childhood and family life. After meeting his parents, I was curious to know more. But when I'd ask, he'd make a few short remarks and then grow quiet and sullen. The same happened when I asked him about his marriage and divorce. No, he'd say, he didn't want to talk about it - it was in the past, and then he'd change the subject.

"What about life and death," I asked him on one trip. "What do you think is the purpose of being alive?"

"I don't know," he answered with a blank look on his face. "I never really thought about it."

Did he have any fears, I wanted to know? No, he wasn't afraid of anything or anybody. End of story. Did he have any hopes? Yes, he hoped he'd find some nice property. End of story. C'mon Larry, I'd say to myself, open up for once - let me know what's under that exterior of yours. I knew there had to be a way in - but I never found it. We never got past chit chat. We talked about the scenery, the weather, tennis, other people's problems, but never the deeper recesses of our own lives.

I became frustrated and gave up trying, wondering what happened to that friendly man who seemed so interested in sharing himself with me in the spring? Perhaps I was being too pushy. Maybe he just needed more time and loving support from me to open up the way I wanted him to. I decided to back off.

Once I asked him to describe the house he saw us building on the property we were looking for. What he described was nothing less than a country mansion with several floors, a circular staircase in the middle, separate bedrooms for all the kids (his and mine), a rec room with a pool table, an exercise room, a den, a TV room, maybe a swimming pool, a few nice cars and of course a motor boat in the yard as well as a snowmobile or two for everyone to play with! He was serious too. This wasn't his plan for when he won the 649 - this was his plan for the very near future, period. As far as he was concerned, it was going to happen, with me and the kids filling up the house and coming to meet him after work, calling out "Daddy! Daddy!" This was what he saw in his future.

I fought against my urge to tell him this was simply not going to be happening. Let him have his dreams, I told myself. They're too far fetched to ever become reality anyway, so let him dream. We continued to look at property and actually found a few pieces that were worth phoning a real estate agent about. He'd always ask me to call. I wondered why - but I didn't think too much about it. I'd just call and let Larry know what they said.

On one of our trips, we found an exceptionally nice piece of property. We walked all over it and then sat down on an old log to rest. "What would you do if we did find the ideal property for a good price?" I asked Larry. "How are you thinking we'd pay for it? The only money I have is tied up in my house and I'm not willing to borrow against it. I can't chance it and I really doubt that you could get a mortgage when your job is so seasonal. Do you have a store of cash you haven't told me about, or what were you planning to do?"

"No, I don't have a store of cash," he said. "I wish I did. And I know I couldn't get a mortgage. I don't even have a credit card or credit rating."

"You don't have a credit card!" This came as a surprise. "Why not?"

"I just never bothered to apply for one. I've always paid cash for everything I've needed." And then more quietly, "Besides, even if I applied for one, I'd never get it until I took care of my income tax."

"What do you mean, 'took care of your income tax'?" I didn't like the sound of this at all.

"Just that I haven't actually filed my income tax returns for several years now. It's not that I owe them anything, because I've never made enough money for that. I just never saw the need for filing a return when I don't owe any money, so I didn't. They write me the odd letter, but that's about all they ever do."

I was shocked! Not filing your income tax was against the law! I'm not Miss Prim and Proper, or anything like that, but not filing your income tax was definitely a no - no in my books, not to mention how many doors it shut financially for Larry, that I had assumed were open.

"You've got to take care of this Larry," I said. "There's no way I'm getting into any deals with you until you do."

"Yeah, I know. You're right...it does need to be done. Now that I'm not so busy with tennis, I'll get out all the paperwork and get it done right away."

"So, if you don't have a credit rating, a credit card or the possibility of a mortgage and I don't have any cash, how do you think we're going to finance property, if we find some?"

"Well, I've got a lot of rich friends. I'm sure I could get interest free loans from them. Some of them might even just give me the money if it's not too much. As far as I can see, finding the money's not the problem - it's finding the right property that's hard."

"You really think people will just give you the money? We're talking about a lot of money when it comes to buying land and building a house."

"One thing at a time and one day at a time, Sharon. Nothing is impossible."

He was right. Nothing is impossible, but what he was talking about seemed highly improbable to me. Now that I knew his financial situation and plans, I lost my interest entirely in looking any further at property. To me, it seemed like a huge waste of time because I just couldn't see it happening, plus my hidden agenda of getting to know each other better had also not materialised, so what was the point? I told Larry that after thinking more about moving into the country, I realised it would not work for me or my kids because they were all involved in activities they needed to be able to get to by bike or walking, which meant staying in Vernon. But he didn't seem to hear what I was saying - it went in one ear and out the other. He continued looking in the country saying that we could move here or couldn't move there depending on the availability of a school bus. He became a man with a vision that had blinders on both sides. I just let it go. I knew that even if he found a place, his friends would never lend him the money anyway, and I had made up my mind not to borrow against my property, so I knew it wasn't going to happen. As winter approached the property hunt died down and we turned to other activities.

Skating was one of the winter activities we thought we'd try with Joey and Daisy. Larry said he was good at it, but didn't have skates and neither did Joey. Daisy was going to need a pair as well. I'd gone out and bought myself a pair of skates the weekend before instead of renting, simply because I wanted to get back into skating. I was a figure skater in my high school days and thought it would be good exercise to start skating again on weekends with Larry, and at the same time teach Daisy how to skate.

We got to the rink and laced up, full of anticipation. It had been many, many years since I'd skated and I wondered how I'd do. Larry was the first one laced up and on the ice with Joey to follow. I looked up from helping Daisy lace her skates. "What's this?" I said, rather surprised. "I thought he said he could skate!" He was going forward, but with the grace of a broomstick. He didn't seem to be able to bend his knees and balance at the same time. Joey wasn't doing too badly, but it was obvious that he hadn't spent much time on skates before either. Daisy and I got out on the ice as well and they came to meet us.

"Whoa, I'm not used to this anymore," he said.

"Let's just skate together slowly so we can get our skating legs back again." I said. Joey and Daisy grabbed a skating walker and started to propel themselves around hanging on to it, while Larry and I skated. It felt good to be on skates again and a few times I let go of Larry's hand to skate around the rink on my own trying to recapture the previous joy skating had always brought me. After half an hour, I realised he wasn't going to get his skating legs back because he never had them in the first place. Joey and Daisy came up to us and Joey wanted to show Larry how he could skate backwards and then wanted Larry to try. Frontward had been hard enough - backward looked impossible, even though he was trying his darndest in front of his son. Being an athletic tennis player, I thought he'd be able to learn to skate quite well over the winter, but there was a little niggly voice inside me asking, "Why'd he tell you he could skate, when he couldn't?"

The next weekend, and the weekend following and every weekend after throughout the winter, Larry always managed to come up with what sounded like a legitimate excuse as to why he couldn't go skating and because I spent my weekends with him, I ended up not going either. It was disappointing, but we did other activities that were enjoyable, so I didn't dwell on it. As long as we spent our time together, what did it matter what we did, I told myself.

Sometimes, on the weekends, I would try to teach Larry about computers. I had one for my family and all of us knew how to use it. Larry was not overly interested, but he was willing to spend some time trying to sort out the basics. I tried to be patient, just like he was teaching me tennis, but it soon became obvious he was not a quick learner when it came to computers. He couldn't seem to grasp basic steps and needed the same instructions repeated endlessly.

"I'm not very good at this, Sharon, as you can see," he said one day as he turned to look at me. The way the light caught his face I could see a scar beneath his eyebrow.

"Don't worry about it. A lot of people have trouble getting the hang of computers at first. You'll get it." And then I asked him, because I was curious, "What's that scar under your eyebrow from?"

He acted as though he hadn't heard me and squinted at the monitor. But then he said, "Surgery."

"What do you mean, surgery?"

"See - I've got one under the other eyebrow too." I looked and sure enough, I could see one there too, but I had no idea what he meant. I must have looked confused as he continued on, "After I left Theresa, I didn't feel very good about myself and I wanted a little pick me up - you know - something to make me feel better about my appearance and the way I felt. I had a little bit of money left so I decided to go for plastic surgery and have my saggy eyelids tightened, and that's what the scars are from."

I felt instantly sick to my stomach, but my curiosity was piqued. "You're kidding!" I said. "How much did it cost?"

"Two thousand dollars."

"You spent two thousand dollars on your eyelids!?" I wanted to add 'Are you crazy?' but said instead, "Did it at least work...did it make you feel better about yourself?"

"Actually it did work. I felt as though I looked ten years younger and that gave me the courage to act ten years younger and start dating women again. I started to work out in a gym to build up my upper body muscles and that's when I started to shave the hair off my chest so that I could see my muscles better. I was working out, feeling good - I dated lots of women and had a good time, so as far as I'm concerned it was two thousand dollars well spent."

I'd never been able to understand plastic surgery and why people would go through the pain of it just to change their appearance. Probably because I've never been able to fully comprehend just how important appearance is to some people. I certainly hadn't realised before how much importance Larry attached to it. It explained the dyed hair, the shaved chest hair (I'd always thought he shaved it because it was grey), and the skin tight jeans he'd force himself into. He thought it made him look younger, which to him, was better and that's why he didn't want to tell me his age. After a bit of personal reflection, I didn't feel it was right for me to pass any judgements on him. My rights and wrongs, I reasoned, didn't *have* to be his rights and wrongs…everyone's different. He did what he did and he had his own reasons for it. Plus, it was a long time ago. That little bit of denial worked pretty well at keeping my inner voices at bay, but it didn't stop me from feeling sick to my stomach whenever I thought about the surgery.

Later that winter, we decided to go cross country skiing. This was something Larry had never tried before, so we rented equipment for him. I had my own equipment from previous years of skiing. We went up to the local ski hill and clicked on our skis. I gave Larry a few lessons on how to step and glide, and then we were off on the trails. He did pretty good for his first time, but as all first timers, he was slow. Painfully slow. I just wanted to get going and ski. But I could see that with a little practice he would be able to pick up the technique quickly and would easily keep up and probably soon be passing me as physically, he was much stronger than I was. So I was prepared to wait for him. He'd been more than patient with me and my tennis. I felt I owed it to him to be patient as well.

At the end of our ski, he said over and over how good it felt and how much he enjoyed it and that he'd look around Kelowna for a second hand pair of skis and boots so he wouldn't have to keep renting. We decided to go up again the next weekend to continue with the training. As for me, I was excited to have a partner to ski with.

However, when the following weekend came, Larry said he didn't think he'd be able to continue skiing because when he went to look at skis, he found he wasn't able to afford a pair and he knew he couldn't afford to keep renting equipment, so he didn't see how he'd be able to continue skiing. I was disappointed to say the least, but…he was my man and I thought it was only proper to stick with him instead of taking off on my own to ski, especially since he never went off playing tennis, leaving me behind. He'd always been there for me, so I was going to do the same for him. Besides, I thought, we can always try again next year.

Christmas was coming fast. Every second year Larry would take his kids and they would all fly to Saskatchewan to spend Christmas with his Mom and Dad. There was only Larry and his sister in the family and she always flew back with her husband and children for this special Christmas as well. It was a family tradition, Larry told me, which he did not want to break. I had my own Christmas traditions with my children, so Larry and I spent our first Christmas apart.

"You have to write down how you make your pancakes before I go, Sharon. I want to make them for everybody for Christmas breakfast, but I don't know how you do it."

I was flattered. I wrote the recipe down and instructed Larry on exactly how to make them. I drove him and his children to the airport and found I was sad to see them going away from me on a special occasion.

I spent the week they were gone with Larry constantly popping into my mind. It was the first time we'd been apart for more than a few days since we'd started dating in April and I missed him terribly. It was like my life had been cut in half, with one half missing, and I ached from the emptiness. I'd have conversations with myself about him calling me from Saskatchewan - will he, won't he, why should he, why shouldn't he, and on and on. I was pleasantly surprised that I felt as strongly as I did about him. I hadn't realised I'd become so attached to him until we were separated. Just like in the song… *"You never miss the water till the well runs dry."*

So you can imagine my happiness when the phone rang late one evening and it was Larry. "Your pancakes were a hit, Sharon," he said and I laughed. We talked a long time. He was missing me too, he said, but he'd be home in three more days.

I imagined what it would be like at the airport. He'd be as anxious to see me as I was to see him, and he'd be searching for me the second he was inside the terminal, and then he'd see me and I'd see him and we'd quickly make our way through the people between us and we'd hug and kiss and it would feel so good to have him with me again. I've always liked romance. The result of too many fairy tales when I was young, I think. I anxiously awaited his return, running airport scenarios through my head several times a day.

Finally, the day came. I arrived early, only to have to wait quite some time for the plane to land. I watched the plane touch down and then taxi and I knew I'd see Larry soon. My legs felt weak and my heart started pounding. I looked for him as everyone filed through the door and then I saw him, with his kids behind. Then I heard that familiar voice in my head: "What are you doing, Sharon? Look at him - he's not your type. Get away from him." Go away little voice, I answered, I don't want to hear you now.

I saw him looking around - no doubt searching for me. I made my way through a crowd of people and came up to him ready to throw my arms around him.

"Oh there you are." He came forward and brushed a quick kiss on my cheek. "Boy, that was a long flight. Let's get our luggage and get out of here." He turned to go with his kids following close behind. All I could do was follow, at least, that's all I thought I could do at the time, so I did, dutifully and respectfully, a few feet behind everyone feeling like I'd been hit with a sledgehammer.

We drove straight to Penticton to drop Larry's kids off at his ex - wife's place. But when we got there, Theresa wasn't home. We'd arrived an hour earlier than he'd told her, so the fact she was out was understandable, but he was upset that she wasn't there anyway. Then we drove around to a relative's place to see if she was there, which she was not. Larry was frustrated that he had no where to leave his kids, which, it was becoming obvious, was something he dearly wanted to do and the sooner the better. When Joey and Anna started to bicker in the back seat, he decided to ask the relatives if he could leave the kids with them until Theresa could pick them up. They didn't mind at all, they said, so that's what Larry did. Of course, this was not the "fatherly" thing to do, but Larry didn't even hesitate. He came back to the car saying, "You're staying here until your Mom comes home and then she'll pick you up. Out you go."

I felt sorry for the way he'd treated his kids and sorry that I was, in a way, an accomplice, simply because I was his girlfriend and because I was present and because I said nothing to change the situation. His limit for kid tolerance had obviously been reached after spending a week with them and I wondered if he ever considered what it was like for Theresa to have the kids all the time, except for the odd time when he felt like taking them for a weekend. But that was not a question I dared ask him right then and there. He was wound up far too tight to handle any questions that he might consider an assault on his decency.

Maybe it was because I'd placed too much importance on how much I'd missed Larry while he was in Saskatchewan - thinking it was a sign of how much I loved him, or maybe it was because I'd anticipated his homecoming to be incredibly romantic only to be horribly disappointed, but whatever the reason, his actions that night felt like a slap in the face. I found it to be a rather rude awakening - sort of like having the lights switched on when your eyes are accustomed to the dark. I finally saw that I'd been making excuses for Larry's bothersome behaviours to myself and others all along. And I knew I was no longer willing to do that.

What surprised me though, was that there was still a part of me that felt attracted to him, even though I could clearly see all sorts of disagreeable faults I'd ignored before. Try as I might, I was unable to figure out why I still felt an attraction. How could it be that I could feel a push and a pull all at the same time? I dearly wanted to sort these feelings out, so I decided to spend some time examining my own thoughts and emotions, as well as Larry's behaviour - what he did, what he didn't do - trying to figure out what it all meant. I kept this to myself as I didn't want Larry to be on guard and change his behaviour just to please me. I wanted to see him as he was, from eyes that were finally looking. It seemed I had discovered the true meaning of "love is blind."

As the months progressed, it became more and more evident to me that our relationship had little chance of developing into anything lasting. I felt as though I'd "grown up" since I first started dating Larry - I no longer felt a strong desire or need for his affection and I no longer felt a comforting satisfaction in caring for him.

Larry's behaviour had changed somewhat from when we first met, but I realised it was not so much that he'd changed, but that his true personality was now showing through. Quite frankly, I did not see Larry as my equal anymore, or perhaps it would be more appropriate to say that I did not feel we were on the same wavelength anymore. I started to feel crowded by his presence every weekend, thinking of so many other things I could be doing if he wasn't there. The time we did spend together felt more like wasted time to me, rather than enjoyable time. The massages had stopped a long, long time ago and our sexual desires had already reached the point of satiation. "I love you," hadn't been said by either of us for months on end and it was certainly not something I could have said anymore. Even Daisy started to find Larry's tickling bouts too much for her. He never seemed to know when to stop and it always ended up in crying. They were just too much. My older kids had wanted nothing to do with him for quite some time and I guess Daisy and I were just catching up to them.

The hardest thing to let go of though, was being a couple. That was the part I'd really liked because of the security and self - confidence it gave me. I'd landed a man, you see - the very thing I'd been taught was most important to a woman. But, I discovered, as important as that was to me, it wasn't half as important as my sense of self - respect. I knew that staying in a relationship with someone, even though I knew I didn't love them, was too low for me.

By the time spring rolled around, I knew I'd fallen out of love with Larry and that I simply couldn't continue on with our relationship. But that decision left me face to face with the hard reality of having to tell Larry. The last thing I wanted to do was hurt him, but I couldn't figure out any way around it. I just couldn't keep sweeping and sweeping everything under the carpet.

I became a nervous wreck…knowing that I had to, but not knowing if I could get the words out of my mouth when the time came to say them. As you've probably gathered by now, I disliked confrontation enough to avoid it at all costs. I rehearsed what I'd say over and over in my mind. I practised in front of my mirror. I talked to my friends about my difficulties. They were unanimous: "You have to tell him Sharon. You simply have to spit the words out. You can't go on like this, that's for sure. You don't love him…so you don't love him. It's not that big of a deal. People are breaking up every day," they'd say.

"Yes, I know. I know I have to tell him. It's just so hard for me to do," I'd answer. They were certainly right about one thing - I couldn't go on the way I was. I felt sick to my stomach just thinking of seeing him again and pretending nothing was wrong, and sick to my stomach thinking of seeing him again and telling him I wanted to end the relationship. I had to put an end to it. Enough, I decided. Tomorrow is the day.

In the morning, I called Larry at the gym and told him I needed to talk to him and I'd meet him at the gym after work. I packed all the things he'd left at my house into my car so that I could give them back to him, and drove to Kelowna. It was the beginning of April. Two weeks shy of a year since we'd first met. Steve had been right after all, I thought. We didn't last a year.

When we met, Larry said he needed to go to the bank first. I went along. He held my hand as we walked which made me feel like a traitor, but I knew if I refused to hold his hand, he'd want to know why and then I'd have to tell him right there on the sidewalk, which was not how I planned it. So I held his hand, knowing it would be for the last time. When we were done at the bank, he asked where I wanted to go for our "talk." He seemed quite excited about it, as though I had some mysterious good news to tell him. I knew I was not acting mysterious and excited by any stretch of the imagination - more like death warmed over. I was disappointed by how out of touch he was with my feelings, which gave me some last minute confidence to carry through with my plans.

We chose an outdoor rooftop restaurant not far from the bank. The sun was shining directly on us and a warm spring breeze made it comfortable enough to sit outside. Baskets of greenery dotted with brilliant colours hung on wooden posts. The waitress brought us each a glass of red wine in a heavy long stemmed glass. Everything was so perfect - it could have been a movie set.

I took a long, slow sip of wine. I was extremely nervous and didn't know how to start. Then Larry said, "So what is it you needed to talk to me about? You're looking rather nervous. Whatever you have to say can't be that bad...Why don't you just tell me?"

"Okay," I said and I looked straight at him. "Okay, I will. I've fallen out of love with you Larry." And as if it wasn't enough to say it once, I added, "I just don't feel like I love you anymore. I want to end our relationship." As soon as I said it, I felt a tremendous surge of relief come over me and I took another large sip of wine.

He was shocked and just sat there staring at me. This was obviously not what he had expected to hear. The only thing that moved were bits of his light blond hair from the breeze. It seemed like an eternity passed before he spoke.

Then he started slowly, "If that's how you feel, Sharon, then that's how it will be. I've been the one to end a few relationships in the past, so I know how difficult it was for you to do this. And I want you to know that I accept your decision."

Thank goodness, I thought. It looked like it was going to be a friendly parting.

We sat in silence for awhile, sipping our wine, each busy with our own thoughts. Then Larry began to talk, hesitant at first, and then with more certainty as though he was speaking from a place deep inside. He talked about how he felt about his life and how he felt about having me in his life. He seemed to be sharing his thoughts with me, offering them to me, rather than confronting me with them.

"You are one of the most warm, understanding and kind human beings I have ever come across and I consider it a very deep privilege to have been able to spend the time with you that I have. I've dated many women, but they were plastic compared to you. You're the real thing and you must never settle for anyone who believes anything less. I thought we could make a go of it, but I can see I was never up to your calibre. I have no money, only love to offer you and you deserve more than that. I love you, probably more than you'll ever know and I know at one time you loved me. I could always feel it in your eyes and your touch. It will be hard for me to get over you, but I accept your decision." We looked straight at each other. His eyes were glistening. I could see he was trying to cover a pained expression with one of honour, and wasn't doing a very good job of it.

My first thoughts were, Oh my God, he's not making this stuff up! This isn't just a "line" he's handing me. He's talking straight from his heart. Why, oh why didn't he do this before when I'd tried to reach inside to find his vulnerabilities, his desires, his fears? This wasn't what I'd expected from him now. He was supposed to get mad and walk out on me, or something like that, not expose himself. My determination faltered. I became confused. Maybe I shouldn't be so hasty in ending this relationship after all, I thought. Maybe we could work something out together. Somehow he'd found the only spark left in my fire, and was blowing on it to get it going again.

Larry continued on, "I want to wish you all the luck possible Sharon, in any relationship you enter into in the future, and just remember to never settle for anything other than the very best, because that's what you deserve."

It was my turn to speak now. "Well, Larry," I started, "I've been sitting her listening to you saying all these wonderful things about me - about us. Quite frankly, I didn't think you were capable of speaking straight from your heart. I'd given up the hope of us speaking like this a long time ago. But I see now that it *is* possible, and that's making me feel confused. I'm not sure anymore if breaking up is the right thing to do. Will you let me think about it for awhile? I just need some time to sort it all out and when I've figured it out, I'll give you a call and let you know one way or the other. It's just that you've thrown me for a loop here. I've never known you to be so open and honest and real and I find myself feeling very attracted to that part of you, so I don't want to make the wrong decision and have both of us regret it."

"That would be wonderful, Sharon. Take as much time as you need. There's no pressure from me. I'll be waiting to hear from you." He seemed relieved, but not ecstatic. We sat for a little while longer nursing our wine and our emotions.

I went home and I thought and I thought. I read book after book. This was a big decision. Sometimes I would be absolutely sure that it wouldn't work and then the next day I would feel the complete opposite. There were just so many factors to consider. On the negative side most of my kids did not like him, he had difficulties with his own kids, we had different tastes in clothing and music, very different financial situations, and he had little to offer in the way of assets or stability. On the positive side he was a patient man, who basically had good intentions, and who could probably become ambitious if he wanted to. I could also now add to the list that he did indeed have some emotional depth to him, an ability to express himself, and a strong love for me. The difficulty lay in getting enough perspective to make a good decision. There were too many of my own emotions to wade through before I could even look at the facts realistically. I was trying to see if the future could possibly be okay, given what the past was like. I didn't want to give up on the relationship if there was a chance it could work. But on the other hand, I didn't want to be drawn down the road of compromising myself again.

After several days of deliberation I finally made my decision and during those seven days Larry had indeed kept his word and never called me once. I took this as a sign of respect. I sat at the table on my deck and began a long letter to him, starting with - "If you are willing to try again after reading this letter, then so am I." I continued on, describing all the things about him and our previous relationship that I did not like. Things that would most definitely have to change. I did not sugar coat anything, but laid it out exactly as I felt. I figured if he could hear me say these things about him and still want to try again, we might have a chance. I ended by saying that if we did agree to try again, there would have to be a great deal more talking between us so we would know how we were both feeling.

I'd just finished the letter and was about to go to mail it, when the phone rang. It was Larry. "Hi, Sharon." His voice was shaky. He didn't sound at all like himself. "I'm sorry I'm calling...I know I said I'd wait to hear from you...but I'm not calling to ask you if you've made your decision. I just wanted to know if it was okay with you if I took Daisy to Dairy Queen for an ice cream?"

I didn't keep him in suspense. "You must be psychic Larry. I just finished writing a long letter to you and was on the way to mail it when you phoned." Dead silence. I could almost hear him thinking - A letter! Oh no, that sounds like dear john.

"I'm willing to try again, if you are," I said and I could hear a tremendous sigh, "But...you have to read my letter first because I've said some things in it that you might be very offended by and you might find that it's you who never wants to see me again after you finish reading it."

"Oh, no...that's not possible. I'll do anything. I'll change anything. I don't care - I just want us to be back together again. I've been going through hell these past ten days. I haven't been able to sleep or eat. I've even lost ten pounds. The weirdest thing was, I never knew I felt so strongly about you until I thought I could really lose you. It was driving me crazy. I love you...I know I love you...after being through this, I know it with absolute certainty, inside and out. I even called an old girlfriend and asked her what I should do. She's the one who suggested I call and ask if I could take Daisy for an ice cream. I had to do something, Sharon. I had to talk to you. Oh, I'm so glad you've decided to try again." It was like a damn had burst inside him and everything came tumbling out. "When can I come and see you?"

"But Larry, remember, you have to read my letter first. You may not feel this way after you read it. I'll go and mail it now so that you get it in a couple of days and you can think about it and then give me a call. Good night, Larry. Get some sleep." I was sure he would not be so ecstatic the next time he called.

A few days later he called back, "I've read your letter over and over and yes, there are parts of it that hurt. I've written down some things about you that I think need discussing as well, but I want to try more than ever. We can do this Sharon, I know we can. We just need to talk it out. I want to meet with you as soon as possible. When can you meet me?"

"I can get away tomorrow afternoon. I'll meet you where we first met - by the sails sculpture in Kelowna. Then I have to do some grocery shopping."

"I'll be there. See you tomorrow. I love you."

I couldn't say I loved him back. I didn't. Not yet anyway. Maybe it would come though.

When I got to the sails sculpture, he was already there. You couldn't miss him…he was shaking and smiling and crying all at the same time. He looked like he was going to burst at the seams. He walked up to me, tears running down his face and he hugged me and hugged me for such a long time, whispering over and over that he would never, ever let me go again. People were staring at us, but he didn't seem to care. He just kept on holding me, laughing and crying. We were quite a sight, I'm sure. I was happy too, but not as much as he seemed to be. I knew how much work was ahead of us. Besides, my neck was getting sore from being held so tightly for such a long time.

"Larry, let's sit down. We need to talk things over," I said. We found a park bench under a tree and he took out the letter. We went over every aspect in great detail. The biggest problems to solve were with the kids. We had to do something to work towards a harmonious relationship between Larry and my kids or at least a liveable one. He agreed to quit being such a "know it all", but we both agreed that would not be enough. We decided we'd each get some books on step - parenting to see if we could shed some light on this problem and maybe even counselling if that became necessary.

Finances were another big issue. Larry agreed with me. He knew it was time he did something to take care of his future, whether we ended up together or not. His knees had been giving him problems playing tennis, so he was well aware that he needed to find something else to do. He'd spent some time thinking about it and had decided to enrol in a pharmacy technician course as soon as possible. That way, he could be a pharm - tech and still teach tennis for extra money. He also agreed to get his income taxes in order first thing, which was another stipulation I'd put in my letter.

What he wanted from me in return was an assurance that I would not keep my feelings to myself, but instead talk to him about whatever might be bothering me so that nothing would ever be allowed to fester in my mind. That way, he felt we would be able to avoid what we just went through. I agreed. He was right. This was one of my old habits that I'd found hard to shake. It felt very good to be able to open up and talk with each other. It was like getting to know each other all over again, but better.

We agreed to not discuss marriage as there were so many things that needed to be put in order before it could ever be a consideration for us. He made it perfectly clear to me that he wanted to get himself well established and on his own two feet before he'd even consider us living together. That was more than fine with me, and I considered it very noble of him to feel this way. When we were both satisfied with our discussion, we left to do the grocery shopping.

He was feeling just as ecstatic as when we first met a few hours ago, and I wasn't far behind. Several times during our shopping, he would come up to me in the aisle and start hugging and kissing me, telling me how much he loved me. Shoppers stared at us as they pushed their carts around us. I couldn't decide if they were jealous or embarrassed. Maybe a bit of both.

Our relationship continued in a well intentioned manner for the next several months. You were wrong after all Steve, I thought. We did make it past a year and if everything goes right, we'll make it much farther.

We often went for walks in the evening. It was a chance for us to talk privately about how we were doing. We'd talk about different ways to improve the relationship between my kids and Larry. Counselling was an option, but we decided not to go that route yet. Instead, we decided to first try and learn what we could from books on step parenting. I bought a couple and offered one to him, but he said he'd wait until I'd finished with them and then he'd read them.

As planned, Larry enrolled in a pharmacy technician course. I tried to give him all the support I could as he became very busy trying to juggle teaching tennis, going to school and studying. I was busy as always with my job, my kids and my house. With winter being over, I tried to drive out to the resort as often as I could to help him in whatever way I could. He seemed overwhelmed at first with all the work he had to do for his course, especially all the difficult math work. I was glad it was him and not me that had to deal with it. We were both feeling positive about our relationship and our futures. I felt close to him again. I loved watching his personality change - he walked with purpose and ambition. Like a man who had things to do and places to go and I found that very attractive.

We started to look for different ways to have fun - different ways of sharing time together when we had some time off. Dancing lessons came up in our discussions. Larry said he'd taken two step lessons a long time ago and would like to learn it again. I was all for that, but we couldn't see how we could fit it into Larry's tight schedule. Instead, we went every now and again to a local bar to watch the two steppers do their thing. I wanted to get up and try it, but Larry didn't feel he could carry it off. He was going to need to take lessons first, he said, before he got up on the dance floor, unless I wanted him to make a fool of himself. No, I didn't want that, I said. So we watched and hoped a time would come when we'd both have the time to take lessons.

As busy as we were, we couldn't miss a weekend tennis tournament that Joey was playing in. Joey and Larry had been at my place for the weekend and we'd promised Theresa we'd have Joey in Kelowna in time to play at the tournament. Daisy came along too. We made it in time and met up with Theresa, who had Joey's gear. Daisy and I went to find a spot to sit, while Theresa and Larry got Joey ready. Both being tennis pros, it was important to them that Joey did well. And he did do pretty well too. He wasn't as strong as some of the other kids, I noticed, but he hit a good ball.

After the game we were all standing around talking when Joey asked his mother, in the innocent manner kids use when they know they have allies close by, if he could have one of the kittens I was trying to find a home for. I was as surprised as Theresa at this. She said no, and he said but why not, and she said you know why not and he said no I don't. On and on they tussled while Larry and I listened. I'd been through the same kind of arguments more than enough with my own kids and I felt sorry for Theresa that she had to go through it in front of me.

"Joey, you're not having the kitten and that's that. I can't afford the food or the vet bills if the kitten gets sick right now and you know that. We've been through this before." Her voice became a little louder. "Now if your Dad was to finally pay the child support he still owes me," and she looked straight at Larry, "maybe we could."

"Don't get into that Theresa - not here, not now," Larry said.

Theresa didn't seem to care, though. I was embarrassed because people were starting to turn their heads to see what the commotion was, but she forged straight ahead. "Why not? Are you afraid Sharon's going to hear?" I began to think the rumours I'd heard from Larry and others about Theresa being one tough lady to get along with, were true. She turned to me and said, "I'm not asking for anything he doesn't owe me - just the arrears. You must know how tough it is to raise kids by yourself."

This was not a battle I was going to let myself get dragged into. I told Larry I'd take the kids out to the car and wait for him there. Much to my surprise, Theresa followed me saying she needed to get her cigarettes. My plan to get away had actually trapped me! When we got to the car Theresa wanted to talk. I put the kids inside because I wasn't sure it would be good for them to hear what she was going to say. But she was civil enough. She told me how Larry had not paid child support for several months while he was on welfare his first year in Kelowna, and now that he was back on his feet she thought he should be paying the arrears back, but that he had refused whenever she asked him. This was all news to me, I told her. I didn't know about the arrears or that he'd even been on welfare, but I did agree that losing out on monthly child support was unfair. I thanked Theresa for telling me about the arrears and said Larry and I would be discussing it for sure. I went to sit in the car with the kids and she went to get her cigarettes.

A few minutes later Larry came out to the car and asked, as we drove off, just what Theresa had done. "Nothing," I said, "except tell me a few things that you neglected to tell me." When I asked how he'd managed to accumulate thousands of dollars in child support arrears and how he felt about owing her this money, he told me the whole story. According to him, when he first came to Kelowna he still had some money from the property division of their divorce. But having no job and dishing out rent money and child support payments every month, soon ate whatever money he had left. And because he couldn't seem to find a job, he had to go on welfare, which did not allow him enough money to pay child support and that's when he racked up the huge debt. He thought he'd be able to get a job easily if he became a hairdresser, so he took a hair dressing course, but quit after a short period of time because he found he really didn't like it after all. And that's when Connie from the resort heard about him and told him to come out to the resort for some tennis. She liked his style and ability and talked to the manager and that's how he got hired on at the resort. He had always hoped he would make enough money to pay Theresa at least some of the arrears, but he never seemed to be able to come up with enough extra on top of the monthly child support payments to pay her off, and after a few years of her badgering him, he decided to dig in his heels and say he wasn't going to pay it back.

I didn't agree with his reasoning, and told him so. "It's a debt that you need to take care of, Larry. Even if it's only a little extra every month. It's like your income tax. You have to take care of these things. Speaking of which, have you done your income tax yet?"

The sheepish look and hesitation told me right away. "No, I haven't. You know how busy I've been with school and everything."

Yes, I did know, but I also remembered him telling me it was one of the first things he was going to take care of when we got back together. It was also one of the stipulations of getting back together. The fact that he hadn't done what he'd promised to do, was the first bump in what had been a relatively smooth ride so far. The way I saw it, I had three choices: either I could start nagging at him to do it, declare an ultimatum that either he do it next week or we were through, or let it go for now as finding the time to do it with his busy schedule would be next to impossible. Being the type of person I was, I chose the latter. I did ask him a few more times as months went by if he'd had any time to get at it, but he always had an excuse, which left me feeling annoyed with the situation.

When the summer holidays arrived, Larry became even busier with the extra demand for tennis lessons at the resort plus exams to study for in his pharm - tech course. He was stressed out. Sometimes he would be quiet and withdrawn and other times he would be irritable. I'd never seen him like that before. We had agreed to discuss our feelings openly with each other though, so one day I said to him, "Larry, something seems to be bugging you lately. You hardly talk anymore. It's as though you're closing yourself off from me again. What's up?"

But my question upset him. "You're expecting too much from me, Sharon. I'm doing my best here. I'm taking this pharm - tech course, trying to keep up tennis full time, plus trying to find time to spend on a long distance relationship with you. What more do you want from me?"

I guess I was expecting too much from him. Obviously, he had more on his plate than he was comfortable handling. I decided to drop the subject, thinking that we could get back to discussing whatever problems we had when his stress level went down after exams and a busy tennis season.

But, as the summer continued and his stress level increased, surprising new aspects of his personality began to show up. The most surprising one was that he started to argue with me, for no other reason than to simply argue. He had never argued with me before - not even once. Now, over something as inconsequential as the name of a particular colour, he would become adamant and defensive, eyes glaring at me, insisting that he was correct. It got so bad that one day, what started as a friendly discussion as to whether or not we should put a roof over my sundeck, ended with a matter of fact statement from him that it would be the ruin of the deck if we did. A few days later, somehow the subject came up again. This time he was adamant that the deck needed a roof. Very cautiously, I told him that he'd said the opposite a few days earlier. He became quite upset at being questioned by me, and said we'd never even discussed the deck before and if we had, obviously I'd misunderstood him. And why, he wanted to know, was I saying we had discussed the deck before, when he knew we hadn't? I shrugged the question off and quickly changed the subject. I didn't want to carry on with such a senseless argument, but I made a mental note to watch out for an increase in this new characteristic that seemed to have popped up out of nowhere.

It wasn't that he argued all the time - maybe only once in two weeks. He just seemed to pick out certain things and get defensive about them. There was no rhyme or reason to it - so I never knew what was going to set him off. His nice side was still very nice, but when this nasty side came out, I just backed off. There didn't seem to be much use doing anything else.

I was equally surprised when Larry started making rude comments about people he saw on the street. He'd never made racist comments before in our relationship and why vindictive statements would pop out of his mouth now, I wasn't sure.

I was perplexed. This was not the Larry I had come to know so well the past few months. I'd never heard him argue with anyone, especially me, or be critical about anyone. In fact, we often talked about how nice it was to be in a relationship where there wasn't a lot of arguing and complaining. However, the arguments and nasty comments were few and far between and I found I would often forget about them, until the next one happened. I told myself, it's all from stress - just hang in there and be patient - he'll come around as he gets it together. Exams were almost over and tennis would eventually wind down.

Then it came time for Larry to do the practicums for his pharm - tech course. He was to choose two places and the school would help to place him. We'd talked about it often. Where would be the best place to do a practicum? What would give him the best shot at getting a job? Kelowna or Vernon? Should it be a small drugstore or a large pharmacy?

"Larry, why don't you do up your resume?" I asked one day. "I'll type it up on my computer for you, and you can take it around to all the pharmacies you can think of and let them know you're looking for a place to do your practicum and that you'll be finished the pharm - tech course soon and looking for employment? That way you won't be wasting your practicum on a pharmacy that's not interested in hiring you at the end."

"I don't want to do my resume yet."

"Why not?"

"Because I want to do it after I'm finished my course so that I can put down the mark I get. That way, when people see how good I did at my course, they'll be very interested in hiring me."

"But you could just tell them that you're almost finished and have been doing very well up until now and if they'd like to speak to your instructors, they could."

"No, I want to wait so that I can include my official accreditation. I've talked to my instructors and they said that it's always useful to get training in a hospital setting, so I've put my name in for the hospital in Vernon. That way we'll be able to see each other at work too."

"But what if they're not hiring?"

"Then I'll put my name in for my second practicum with someone else, either Vernon or Kelowna or any place between who is."

"Okay," I said. Obviously he had his mind made up. "So that means we'll be working together. You're going to get to know your way around the hospital really well, I'm sure. We'll probably meet in the hallways since I have to run down to the pharmacy in the basement quite often. It should be nice to work in the same building."

"That's one of the reasons why I chose it."

The following week Larry started his practicum. When I would come to work in the morning I would see his car already in the parking lot, right beside my parking spot, which gave me a comforting feeling. I'm not alone in the world, after all, I thought. I'd often leave him a note on his car when I'd go home after my morning job. Looking forward to seeing you tonight...Hope you had a good day...Come for supper...that sort of thing. And when he would come over, we'd talk about everything that happened for him in the day while having supper and then he'd go back to the resort to teach tennis in the evening. He was excited about working in a new field, but like anyone starting a new career, he was also nervous, unsure of himself and feeling stressed.

The first time I ran into him at the hospital was when he was working on the pharmacy computer. He smiled as he said hi to me, but underneath the smile, anguish was written all over his face. Computers were obviously not easy for him, and I noticed the person teaching him was looking quite frustrated. I gave him a smile and headed back to my office, thinking that I'd teach him some computer basics after work.

By the time he finished work and came for supper, he was wiped out. All the nervousness and tension of trying to keep up and learn in a hectic new environment, had certainly taken its toll on him that day. I asked him if he wanted some help on the computer. He looked at me with a look of horror. He didn't want to ever look at another computer again. But he knew he couldn't avoid them, so we went to sit down for awhile at my computer to see if there were any questions he had that I could help him with. I discovered he had a great fear that he could blow the computer up or wipe out every bit of data with one wrong stroke, and he was terrified that he would make that one wrong stroke, no matter which key he touched. It became obvious that his fear of computers was going to be a problem for him in any pharm - tech job he'd apply for and I couldn't see any way to help him get over that fear. The more I tried, the more frustrated he became, until he said, "The computers at the hospital are different from yours, Sharon, and I just can't learn everything at once. I'm going to learn what they teach me at the hospital and that's all I can handle right now. I'm going home to bed."

I felt sorry for him. Information overload was probably the reason he couldn't remember any of the simple steps I repeatedly showed him on the computer. Maybe he was just stressed out and not slow at learning after all. At least that's what I hoped.

As his practicum continued into it's second week, I had the opportunity to see him on several occasions in various parts of the hospital and every time I ran across him, I would watch to see how he was fitting in. Sometimes I would meet people who worked in the hospital pharmacy and I would ask them how he was doing. The answer was always the same. They'd say he was doing pretty good, although he was slow to catch on to some things, but he tried very hard to do everything right and that he liked to joke around so everyone seemed to like him. They certainly weren't jumping up and down about him. However, I realised the fast pace of a hospital is difficult for anyone to get used to and I hoped his next practicum would be easier for him.

Dieter and Vicki had invited Larry and I to a special dinner in Kelowna. It was to be just the four of us. Both Larry and I welcomed the invitation. It was always delightful to see Vicki and Dieter, and the thought of dining in an exclusive restaurant, something neither Larry nor I could afford, made our anticipation even more exciting.

It turned out to be a lovely dinner, with Dieter pausing in conversation to make the occasional aristocratic toast in his "proper German English". To which we would all nod, clink our goblets together and then empty them of their fine wine, only to have a persistent waiter come along to fill them up again. It was several hours before we reached dessert, and when we did Dieter brought out a beautifully wrapped gift and placed it in front of Larry.

"What's this Dieter? What are you up to?" Larry asked suspiciously.

"Now, my friend," Dieter began. "I have a little gift for you and I want you to open it. In a few days, I fly to Germany for a doctor's appointment...it's nothing...it's not important, but I wanted to give you this before I left. You have been a very good friend to me...a very good friend indeed and I wanted to show my appreciation for everything you've done for me, so...I went and got you a little something. Go ahead, please, open it."

Larry looked at Dieter. "Dieter, you don't have to..."

"Please, my friend. Just open it. This is something I want to do."

"Alright, Dieter. I will."

We all watched as Larry very carefully untied the delicate ribbon and slipped the fancy wrapping paper off. Inside was a small box, definitely a jeweller's box. I held my breath as Larry opened it. It was a watch. An absolutely gorgeous, gold watch!

"Dieter...this is too much. You don't have to do this to show your friendship. I know you are my friend and I will always be your friend too, but please, Dieter, this is too much...you..."

"Larry," Dieter interrupted, "you have been my friend from the first time we met and I know in my heart that you are a true and honourable man. I am also an honourable man and I am showing you my appreciation with this watch. Please, you must accept it. It would mean a great deal to me if you did. Look, turn it over, there's an inscription."

Larry looked at the inscription and then at Dieter and then he looked at me. I had tears in my eyes. Dieter's thoughtfulness and caring was straight from the heart and I couldn't imagine anything more touching than Dieter's display of friendship for Larry. We were all waiting to see what Larry would say. He cleared his throat. "Dieter, you have been a true friend to me as well and because of that, I do accept your gift and will wear it with great pride. Except...I think I'll take it off when I play tennis. I certainly don't want to lose it." We all laughed.

"Put it on, let's see how it fits you," Dieter said. "I had to guess at the sizing. You may have to take it in to my jeweller to have some links taken off or put on. Yes, I see you will. It's a little too loose. Here, I will give you the name of the jeweller where I bought it and you can have that done whenever you like."

Larry passed the watch to me to have a closer look. It was absolutely exquisite, and knowing Dieter, probably very expensive. I handed it back, wishing I had a friend like that. It looked very nice on Larry's muscled, tanned arm. We continued on with the evening, more toasts and more wine with our good friends.

As we were driving home that night, Larry confessed to me that he was not used to wearing something so expensive. "It's not really me," he said. "I'm not sure what I'm going to do with it. I'm afraid to wear it in case I loose it."

"After you have it made smaller, it will probably feel better and you can always save it for special occasions." I said.

"But I never have special occasions and what if someone breaks into my apartment and steals it and then it's gone for good." He thought for awhile. "You know what I think I'm going to do?"

"No…what?" I didn't like the tone in his voice.

"I think I'm going to take it to another jeweller and have it appraised and see how much it's worth."

"Why do you want to have it appraised? What you are planning to do?"

"Well, I don't want to wear it and I don't want it stolen so I thought if it was worth it, maybe I'd return it for the money instead, which I could use a whole lot more than a fancy watch to worry about, stashed in some hiding spot."

Was it the wine, I wondered, or did he really just say he was going to sell the watch? This most special of special watches given in friendship! "Larry, Dieter gave you this watch as a token of his friendship. It's a symbol of how much he values you as his friend. That's not something you can trade in for money. What kind of a friend would you be if you did that? And how would you ever explain to Dieter that you had sold his watch? It would be like saying you sold your friendship. You can't be serious about this."

"It's just a thought that crossed my mind. I probably won't go through with it. I'll take it and have it shortened though, and maybe appraised, just so I know."

I couldn't understand how Larry could even consider selling the watch. It must be the wine that's muddled his thinking, I thought. Tomorrow he'll have forgotten all about selling it.

It was time for Larry's second practicum. Once again we went through the same discussions of getting his resume ready first and checking out which pharmacies were looking for a potential employee and once again, Larry refused to do his resume and call around to various pharmacies. He felt that getting experience in larger pharmacies would be worth more than finding a pharmacy that was hiring. He wanted to get as much experience as possible, finish the course and then do his resume and take it around to all the pharmacies. It wasn't the way I would have done it, but it was definitely the way he wanted to do it, and since it was his career on the line, I didn't argue. He chose a large supermarket pharmacy in Vernon. Once again, he would be driving every day to Vernon.

According to Larry, this job was less stressful than the hospital, but not by much. Here there were customers to deal with, which he thought would be easy after his own dealings with the public, but it soon became clear to him that they wanted service and they wanted it quickly and professionally from a pharmacist. After all, he wore a professional white medical coat, so customers automatically assumed he could answer their questions. And then there was yet another computer system to learn, plus the phone ringing all the time bringing more questions and problems to be dealt with, not to mention learning how to run the computerised cash register. He was stressed again.

Every now and again, I would go into the store for groceries, and I would stop and watch him without him knowing I was there, just to see how he was fitting in. He was trying, there was no doubt about that, but he just didn't seem to have the right personality for the job. He seemed too slow and too nervous - not confident at all.

One night he came over to my place after work with pages and pages of hand written notes. "Sharon, can you type these up for me by the end of the week?"

"Why? What are they? Let me see."

"I've been going around on my lunch hours and writing down the name of every medication on every shelf of every row in the pharmacy. I was hoping you would type them up so I could give them to the pharmacist to impress him."

I looked at him. Surely, he must realise that the pharmacist already knows where everything is on his shelves and surely, he must realise that items get moved from time to time, so this list will not be accurate for long. Surely he must see that this would be appropriate for someone learning to stock shelves, not a pharm - tech. But I could see this childlike eagerness to please on his face and I didn't have the heart to say no. He'd had a tough time of it, I figured. Getting a taste of the workforce again after fifteen years of teaching tennis and running your own show had to be difficult.

"Sure I'll do it for you Larry, but there's a lot of typing here. It may take me a few days."

"Thanks, Sharon. I knew you'd help me. I'm going to need it the day after tomorrow though. Actually, I'll need it tomorrow night, because I want to give it to him first thing in the morning and that's my last day. Do you think you can do it?"

"If you help me we should be able to get through it."

And we did. I typed till midnight with Larry spelling out the Latin words of some of the drugs for me. I had no idea a pharmacy carried that many medications. Larry was so proud of himself as he left for work the next morning with his papers in hand. I wondered just what the pharmacist was going to say when Larry handed over those papers like an elementary student proudly handing in his report. By now it was painfully evident to me that Larry was going to have difficulty being accepted back into the workforce. He'd simply been out of the fast, demanding pace for too long. I wished it wasn't so after all the hard work he'd put into the pharm - tech course and his plans for the future, but deep down I knew it to be true.

Summer holidays were coming to an end and I needed to drive to Saskatchewan to pick up my daughter Billie, who had been staying with my brother and sister - in - law for some of the summer holidays. I told Larry about my plans to go and that I'd be gone for approximately a week.

"Maybe I'll go with you," he said.

"Go with me! How would you manage that? Aren't you still in your busy time of the year? Plus what about making up for all the money you lost teaching tennis while you were doing your practicums? Don't you need to make that money back to tide you over the winter?"

"I can probably get Danny to cover for me for a week. He'll be glad to make extra money teaching tennis at the resort. Besides Connie will probably let him stay with her and she'll feed him too, so he'd be more than happy to do it. And don't forget that I'm going to be getting a job as a pharm - tech soon so I won't need to rely on tennis so much anymore. Plus, lately I've discovered that it's become more important to me to spend my time with you, rather than worry about making money."

What was he thinking? He hadn't made much money all summer long and he had no jobs on the horizon that I knew of. "Are you sure about this Larry?" I asked. "Won't the manager of the resort be ticked off with you if you take even more time off from teaching tennis? That is what he's hired you for, after all."

"Ted's a good guy. He'll understand. He likes me, especially since I drive his son into Kelowna every morning in the winter, give him a tennis lesson and then drive him to school."

"Yes, but didn't you say this kid was going to be getting his drivers license soon?"

"Yeah, I suppose he will."

"Then he'll be able to drive himself around and won't need you to take him into Kelowna pretty soon?"

"Yeah, I imagine Ted will let him do that. Maybe not in the winter though. The roads can be pretty bad between the resort and Kelowna early in the morning."

"Larry, do you have a signed contract with Ted to let you stay in your apartment for a certain period of time?"

"No, it's just always been word of mouth and a handshake, which is good enough for me. He told me that as long as I'm the tennis pro here, there'll always be a place for me to stay for free and he knows I have kids that visit, so he lets me have my own apartment rather than asking me to stay where the other employees do."

"I wouldn't rely on Ted too much if I were you. I can see the day coming when he won't need to be so nice to you because he won't need you as his son's ride anymore and then he may ask you to move."

"No…no, he'd never do that," Larry said. "At least, I hope he wouldn't. Ted's always liked me and I've been a good asset to the resort."

We walked on in silence. I wondered how much Ted liked Larry's increased absences or how much he liked the unkempt state of Larry's apartment, not to mention all the money the resort was losing by not being able to rent Larry's apartment. And then there was the problem of

Larry's long distance phone calls to me. Larry had tried to tell Ted they were professional calls at first, but it became obvious to everyone that he was abusing the phone privileges he'd been given to promote himself and the resort professionally, and was asked to pay up. I couldn't see Larry's living arrangements continuing on with any certainty when his commitment to being the resort's tennis pro was dying out. I knew if I was Ted, I wouldn't feel like I owed Larry too much and I would be seriously considering asking Larry to move, for the winter at least.

"Oh, I forgot to tell you Sharon. I had Dieter's watch shortened last week and while I was there the jeweller was telling me about it. You know how much it cost?"

"No, I haven't a clue, but I imagine it was close to a thousand dollars."

"Try doubling it. It was over $2,000.00!"

"Wow, I can't imagine spending that much money on a watch. Dieter must really appreciate your friendship. You've got it in a safe place don't you?"

"Yes I do. No one will ever find it where I'm keeping it."

I wasn't sure what he meant by that, but I didn't pursue it. "Getting back to Saskatchewan Larry…I'm not sure yet when I'm going to go. When I decide I'll let you know. It's going to be pretty squished in my little Nissan with Daisy and then Billie as well on the way back. Are you sure you're up to a long, hot drive with two young kids packed into a small car?"

"Yes, Sharon. I'm sure. The main thing is that I'll be with you. The drive there will be fun because there'll only be the three of us and I'm sure we can all put up with one day of cramped driving on the way back. I'd offer to take my car, but with its 300,000 kms plus, I'm not sure we'd make it all the way. Besides we'd all be deaf by the time we were done, unless I broke down and finally put a muffler on, which I don't really want to do. I like when my car sounds like a jet engine."

"Yes, I know how your car sounds and I'll be glad when you do put a muffler on. Then maybe we could actually talk while we drove. But, seriously Larry - shouldn't you be using this time to go around job hunting since you've just finished your course? Isn't that the best time to look for a job?"

"I can't go job hunting without a resume and I still can't do my resume because my marks and certificate aren't done up and may not be for a few weeks yet, so I have to wait until then. I could use a holiday after all I've been through this summer and I want to be with you, Sharon. That's what's important to me."

I quit arguing. It was his life and if he was going to get a job the push had to come from him, not me. I wasn't his mother - I was his girlfriend. What I couldn't understand though, was how easily he gave up teaching tennis. In our first year together, tennis was the centre of everything for him. His life revolved around it, our relationship revolved around it, and here he was willingly throwing away a weeks worth of tennis lessons as if it was no big deal. I couldn't help wondering what was going on in his mind.

I also found I wasn't feeling too excited about going to Saskatchewan with him. I used to look forward to spending time with him, but I was starting to wish I had some time to myself for once. I couldn't see myself saying no to him, though - he was too enthusiastic about going and I could certainly understand his need for a holiday after the stress of his course and practicums. He did indeed manage to get Danny to do his tennis lessons for him, I got my car checked for the trip, we packed up and left the following week.

We left early in the morning so that we'd have some time to try out Larry's new binoculars at a bird sanctuary on the way. We all took turns looking at the hundreds of birds on either side of the road. The binoculars made it well worth the stop as we could see all the birds in such great detail. Then we continued on and made it to Larry's parents place in Moose Jaw in the late afternoon, where we planned to spend the first three days.

We got out of the car and stretched. It had been a long drive. They lived in a quiet neighbourhood on the outskirts of Moose Jaw with a park nearby. On our way in to meet Larry's parents, Larry said we'd go to the park after supper for a walk. We were met at the door with handshakes and hugs and then we went to sit in the living room. No one seemed to have too much to say after a short while. We all just sat there and I felt a sudden sense of unease sweep over me. The silence wasn't right somehow. There was too much tension along with it. Too many unspoken words. Finally, Larry grabbed the remote and turned on the T.V. At this, Daisy perked up and went closer to the T.V. to watch as well. I moved around the room, looking at the various pictures and momentos that were everywhere.

After supper, Larry, Daisy and I went for our walk in the park. While Daisy was off in the playground, I asked Larry about his Mom. "She doesn't seem to be any better, but is she getting any worse?" I asked.

"Not really," he said. "There's something you should know, Sharon…My Dad doesn't always tell my Mom everything. He doesn't want her to worry unnecessarily. I don't think anyone has ever told her that Theresa and I are divorced, so she may be wondering why you're still with me."

"You're kidding, right?"

"No, I'm not. Mom can't handle upsetting news, so no one tells her anything upsetting. Her health is too fragile."

"She certainly didn't seem too fragile to me when we drove into Vernon together when they were visiting. She talked a mile a minute and made a lot of sense as well. I don't think she's as fragile as everyone makes her out to be."

"You could be right, but that's the way it is around here. I'm just letting you know in case something gets said."

We played catch for awhile in the park and then headed back to Larry's parent's place. Larry's Dad had finished the dishes and both his Mom and Dad were sitting in the living room watching T.V. We watched for a little while with them and then we all went to bed at an early hour.

The next day Larry, Daisy and I went to visit Larry's Aunt and Uncle. Afterwards, Larry's Uncle gave us a tour of the brick factory where Larry had grown up. It was being fixed up for public tours. I found it very interesting, especially with Larry showing me the things he remembered. After the tour, we walked over to the house where Larry had grown up. It had been abandoned for quite some time, but you could still go in it. It seemed to bring back a lot of memories for Larry as he told me about the mischief he had got into as a kid. From there we walked towards the rolling hills directly behind the family home. They were the kind of gentle hills that just beckoned to be walked about on; short golden grass, the odd grove of bushes here and there, and many well worn cow trails. There were no dangers to these hills other than the quicksand Larry told us to watch out for in certain low lying areas. We walked for hours over the hills, the same hills where Larry himself had spent countless hours roaming as a young boy, gun in hand, searching for gophers or birds to shoot. As we walked, Larry told me that throughout his childhood he considered himself to be a loner, not that he wanted it that way, it just seemed to come from living in the country. He had been happy to spend his time alone, walking these hills when he was young, but as he got older, he wanted to go out with the other boys in his school instead.

"I wanted to do things with them," he said. "I wanted to be like them. But the only way I could do that was to get my Dad's car and he would *never* lend it to me. Never. It used to make me so mad and I could never figure out why he wouldn't let me borrow it. He'd always lend it to my sister, but whenever I'd ask, he'd always say no. I still don't know why he wouldn't trust me with his car."

"Did you maybe do something, like have an accident or something that would make him not trust you?"

"No, I never did anything like that. I never had the chance to. He just never seemed to trust me. I don't think he even liked me. I know I disappointed him," he said sadly, but then he became quite excited as he said: "And then this morning, he tells me that he gave my gun away. Can you believe it? He said he gave it to another relative. How could he do that? That was *my* gun! It was the gun I always used when I went hunting here. I'd always planned to give it to my son, to Joey, and now I find out that he never even kept it for me! It's gone."

"Did you ever tell your Dad that you wanted it?"

"No, I didn't. But he should have known that. He should have known I'd want it. It was a big part of *my* childhood." When he looked straight at me I could see hurt and anger in his eyes. "It wasn't his to give away," he continued, "and now it's too late…the damage has already been done."

I didn't know what to say. He was right - the damage had already been done and there was nothing that I could say to make it go away. Somehow he was going to have to accept it and let go of it, but I couldn't see him doing that any time too soon. I was reminded of how powerful family dynamics can be, even years and years later when everyone is grown up. Some hurts just never stopped. I decided not to dig any deeper into Larry's pain, mostly because I was afraid of what I might find out. There was only so much I was ready to know.

We left Larry's parents and drove to Southey to join my family for a few days. Since Larry had already met my parents and my brother's family during their vacation to my place a year before, I wasn't too worried about everyone getting along. But, he hadn't met the rest of my relatives, of which there are many. My brother and sister - in - law had organised a backyard party at the farmhouse where I grew up. Hot dogs, beer, softball and fun. I thought Larry would really enjoy it as he'd always seemed outgoing and interested in meeting new people before at parties. Much to my surprise, however, at this party he became quiet and withdrawn and seemed very uncomfortable as though he felt terribly out of place. He just sat on the picnic bench, both hands tucked under his thighs, glancing around with a very nervous smile on his face. If someone tried to strike up a conversation with him, just by the way of being friendly, he'd give them a short answer that usually stopped the conversation dead.

I'd never seen him act this way around people before and wasn't sure what was going on with him. Maybe he was comparing our families, maybe he was feeling outnumbered and insecure, maybe he felt out of place. I'm not sure. We never had a chance to talk about it. But, whatever the reason was, he was very glad when the party was over. For the rest of the time at my parents, however, he was very pleasant. He was talkative, helpful and happy - much more like his normal self. When it was time to go, I didn't have to do anything. He packed the entire car for us and was ready to go.

The trip back was long, hot and cramped. My car didn't have air conditioning, so none of us were very comfortable. No one talked much. Larry and I took turns driving and since we couldn't find anywhere to stay for the night, we ended up driving all the way through to Vernon, kids fast asleep in the back. We arrived in the wee hours of the morning, exhausted. It wasn't that I was hoping for some time to myself anymore - I *needed* some time to myself now.

I went to work the next day and Larry went out to the resort to see what he could salvage in the way of tennis lessons. When he called that night, he said that Danny seemed to have done a good job but there weren't many people left at the resort wanting lessons. Now that he was back, he knew he should start trying to promote the tennis aspect of the resort, but he'd lost his enthusiasm, he said, and the season was almost over anyway. Pretty soon people would be heading back for the start of school, so why bother. I didn't like the sound of this. Where was he going to get money from for the winter, I wondered?

"What about doing up your resume then, Larry? I asked. "I can help you with it, if you want."

"I thought about it," he said, "but, I still can't do it. I haven't received my marks yet."

"Are you sure you need your marks? It's getting later and later and if you wait much longer, everyone from your class will have jobs and there'll be none left for you."

"Okay, okay…let's do it, and then we can finish it when I get my marks back. "Great," I said. "Bring your stuff over and we'll do it tomorrow night."

"I'll get all the papers together tonight. By the way, Steve called from Vancouver to tell me that he's finally selling the car I've always wanted. I told him a long time ago that when he was ready to sell this car, he should call me first. So that's what he did. He wants to know if I still want to buy it. It's still in excellent shape too, he said."

"So, are you going to buy it? It sounds like a great opportunity for you since your car may not last that much longer."

"I don't have the money. He wants four thousand for it, which is a good deal because it's such a nice car, but I just don't have the money, so I don't see how I can even consider it."

"Larry, you always told me that if you ever needed money, you were sure Dieter would be willing to lend it to you. Maybe now is the time to ask him, because you do need a new car. Yours could go at any time."

"Maybe you're right," he said. "I'll ask him tomorrow morning."

After their tennis lesson the next day, Larry and Dieter went for coffee. Larry brought up the subject of the car by telling Dieter about this great car a friend of his was selling in Vancouver. Dieter looked straight at Larry. He knew exactly why Larry was telling him about this car. He also knew very well the state of Larry's financial situation.

"Do you need some help buying this car Larry?" Dieter asked.

Larry looked at Dieter, hesitated for a bit, and then said, "That would be very nice."

"I'll tell you what I'll do," Dieter said. "I'll give you four thousand dollars that will be worked off in tennis lessons between us and I will give you an extra thousand for free so that you can buy some new tires for this car. Agreed, my friend?"

"Yes, Dieter," Larry nodded. "Agreed."

Dieter took out his cheque book and wrote a cheque for five thousand dollars right then and there and handed it to Larry. "Thank you Dieter. You are a true friend."

Larry was so excited about the cheque that he brought it to my place that evening to show me. "Look at this," he said, "five thousand dollars payable to Larry Scott. This is going to look very good in my bank account."

"So when are you going to Vancouver to get your new car?" I asked.

"I don't know. My Nissan's still running so I think I'll wait awhile. No sense getting rid of it while it's still going."

"But, won't Dieter be wanting to see your new car soon?"

"I suppose. He never said anything. I'll probably go next weekend and get it." But when next weekend came, Larry said he still wasn't ready to give up the Nissan. It was a sentimental thing, he said. He'd had the Nissan for so long and driven so many places with it, he found it hard to just give it up. Every time I'd ask Larry when he was going, he'd always give me the same answer. After a few weeks, I quit asking. I figured he was going to do it when he was ready to do it and not a minute sooner. I never understood men and their cars anyway.

It appeared to me that Larry was floundering. He was not busy by any means, yet he made no effort to look for a job as a pharm - tech, even though his resume was done, and he had no plans to go to Vancouver to get the car, plus he showed no desire to drum up some business teaching tennis. To top it all off, he told me that Danny's bid to teach the juniors again during the winter had not been accepted, which meant that Larry would not be teaching them either, since he worked for Danny on that job. He started to show up in Vernon several times a week. He'd call me from different places and say he was in Vernon and would I mind if he came over. I'd let him come because I knew he wasn't quite himself, but I was feeling smothered. He was coming far too often.

My second oldest son Matt, had decided to go and live with his father in the Kootenays. Jake, my oldest son had already moved there a few months before. I'd made arrangements for us to all meet in Nakusp, a halfway point, the following weekend to transfer Matt's belongings. It also happened to be the weekend of my birthday. This would be my time away, I thought. A birthday present to myself - a weekend away from everyone. Maybe I'd go to the hotsprings, or maybe I'd just go sightseeing. Who knows, I'd do whatever I felt like doing, whenever I felt like doing it.

But, when I told Larry I'd be gone on the weekend, my heart sank. He said he'd been making plans to go to Nakusp as well, and wasn't this a coincidence. He was planning to go to pick pine mushrooms to make some extra money, while he waited for his certificate to be ready. He'd already started getting together the things he'd need to stay for two weeks. "This is great," he said. "We can take both cars and pick together on the weekend, and then you can come home and I'll stay and make my fortune."

Oh, God, I thought. How am I ever going to get some time to myself? At least, we'd only be together for the weekend and then there'd be those two weeks while he stayed and picked. And I was glad to see him finally taking some initiative about doing something other than moping around, so I bit my tongue and bided my time.

116

We packed up both cars. Larry's was packed to the brim with camping equipment and food and my car was full of Matt's mountain bike and his gear. It was a sad drive to Nakusp for me. I didn't want Matt to leave. I wondered, as did everyone else, if he was leaving because he was afraid Larry was going to move in with us, but I was afraid to ask him, in case his answer was yes, which would have caused tremendous guilt for me. We met up with Jake in Nakusp and transferred Matt's belongings and said our farewells.

Larry and I headed out to look for a good site to pick mushrooms. We had to go a few different directions and stop and ask around. By the time we found a good area, it was almost dark. We drove back and forth on an old logging road looking for some place to pull off to camp for the night. We took a chance on a narrow trail that led off the road. After a few hundred metres, it opened up into a large flat area. From what we could see with our headlights and flashlights, we'd lucked into what was once an old homestead. We decided this would be home for the next few days and Larry proceeded to set up his tent, with me holding the flashlight. In the morning, we saw, to our delight, that our campsite was perched on the edge of the shimmering, blue lake. The site was secluded, had it's own firepit and an old wooden electrical spool tipped on its side for a table, not to mention an old apple tree complete with a barrel underneath it for a seat. A perfect invitation to sit and look out over the lake, coffee in hand, after a satisfying campfire meal. On one hand I would have liked to enjoy the beauty in solitude, but on the other hand, it was bear country, so I was glad to have Larry around, although I really had to wonder what he'd do if a bear did show up. He was definitely a city guy and not a woodsman. Still, I found it comforting to not be alone.

All day Saturday we looked for mushrooms. We tried this road and that road and walked and walked, but we didn't find very many mushrooms. We weren't sure if we were too early in the season, or just not looking in the right spots. We talked to others who'd been out picking and according to them it was probably a bit early, but they could start coming anytime. A few days can make all the difference when it comes to pine mushrooms. One rain is sometimes all it takes. I didn't care. I wasn't there to make money. Just roaming around the beautiful forests was good enough for me. It gave me time to think - to sort out how I was feeling about Larry and I.

What I came to realise was just how different our relationship had become since our near break up in the spring, and especially since we'd first met the previous spring. There was a time in our relationship when I would have been very sad to know we'd be separated for a while. That feeling certainly wasn't with me any longer. Instead, I was looking forward to us spending time apart. Did I change? Did he change? Obviously, we'd both changed, or perhaps it wasn't change so much as getting to know each other much, much better. It takes time for the real person to filter through all the good intentions and favourable impressions that automatically come with a new relationship. I was now seeing Larry under stress, when the chips were down and, quite frankly, I didn't like what I was seeing. No two ways about it - he lacked ambition and drive, two characteristics I considered very important in a partner. I realised he'd be fine again if he could get his life back together, but the question was - could he get his life back together? I wasn't so sure. I knew I needed some space from him, but I also knew I didn't want to be rid of him completely. Mostly, what I wanted for us, was for him to get back into his own life, working on his own career, taking care of his own finances and future and being content within himself. If that happened, then I could see us making a go of it. And I knew if there was any way I could help him get his self - confidence back, I would do it without hesitation. But for the moment, I just wanted to be alone - even for just a few days.

The first thing I saw when I opened my eyes was Larry looking down at me, waiting for me to wake up so he could give me his present. It took me a second to realise where I was. This was a tent, not my bedroom and yes, now it's coming back to me - it's my birthday. Larry was like a little kid, "Open it, open it," he said. His eagerness made me dread opening his present all the more. I remembered the disappointment at my last birthday, and then there was the bottle of hair conditioner with a fifty dollar bill taped to the bottom of it for Christmas, so I hadn't been expecting too much in the way of a present.

I unwrapped the paper very slowly. There were two presents. Several pairs of silk panties slid onto my lap - beautiful rich colours, trimmed with lace. Unfortunately they were too small, but that was okay, I told Larry. I would exchange them for a larger size when I got back home. The other present was in a jeweller's box. It was too big for a ring, thank goodness. I lifted the lid a little and peeked inside. It was a watch! A rather expensive looking watch with a band of shiny brown imitation alligator skin. A very thoughtful gift and far too expensive for Larry's financial situation, but truthfully not the type of watch I would have ever picked out for myself. I looked up at him. He was eagerly waiting for my response. I couldn't tell him the truth. I couldn't hurt his feelings. And because I couldn't be honest, I knew I was going to have to wear this watch, no matter how tacky I thought it looked. "It's lovely Larry. Everything's lovely. Thank you very much." I put on the watch and held out my hand to look at it. It was definitely not "me", but it was Larry and a giant leap forward from the effort he put into other gifts. "Thank you, Larry," I said once more as I hugged him. "These are very nice gifts."

After breakfast, I went to sit on the barrel under the apple tree to relax and look out across the lake, admiring the way the morning sun worked at warming the night air.

Larry had finished what he was doing and came to stand beside me. "It's beautiful out here, isn't it?

"It certainly is," I answered.

Larry turned and looked at me for a long while, as though he wanted to say something but didn't know how to start.

"What is it Larry? You look like you've got something on your mind." I thought maybe he was feeling the same way I was about our relationship and wanted to talk about it.

He hesitated for awhile, kicked a stone into the lake and then said, "Nothing. It's not important." I didn't push. The last thing I wanted was to have such a gorgeous view ruined by unhappy feelings.

We stayed there for another half - hour, each contemplating in silence. When the sun had warmed our faces enough, we decided it was time to go and hunt for mushrooms. It was another glorious fall day of traipsing through the forests. We were finding some pine mushrooms, but not the great amounts we had hoped for. When we took them to the buyer, the prices were still low, but still, we made more money than we would have just going for a walk through the forest.

It was late afternoon, and I told Larry it was time I left him and headed back to Vernon. I didn't want to come home too late, as I knew my kids would have made a birthday supper for me and they'd be eagerly waiting for my car to pull up.

"You know, Sharon…," Larry said. "I think I'll come back with you. The mushrooms aren't a very high price right now and they don't seem too plentiful either, so I think I may as well head back with you instead of hanging around here."

No, no, no…this can't be happening. "Are you sure Larry?" I was desperate. "The forecast is for rain you know, so the mushrooms may start to come out and the prices may go up in a few days. You know how quickly the prices can change. Plus…plus you're all set with a good campsite and you've got lots of food and gear with you. Why don't you stay for a little while anyway and see how it goes?" Please, please stay, I thought. This isn't fair. I want my time alone.

"No, I don't want to climb around the hills all by myself. It won't be any fun without you here. Maybe we can come back together later, if things pick up."

No fun without me! Come back together! Did he have to be with me all the time? Couldn't he do anything by himself anymore? I felt so frustrated, but I could see his mind was already made up and short of me saying, "For God's sakes Larry, leave me alone for awhile," he was going to be coming back home with me. At least, I thought, we'll be in different cars.

We packed up quickly and I drove out first, with him following. I was in no rush to end the solitude I at least had in my own car so I drove the speed limit and contentedly stayed behind cars that were going the speed limit in front of me. Not Larry, however. He pulled out to pass me and the three cars in front of me on a solid line! By the time he passed the last car he was halfway into a blind corner, going uphill with black smoke billowing out of his tail pipe. He was an accident waiting to happen and I wondered what he was trying to prove by this little demonstration. I was certainly glad I wasn't a passenger in his car and I was very glad to have him zooming off ahead of me, rather than tailgaiting me. I dropped my speed even further, to let him get far, far ahead. I relaxed back into my seat, turned my radio on and was treated to the most wonderful jazz I'd heard in a long time. Not Larry's type of music at all, and I knew if he'd been riding with me he would have turned it off saying what junk it was. I drove slowly and relaxed the entire trip back. It was a most wonderful three hours.

When I pulled into my driveway, I saw Larry's car parked there. Damn, I thought. I wish he would have just gone to his place. The three kids I still had left with me came running out of the house saying happy birthday and telling me to come in, come in - there's a party waiting for me. Such great kids, I thought. Unfortunately, Larry was also waiting for me.

It was indeed a nice birthday party. The house was decorated, a delicious supper was served and for dessert, a forty - one candle cake complete with presents!

Larry wanted to go home after the party, rather than staying the night. He had some things he wanted to take care of, he said. I didn't ask him what they were. I was just glad he was going home instead of staying. For the rest of the week, Larry stayed at his place and only called occasionally.

Finally, some time to myself to think, which was something I certainly did. I had many discussions with myself, all pertaining to Larry and I and my kids. What was to become of us, I wondered? I believed the natural progression of a relationship was to go from dating to living together, so obviously living together was on my mind. That was the next step - but could I actually live with Larry? There were problems everywhere I looked if we did; financial problems; kid problems; ambition problems; space problems in my house and in my life. Did I really think we had the kind of relationship where we could discuss these problems and overcome them? No, not at the moment, but if Larry could get back on solid footing - maybe. And what about my kids? They were leaving me and I felt hurt by their leaving. I knew they'd all leave eventually, and then what would I have? Nothing. So why not partner up with someone now, who wouldn't leave me - someone I'd have when everybody else left? What to do? What to do? Clearly, this was not a predicament that was going to go away any time soon. It required time and more thinking, or at least so I thought. One thing I did know for certain was that nothing was going to work until Larry got himself back on his feet, and as much as he was starting to drive me nuts with his dependency, I was determined to help him do this if I could. I felt it was my responsibility to at least try and make things work.

One of Billie's great desires was to put a fish pond in our backyard. She'd been working at it for the past few months, but was finding it rather hard to do by herself. She was only twelve years old at the time. There was a lot of hard digging needed, plus a two foot retaining wall to keep the dirt from sloughing onto the lawn. I told her that if she does the digging, I'll put up the rock wall for her. Larry offered to help me with this on the weekend. An offer I gladly accepted as it was a large project.

We started eagerly one Saturday morning. It didn't take long, however, to see that we were going to have some problems working together on this project. Larry seemed to assume that he knew more about cement and rock walls than I did, simply because he was a man, and he told me so. He refused to acknowledge the experience I'd had from helping my ex - husband on large rock wall projects in the past. I knew I had more experience than Larry when it came to rock walls and mixing cement, but he couldn't and wouldn't accept this fact. He became sarcastic towards me, making fun of the way I wanted to lay the rocks and telling me I was mixing the cement all wrong.

"Here let me show you how to do it."

"So tell me Larry…how much cement have you mixed in your life?" I asked.

"Back in Saskatchewan I'd help my uncle mix cement for granary foundations."

"Really? How many granary foundations did you pour and how old were you then?"

"I was in my teens and we poured a couple at least and the way you're going about it is certainly not the way it's supposed to be done."

"Well, I helped my ex - husband do an awful lot of rock work and cement mixing for the stone foundation and retaining walls on our house and this is how he taught me to do it, and it always worked fine for us. And don't forget that this retaining wall was my idea and I know how I want it to look in the end and you don't."

We glared at each other for a few moments and then Larry went back to mixing cement and I went back to laying rocks. He mixed and I laid the rocks for the rest of the afternoon, layer after layer, never speaking a word to each other. By the time we finished, though, our egos were back to their proper size and we stood back together to look at our handiwork. We were both satisfied with the end result.

"I think we should let Billie put the date into the wet cement," I said. "After all, this whole project has been her idea from the start."

Larry agreed and we went into the house to tell Billie. Before I could even say anything, Larry blurted out, "Billie, we know how much you've always wanted this pond, so we decided," he glanced over at me...did he see my eyes narrowing...I doubt it because he turned back to Billie, "that you should have the honour of inscribing 1995 in the cement to commemorate the year the pond was built. But you've got to come and do it now before the cement hardens."

The jerk! How could he do this? This was my daughter, my rock wall, and my idea! And he was just taking over as though he had the right to bestow this privilege on Billie. This wasn't even his property! Whose high horse was he on anyway? I was fuming, but rather than embarking on an emotional scene in front of Billie, I just followed everyone out to the pond muttering to myself under my breath. I watched her inscribe 1995 with Larry directing her where to put it and how to put it there, smiling at her, smiling at me, but I wasn't smiling back. I started to clean up and Larry, sensing my seething anger helped till the clean up was done and then said he needed to go to his place and couldn't stay for supper.

It took me three days to forgive Larry, during which time I didn't want to see him or talk to him, I was so mad at him. But after three days, surprisingly, my anger vanished. I decided to chalk the whole experience up to a lesson well learnt. *Never* again should we *ever* try building something together. We just don't work together that way.

I'd calmed myself down, I was going to be okay, it was in the past and I was now ready to go forward once again.

Two days later, I got a phone call from Larry in the middle of the afternoon. He sounded upset. "Sharon, I'm in Vernon and I need to talk to you. Can I come over? I've just had some very bad news."

"What is it, Larry? What's happened? You don't sound very good."

"I'll tell you when I see you. I'll be right over."

What on earth could have gone wrong now, I wondered. He came into my house looking frantic. "What is it, Larry?"

"Ted told me I have to move out. I can't stay there anymore! I think I'm still in shock."

"Oh, no. This couldn't come at a worse time for you," I said. "What did he say? Does he want you to move for good? Is he letting you go completely, teaching tennis and everything?"

"No, he says I can have the tennis job back next summer and while I'm doing that job, I can stay where the rest of the staff stays, but he won't let me stay at the resort for the winter when I'm not teaching and I won't be able to have that apartment anymore. They're going to rent it out next year. I don't know how he can do this to me. He knows I've got two kids that come to see me and he knows I didn't have a very good season. I don't know what I'm going to do, Sharon. I don't have enough money to rent and I don't know what's going to happen with Danny and teaching the juniors this winter. They're still not sure if they're going to give the job back to him or not." He looked so afraid and hurt. "Ted wants me out by mid - October. That's not even a month!"

I felt sorry for Larry, sitting there on the edge of my bed, looking so worried, but quite frankly, I would have done the same thing, had I been Ted. His job was to manage the resort and Larry's half - hearted attitude towards promoting the resort's tennis capabilities over the past summer did not leave the resort looking too good. Plus, if Larry would have stayed another winter without cleaning his room the way he'd been asked to by the house cleaning staff, a fumigator would have been needed to make his room liveable again. It wouldn't have surprised me either, to find out that Ted knew all about Larry stealing toilet paper and soap from the housekeeper's storeroom when he thought no one was looking. And as it turned out, Ted's son was indeed now driving himself to the gym for tennis lessons in the morning - tennis lessons that Larry was probably not going to be teaching unless Danny got the contract again. Ted did not need Larry anymore and I can't say that I blame him. Larry hadn't taken care of his position or place at the resort. Looking at Larry, though, it was obvious he would never have agreed to any of this. He felt he had been terribly wronged and was visibly upset.

"What are you going to do?" I asked him. "Have you got any plans?"

"No. He just told me an hour ago and I drove straight to Vernon to talk to you about it."

Half of me wanted to help and say "move in with me," and the other half wanted to say "you created this problem, you deal with it." My softer half won, as it usually does.

"You can stay with me till you get yourself sorted out Larry. That way you won't be forced to find a place right away."

"Yeah, I thought that would be the obvious thing to do. Why don't we try living together until April and if it doesn't work out between us, I'll move out and never bother you again?"

Whoa! That's not what I said...October till April? That's six months! "No, I don't want to set a specific time, Larry. How about if either of us decide at any time that it's not working, you move out - no questions asked?"

"Sure, okay. But you'll see...it'll work out. The only thing is - I don't want to just move in without it being okay with your kids."

"Right, I'm glad you thought of that. I'll ask them how they feel tonight and let you know."

He was looking much more relaxed than when he first came. I was glad to help him, but I had an uneasy feeling in my stomach that I couldn't ignore. Was it really going to be okay? I wasn't so sure, especially the way I'd been feeling about him lately, and where were we going to put all his stuff? My house was already full with all our stuff.

That night I told Tom, Billie and Daisy what had happened and asked how they'd feel about Larry moving in for awhile. Tom said he didn't care, just as long as I was happy. He added that he didn't like Larry very much, but since he'd be at his friends places a lot, it didn't really matter how he felt. Billie said she didn't like Larry and didn't like the idea of him moving in and being around all the time. She liked it the way it was with just the four of us living together, so her vote was that he wouldn't move in. Tom and Billie's answers didn't surprise me. It was obvious that neither of them liked Larry. I was pretty sure Daisy would want him to move in though. She'd always liked him and often talked about wanting to have a "live in" Dad. When I asked her, she answered with the kind of enlightenment and honesty that a young child often has. "I don't want him to live with us, Mommy. He treats me like I don't know anything, and I know lots. The other night when he was reading me a story, he talked to me like I was a baby. And I'm not a baby. I'm gonna be 7 years old!"

What could I say? She'd hit the nail on the head. He treated us all as though we didn't know anything, whereas he—the man - did.

I called Larry later that night and told him what the kids had said - they would rather he didn't move in. He assumed I was talking only about Tom and Billie. He asked what Daisy had said, and I told him that she also said "no" because she thinks you treat her like she doesn't know anything and the other kids said they want their space to themselves. I felt it was important to tell him exactly how they felt. I didn't want to make excuses for them.

There was silence on the other end of the phone. I knew he'd be upset at this news. How could he not have been? He'd thought for sure Daisy liked him and I knew he liked her.

"Look Larry, I know this isn't pleasant news for you. Just take a few days to think about it. Then we can get together and sort it all out. I'm sure we can come up with some kind of plan."

"Yeah, okay, sure…fine."

"I'll call you in a couple of days, okay?"

"Yeah, whatever. Bye."

I felt awful after I hung up. I understood how devastated he must be. It had seemed pretty certain that he was going to be able to move in with us when we'd talked earlier in the day, and now that appeared not to be an option anymore, and for a reason that must have hurt deeply. He'd certainly seemed to have more than his share of bad luck lately. But then I stopped myself - the bad luck he'd been having was actually nothing more than the end result of his own actions and decisions. He'd caused these problems for himself. He needed to quit blaming everybody else and take some action that showed he could stand on his own two feet. Maybe move in with a friend in Kelowna - or Connie for that matter. She'd probably be willing to help him out till he could find something on his own. It certainly wasn't the end of the world. I hoped he'd be able to see it that way too after he had some time to get over the initial shock.

I let a few days pass. I wanted him to have some time to think things out. The weekend was coming up, which I thought would be a good time to get together and work out our problems and see what could be done, so on Friday afternoon I called him at the resort to set something up for the weekend, just as I had done time and time again for the last eighteen months of our relationship. I could tell that he didn't sound right as soon as he said hello. I asked if I could come to the resort one day on the weekend so that we could talk things over.

"I can't this weekend," he said. "I won't have any time. I'm getting my hair dyed tomorrow and on Sunday I'm going to Salmon Arm to visit with my friends. I'll mail Daisy's birthday card to her."

Never in our entire relationship had Larry said he didn't have time to meet with me. He'd *always* made time for me, plus his friends in Salmon Arm were friends that he'd been anxious for me to meet ever since they'd moved to Salmon Arm a few weeks ago. He'd often mentioned how great it was going to be for us all to visit and get to know each other. And mailing Daisy's birthday card! Her birthday was a week away and he'd always wanted to be there for her birthday before. I didn't like the sounds of this at all. It was completely out of character for Larry.

"What's going on Larry? I asked. "Are you breaking up with me?"

He didn't say "yes" and he didn't say "no". Instead he said, "I've been doing a lot of thinking Sharon, and I realised for the first time that our relationship really has nowhere to go. All you ever think about is your kids and I think you spend way too much time with them and are far too concerned with them."

Tears started coming. This was not what I was expecting. I managed to say, "So, this is it then?" I left lots of time for him to answer. I wanted to hear him say it wasn't over, that we should just take some time and cool down, but he never said a thing. There was just silence. After what seemed like forever, I said, "I guess this is good - bye then," and still I waited for him to say something, but there was nothing. I said good - bye and slowly hung up the phone.

This had been a shocking turn of events. I felt like I'd been blindsided. I sat at my kitchen table for awhile, tears flowing freely, feeling numb, not able to think. Then the shock wore off and anger took its place. After all I'd done for that guy, after all I was willing to do, he turned around and said I wasn't any good! The nerve of him!

I had to do something physical. I went outside and mowed my lawn with a passion - up and down, back and forth, tears still streaming down my face in a combination of hurt and anger. I tried and tried to make sense out of what had just happened. How could he do this to me? Why would he do this? And then - all of a sudden - I saw it too! I stopped mowing. Larry was right! Our relationship didn't have anywhere to go! We couldn't go forward and live together because of what my kids had said about him, and we couldn't go back to where we had been because we could never pretend that none of this ever happened. We were stuck...we couldn't go ahead and we couldn't go back. The only thing left was to split up and go our own separate directions. He was right! He'd been able to see our predicament, while I was still forging ahead, blinders intact, trying to push, pinch and squeeze our relationship into being something it could never be.

I finished mowing my lawn feeling light as air thinking about what my life would be like without Larry in it. No more worrying about Larry's ability to get a job. No more worrying about Larry's living predicament. No more crowding. No more worrying about Larry's lack of ambition, his finances, his emotional state, his car, his kids, my kids, driving back and forth to the resort, long distance phone bills - no more worrying, period. I could even take his watch off and get one that I liked! I was free, truly free...and it felt great!

I wanted to let Larry know that I agreed with him about breaking off our relationship. I was afraid he might have plans to go mushroom picking after coming back from Salmon Arm. I knew a letter would never reach him in time, so I decided to call and leave a message on his answering machine. I explained in my message that I agreed with him about breaking up, that he was right about our relationship having nowhere to go, and that I'd be writing him a long letter to explain more about how I felt. I also told him that I would send the stuff he had at my house to the resort via a mutual friend. Then I sat down to write the letter. It was important to me to explain exactly how I felt so that he would know and have it in writing. When I was done, I went to the mailbox and dropped it in.

I had no idea just how much weight and worry I'd been carrying on my shoulders from the relationship, until it was over and the weight was lifted off. I felt light enough to fly. The bounce in my step and the twinkle in my eyes came back. There was absolutely no way I would ever consider going back into that relationship. It was most definitely over. The relationship had lasted eighteen months, from April 14, 1994 to September 23, 1995.

I went around my house, putting everything I could find of Larry's into a box to give to my neighbour to give to Larry next time he saw him and then, I went grocery shopping. That night at supper, I told my kids my relationship with Larry was over. They were very happy for me, except for Daisy who wondered if she was ever going to be able to have a live - in Dad.

"He just wasn't your type, Mom and we're really glad that he's not going to around anymore," they said. They went on to tell me everything about Larry that irritated them, now that they felt it was safe for them to say exactly how they felt. They hadn't wanted to hurt my feelings before. Most of it I already knew. I just hadn't wanted to think about it. But I was surprised when Daisy told me that Larry would sometimes bite her ear when he was tickling her and she didn't like that she couldn't get away from him sometimes. Now that just sounded weird to me and I wasn't sure what to make of it. Billie was worried that I would have been willing to abandon her in favour of Larry, if it ever came down to having to choose! It was plain to see that Larry's presence had driven a wedge between me and my kids and I was very glad to know this wedge was now gone. I learned that intimate relationships could come and go, but family ties were forever.

I was getting ready for bed, still feeling light and happy, when the phone rang. It was Larry. He'd come back from Salmon Arm and had listened to my message in horror.

"I didn't say I wanted to break up, Sharon. I don't want to break up. How can you say it's over?"

"What do you mean, you didn't want to break up? When I asked you if this was it, you never said anything. How did you think I was going to take that?"

"I don't know how you take anything anymore. I only know I don't want to break up. I don't want it to be over."

"Well, I'm sorry Larry, but for me, *it is over*. I realised that this afternoon after we talked. For me, there's no going back. That's not something I could ever do. I've mailed you a letter that will explain everything."

"I don't want to read it in a letter. I want you to tell me."

"Okay. I'll tell you what I said." If he wanted to hear it from me, then that's how it was going to be. I went on to tell him exactly how I felt. I told him that from the very first I had the feeling that he wasn't my type and that I had ignored that feeling, but it seemed to prove true in the end. I said I felt that he was too old for me in his thinking, that he seemed to be stuck in the 50's and I wanted to be in the 90's. I also said that I found his attitude towards his financial situation very disappointing. It wasn't so much that he didn't have much money, but that he didn't show much drive to improve his situation and as an example I pointed out that he hadn't even taken care of his income tax yet, as he said he would do time and time again. I told him his relationship with his children bothered me, as I didn't like his lackadaisical attitude towards his responsibilities towards them, having them over only when it suited him, and not taking seriously the fact that he owed his ex - wife over $3,000.00 in child support. I also did not like his attitude towards my children and I didn't see him making any changes to try and work things out with them and that because of this discord, I often felt torn between him and my children.

"I've told you all of this Larry, because you need to know exactly how I feel. And that's the key. This is how *I* feel. You are the person you are and I know that people shouldn't have to change to suit someone else. I wouldn't want it that way anyway. There's nothing wrong with your qualities - they're just not the qualities I'm looking for. I'm sure you'll find someone who is attracted to the person you are…it's just not me. You'll be getting my letter in the next few days and then you'll have it in writing too."

"It's not that easy Sharon," he said. "I don't want it to be over."

"But it is Larry. It *is* over. I'm not changing my mind. I'm not coming back. It is over. You'll get my letter and then maybe you'll understand it better.

He was quiet for a moment. And then he said, "Do you remember when we were sitting by the lake in Nakusp on the morning of your birthday?"

"Yeah, I remember. Why?"

"You asked me if I had something on my mind. I said I didn't, but actually I did. I was going to ask you to marry me, but I was afraid you'd say no, so I chickened out. I wonder if things would be different now if I had asked you."

This was a surprise. I had no idea he'd been thinking about marriage at that time. But what was even more shocking to me was the sudden realisation that I probably would have said yes, simply because I wouldn't have had the guts to say no, being the "avoid all conflict" type of person that I was. And where would that have ended up, I asked myself in horror?

"I had no idea Larry," was all I could say. "It just didn't turn out that way."

"About exchanging our stuff…I don't want you to give my stuff to your neighbour to bring here. I've always been a private person and I don't want everybody knowing what happened. How about if I meet with you when you finish work on Monday? I'll be waiting in the hospital parking lot and you can give it to me then. And I'll bring your stuff too so we can exchange things there. Will you do this one last thing for me?"

I didn't want to. I truly did not want to see him face to face. I knew it was a backwards move, but a part of me argued that I owed it to him after what had just transpired between us. Just this once, I thought, just this once and that'll be it.

"Okay, Larry. I'll be finished at 12:30 and can meet you in the parking lot after that. But Larry, remember…it's over. I want to make sure you understand that completely."

"Yes, Sharon. You've made that very clear. I still think you're wrong, though. I'll see you Monday at 12:30."

I put the phone down. It shouldn't be this way, I thought. It's over and yet here I am meeting with him when I really don't want to. I felt the weight settling back down on my shoulders.

Part II

Sharon Velisek

The Stalking

<u>Author's Note</u>

The following section of this book shows the sequence of events as they occurred, to the best of my knowledge. The conversations and information regarding Larry's lawyer, doctor, counsellor and friends is taken from the transcripts and statements issued for the Coroner's Inquest into Larry's death, which took place in the fall of 1996. During the actual time I was being stalked, however, I was not aware that Larry was involved with these people whatsoever. It was only during the Inquest that everything was disclosed. The interaction between the police is taken from my actual police file (see Appendix) and the police testimony at the Inquest.

In Part II I've attempted to put all the events into chronological order to give the reader a "birds - eye" view of how innocently stalking can develop, hoping this will help increase the public's awareness of the dynamics involved in stalking. You will be able to follow the actions of everyone involved, from the break up right through to the emotional turmoil that enabled Larry to pull the trigger.

<u>Monday, September 25, 1995</u>

Monday came, and I was dreading meeting with Larry after work. I had all his stuff in a box in my trunk, hoping it would be a quick "here's your stuff" exchange. As I walked towards my car in the parking lot, Larry saw me and got out of his car. He was visibly shaking from head to toe - obviously very emotionally upset, yet he was trying to smile. He tried to talk, but his voice started to crack. So he stopped, trying to get his emotions under control before continuing on. When I saw how emotional he was, my control broke down as well. I didn't do much better at talking than he did.

I opened my trunk and he opened his. We started to carry things from one car to the other. It was difficult. Breaking up had been so much easier when I was writing the letter, or talking over the phone. He'd put all of my belongings into a box, which I took from him. But he'd also brought back all the firewood I'd split on our mushroom picking trip for some reason. This took awhile to haul back and forth, and by the end of it, my brave front had given way to tears, as had his. He asked me again why I was breaking up with him. He just couldn't understand why I was willing to give up something that was so good. I tried to explain it to him again, but this was so hard to do now that I could actually see the hurt on his face. I needed to get out of there. We said our good - byes once again. As I was driving past Larry, he called out to me. I stopped my car and rolled down my window to hear what he had to say.

"Sharon, I forgot to tell you...look, I know what a nice person you are and that you're probably planning to get me a present for my birthday in October or take me out for supper or something, but I just wanted to tell you not to worry about my birthday and you shouldn't buy me a present or anything like that. I'll be okay. I just wanted to tell you that."

He's sure got me pegged wrong, I thought...I'm not that nice of a person. I'd never even thought about his birthday since the break up, and I had no intentions of ever talking to him again, but I didn't see where trying to explain that to him would do anyone any good right then and there. So I just said, "Okay, Larry. I won't. Good - bye," and then drove off.

"Good - bye, Sharon. I love you," I heard him say as I drove away.

All I could think about on the way home was how glad I was that this relationship was finally over. I didn't need any more emotionally charged meetings like the one we'd just had. Later that night, I called Dieter and Vicki and told them that Larry and I had split up. I asked them if they would offer whatever help they could to Larry, because he didn't seem to be handling it very well from what I could tell in the parking lot. They said they'd already been talking to him and would most definitely help in whatever way they could. I felt much better knowing this, as I knew they meant every word of it.

Wednesday, September 27

I was finishing up at work, doing some last minute photocopying with my back towards the door, when I heard Larry's voice behind me.

"Hi, fatso. I just wanted to bring you back your BC Tel Calling Card."

Shocked, I whirled around and saw Larry standing a few feet away from me, hand outstretched, holding my card. His arm was shaking so badly, the card would have fallen except that he was squeezing it so tightly that his knuckles had turned white. I reached for the card and before I knew what was happening, he grabbed me and pulled me towards him. He put his arms around me and was holding on to me for dear life. I was trying to push him away, but he wouldn't let go. After a tussle, he finally released me.

"Sharon, I need to talk to you. I've just got to talk to you. Come outside where we can talk. I have to talk to you. Please, Sharon. Please come and talk to me...just for a little while."

I told him to sit down and directed him to the chair opposite my desk. "Sit here and wait till I'm finished work. I can't talk to you right now, but if you can be quiet and let me finish what I'm doing, I'll talk to you for a bit. Then I have to go to meet someone." He fidgeted and stared at me the whole time he waited, but he was quiet.

When I finished, I looked at him and asked where he wanted to go to talk. There was no place that I could think of in the hospital where we could talk in private, and I wanted the conversation to be private because I had a pretty good idea how emotional it was going to get. The hallway or the cafeteria was not going to do. Larry suggested his car in the parking lot. I hesitated. I knew it wasn't the smartest thing for me to agree to, but I couldn't come up with a better idea on short notice, so I agreed.

As soon as I closed the door to his car, he reached over and put his hand on my thigh and tried to kiss me.

"Keep your hands to yourself, Larry and don't even think about kissing me."

"Okay, okay. It's just that it's so nice to be close to you again. I miss you and I just want to touch you."

"Larry, it's over. You know that, so stay on your side of the car. What did you want to talk about?"

He put his hands in his lap and hung his head. "I'm not handling this break up very well, Sharon. I can't quit thinking about you. It's driving me crazy." He looked over at me. "You're my only friend, so I'm asking you to be my friend now and help me, as a friend, through this break up. You're strong Sharon. You've always been the strong one. I'm not. If you don't help me, I don't know what I'm going to do." He reached over and put his hand on my thigh again.

"Take your hand off, Larry." I waited until he did. "Look, this break up hasn't been easy on me either, but you're a lot stronger than you think. And it's not true that I'm your only friend. You've got Dieter and Vicki...they've always been good friends to you and you've got your kids too. As a friend, my advice to you is to become involved with your family again instead of looking for someone else's family to move into. When things get tough, families can help, if you turn to them. And what about Connie and Danny. I'm sure they're more than willing to listen to you and help."

"But none of them are like you. You know everything. You know me better than anyone else. No one can help me like you can." And again, he tried to kiss me.

This was becoming difficult. I was trying not to become emotional, but I could feel the tears welling up inside me. I hated being the source of Larry's pain. I felt so guilty. "Larry, please...stay on your side of the car. I don't want you trying to touch me...I don't want you trying to kiss me. I'm just here to talk," I said, trying to be gentle. "I don't think I can be the friend you're asking me to be, but I'll think about it and let you know. I called Dieter and Vicki last night to ask them if they could help you in whatever way they could, and they said they'd already been in touch with you and were more than willing to help, so I know that even if I can't be there for you, they will be. You don't have to be alone."

At this, his mood changed suddenly. He became quite upset. "You talked to Dieter and Vicki? Who gave you the right to talk to them about me?"

"I knew you'd be hurting and I wanted to make sure you'd have friends to help you, so I called them." That seemed to calm him down. He sat there looking so sad, so helpless, so pitiful with tears silently sliding down his face. My emotions were taking over too. I had to get out of that car. "I have to go Larry. I have to pick my sister up from the airport."

"Let me give you a ride home."

"No, I want to walk." As I got out of the car I told him I would think about being his friend and would let him know what I decided. I closed the door, saying good - bye and started to walk away. He quickly made a U - turn and came back to follow me as I walked along the sidewalk. He had his window rolled down and kept calling out to me, "Good - bye, Sharon. I love you...I love you...Good - bye...no one will ever love you as much as I do...Good - bye..." It was torture.

Finally, I was able to cross the street and get onto the hospital grounds where he no longer could follow me. I felt drained, and I knew then and there that I could never handle being the friend he was asking me to be. He was going to have to rely on his other friends. As soon as I got to my place, I called and left a message for him saying how I'd thought about it all the way home and decided I could not be the friend he was asking me to be because it was just too difficult for me emotionally. And that I was sorry, but he was going to have to look to others for friendship and support. I also told him he was to *never* try to contact me again.

I left for the airport to pick up my sister, Jennette. She'd come to visit for a week. She couldn't have picked a better time. I was so glad to have someone to talk to about everything that had happened. It helped me sort out how I was really feeling.

After our discussion at the hospital, Larry drove to Kelowna to see his doctor, Dr. Spelding, for an appointment Larry had made specifically to discuss the problems he was having with the break up. During this appointment, he told Dr. Spelding that we'd had a good relationship for 18 months prior to the break up and that he found himself to be quite devastated by the break up, especially because it had ended so suddenly with no particular warning that it was ending. He couldn't understand why he was having difficulty handling this separation when he had no trouble handling the termination of his ten - year marriage. He felt it must be because it ended so suddenly. They also discussed whether or not I was getting any counselling or if there were any plans for Larry and I to have counselling together.

Dr. Spelding explained to Larry that perhaps I was going through an "awakening", meaning that because I had not been in a relationship for several years since my divorce, I had possibly come to an awakening after 18 months in this relationship, that love and happiness were not all I required - that I needed a partner who could also offer financial stability. Larry agreed that I had indeed stated that his lack of financial stability was one of the reasons I ended the relationship.

They discussed the benefit of Larry taking an antidepressant called Luvox®. It was known to have very few side effects, other than drowsiness. He wanted Larry to try a small dosage and report back to him after a few days to see if the medication was being tolerated and if it was appropriate for Larry to continue on with it.

September 28 to October 1

Larry spent a great deal of time talking to his friend Connie at the resort during this time period. He asked her if she thought he'd ever find anyone who would love him when he doesn't have any money. She was supportive as best she could be and would try to get Larry to talk about other things, but he'd always come back to the break up. She'd ask him to play tennis with her to take his mind off of me, but they usually ended up talking over the net about the break up and would end up going for coffee instead and continue discussing the break up. She asked him to come for supper often, as he was becoming very thin and obviously not taking care of himself, but he always refused, saying that he just couldn't seem to eat. And then one night he called her on the phone: "Listen Connie…Do you want to hear it? Do you want to hear Sharon's voice on the tape?" Larry had apparently not erased my messages on his answering machine.

"No, I don't want to hear that, Larry. You're becoming obsessed with her. You've got to go and get some professional help." But Larry told her that he was seeing a doctor already, which was a great relief to Connie as she knew he needed more help than she could give him.

Meanwhile, I was trying to carry on with my life. The emotions that had built up in me from the last two meetings with Larry and the break up in general, finally took their toll. I had to leave work early one day as I kept feeling like I was going to faint. I knew it was just from all the stress. I went home to lie down for the rest of the afternoon. I was fortunate to have Jennette staying with me to help out and to talk to and I started to feel better towards the end of the week. Together, Jennette and I organised Daisy's birthday party. She was turning seven. I was worried that Larry might try to show up at the birthday party, but he didn't. In fact, the whole time that Jennette was with me, Larry never attempted any contact with me whatsoever. I felt that he must have indeed gone to his friends for support and found the help he needed, for which I was very thankful.

Monday, October 2

Larry went back to see Dr. Spelding as planned. He had taken the Luvox® a couple of times and said he was feeling much better, especially over the last twenty - four hours. However, he stated he did not wish to continue taking the antidepressants and would rather get through this with counselling instead. Dr. Spelding knew that there was no way the Luvox® could have been making any difference yet, as it takes two to three weeks before the benefits would show up. But, if Larry wanted to try counselling and was feeling better, then Dr. Spelding would support him in this. He explained to Larry that he needed to see the positive side of things, instead of the negative, and that the relationship had given him eighteen months of happiness and now he should be looking at developing a plan of action for himself, instead of focusing on the past and the fact that the relationship was over. It appeared to Dr. Spelding from this meeting, that Larry was getting better.

Friday, October 6

As I lay in bed thinking before falling asleep on Thursday night, I decided that in the morning I would get up very early and take my car to Canadian Tire to have the oil and fuel filter changed, a necessity that was already overdue and had become all the more imperative as my car had not been running smoothly at all. As the kids and I were getting ready on Friday morning, I told them that I had to leave very early because I was going to drop the car off at Canadian Tire, then walk to work. I was running late, so I was in a rush when I opened my car door to jump in. I was stopped in my tracks, however, when I saw a white powder evenly scattered all over the front seats and dashboard of my car. It was one of the strangest things…I couldn't figure out what could have happened. I tasted a tiny bit on my finger and discovered it was sugar. I was truly baffled, but I was also in a rush. I brushed the drivers seat clean and jumped in the car and drove to Canadian Tire thinking that maybe they could figure out why I had sugar all over the inside of my car. I arrived shortly after they opened and explained to them about the sugar I had found in my car interior, and asked if they could figure out how it might have got there, as well as do an oil change and replace my fuel filter. I told them I'd be back after lunch to pick it up, gave them my keys and proceeded to walk to work at the other end of town.

When it came close to lunch, I called Canadian Tire to see if my car was ready so that I could come and pick it up. They told me that it was, but asked me why I was calling again.

"What do you mean, calling again? This is the first time I'm calling."

"Well someone just called here asking about your car. They said they were calling on your behalf and wanted to know if your car was ready and how much it was going to cost. It sounded like a woman's voice."

What the heck was going on? First the sugar and now this. "Look, it wasn't me who called you before and I have no idea who it could have possibly been. My concern is that someone might be trying to scam my car. You guys know what I look like, so whatever you do, don't give my keys to anyone else but me. I'm just leaving work now so I should be there in half an hour."

I walked as fast as I could to Canadian Tire, wracking my brain the whole time trying to figure out what on earth was going on. Who could have possibly called in my place and why would anyone have wanted to? It just didn't make any sense to me at all.

As soon as I walked in the door, the service man behind the counter told me a man had just come to inquire as to when I was going to pick up my car and had then gone back into the store to wander around and wait for me. They described him as blond, thin and lanky. I knew at once it was Larry. I was outraged. The nerve of him! This relationship was supposed to be over. I'd told him I didn't want to see him again, yet here he was, waiting for me.

I thought if I could write my cheque quickly, maybe I could get out of there before Larry would see me, but I was not quick enough. As I was writing, he came sauntering up to the counter and said, "Oh, Hi Sharon. I was just here visiting a friend and happened to see your car in the parking lot, so I thought I'd stick around and say hello to you."

It rolled off his tongue so easily, I almost bought it. But then I realised if it was the truth, it meant that Larry drove for an hour and fifteen minutes to visit a friend who was at work and would have no more than a few minutes to spare for a visit, plus, this was a friend Larry had never bothered to visit before, whether at work or not, so why now?

I ignored Larry and asked the men behind the counter if they'd been able to figure out how the sugar got inside my car. They were baffled, they had to admit, but they figured it was probably a prank of some sort - maybe some kids putting sugar in my air vents, or something like that.

Larry listened to us talking about the sugar and acted surprised and very concerned.

"What happened Sharon? What's going on?"

I kept ignoring him and continued discussing the situation with the servicemen, but it soon became apparent that I wasn't going to get any answers from them and I wanted to get away from Larry as quickly as possible, so I thanked them and said good - bye.

But before we dispersed, Larry had to add his two bits, "It was probably just kids playing a prank, you know. Kids do that sort of thing."

I walked outside. Larry followed me.

"Could I talk to you for a few minutes, Sharon? I just have a few questions I need to ask you." And then without even waiting for my answer he started talking quickly. "I'm better now, Sharon. I started seeing a counsellor, and isn't it ironic that all the time I thought it was you that needed to see a counsellor and here it was me that needed to see one? But I have been, and I'm taking medication too and I'm doing so much better with the break up and I just wanted to tell you that. Do you think we could go somewhere and talk? I just want to talk to you for a few minutes."

"No, Larry, we can't. Whatever you have to say to me you can say right here and you better hurry, because I'm in a rush," and I started walking over to where my car was parked.

"Why won't you be my friend Sharon? I don't understand it. Can't you just explain to me why?"

"Just what do you mean by 'being a friend'?" I asked. "Tell me what that means to you."

"Well, you know...a friend. Someone I can call if my car runs out of gas in the middle of the night on Westside Road - that sort of thing."

That was the strangest definition of friendship I'd ever heard. "No, Larry. I am *not* going to be your friend. You have other friends who can help you out with that. I've already told you that."

I opened my car door to get in, but before I could get in, he put his hand on my door and stepped in between me and my front seat. "Wait, Sharon," he said. "I want to ask if you and Billie and Daisy will go to the Armstrong Fair with me. It's coming up soon. What do you think? Will you go with me?"

I couldn't believe what I was hearing. I'd made it perfectly clear on several occasions that I wanted nothing more to do with him, that our relationship was over, that we were through, and yet here he was asking me and my daughters to go somewhere with him! Why wasn't he getting any of this?

I turned to face him. "No, Larry. We will not go with you."

"Why? Why not, Sharon? I want you to tell me why not." He was becoming upset.

"I don't have to give you the reason why Larry. We're simply not going."

"Yeah, well you're not the only one who has something to say about this relationship. I've got something to say about it too, you know. You might have decided to break it off with me, but it's *my* decision to keep it going. As far as I'm concerned, we're still going to be friends."

"But Larry," I said, "it doesn't work that way. In order for two people to be friends, both people have to be willing to be friends, and as I've said before, I am not willing to be your friend."

He took a step towards me and I backed up. "You know, just because you don't want to see me anymore doesn't mean you have the right to keep me from seeing Daisy. That's between Daisy and me and has nothing to do with you." He was becoming more and more agitated. He took another step towards me and once again, I backed up. I felt the car door against my back and realised I couldn't back up any farther.

"It most certainly does," I said, trying to sound strong. "I'm her parent and as her parent, I'm saying that you are not allowed to see her and have no right to see her." I'd never seen Larry act like this before and I was becoming frightened. His eyes looked wild and his face was getting redder all the time.

Another step closer brought him far too close to me, but I couldn't get away. He had me pinned against the car door. He reached out and tried putting both his hands under my sweatshirt on my waist. "Get your hands off of me." This was too much! He was irrational, agitated and pushy and I was scared. With a sudden surge, I flung myself past him and ducked into my car. He backed off and I grabbed my door and slammed it shut. I took off as fast as I could. He must have taken off equally fast from wherever he was parked because he was soon following me, honking his horn, trying to get my attention. I ran the tail end of a yellow light, thinking that would get rid of him, but he followed me right through on the red. He came up in the lane beside me, honking and waving at me. My heart was pounding. I was afraid he was going to follow me home, and then what? I shouldn't have signalled to make the turn leading to my place, but I was so rattled, I couldn't think of anything else to do but head for home. Fortunately though, when I took the turnoff to my place, he kept going. I was tremendously relieved, but I still kept checking in my rear view mirror for him all the way home.

I pulled into my driveway feeling like a wreck. I was exhausted already and it was only mid afternoon. I got out of my car and just happened to glance along the side of the car. I noticed, for the first time, that there were small white clumps all around my gas flap. I reached inside the driver's side and popped the gas flap open and discovered hardened sugar clumps all over. That's when I knew I had sugar in my gas tank. I also noticed there was an area halfway down my driveway that still looked wet, even though the moisture from the night had dried everywhere else.

I went in the house, called Canadian Tire and told them that I had just discovered there was sugar in my gas tank. They were quite surprised as that was something that had not occurred to them to check for.

"What do I do now?" I asked them. "I have no experience with this sort of thing, whatsoever."

"Whatever you do, don't drive your car, as that would wreck the engine completely." They gave me the number of a mechanic who knew how to deal with sugar in a gas tank. I called him right away and explained the situation. He seemed very knowledgeable and helpful and we made arrangements to have the car towed to his garage first thing in the morning. At the end of the conversation, he asked, "So, who's mad at you?"

"I can't think of anybody who'd be mad at me, especially not someone who'd be mad enough at me to do this."

"Have you recently broken up with someone then? Have you got an angry boyfriend?"

"Oh, my God...Yes, I have!" That was the first time it occurred to me that it could have been Larry that put the sugar there. Up until that point in time, I still assumed the sugar was some sort of prank, with Larry coincidentally showing up. I hadn't linked the two.

"Then more than likely, he'll be the culprit. Generally, people think sugar in the gas tank is a common prank, but it isn't. In my thirty years of being a mechanic, I've only seen it happen a few times and never has it been a prank. It's always been planned revenge and usually involves an angry ex - partner. Have you touched the gas cap yet?"

"No, I don't think so. Why?"

"Give the police a call and see if they can come and fingerprint it. That'll tell you who did it for sure."

I thanked him for all his good advice and told him I would see him first thing in the morning. Then I called the police. The receptionist took the information and told me a constable would call me back.

A few hours later I got a call from the police. I explained to the Constable about the sugar in my gas tank and my recent break up with Larry and that hopefully fingerprints could be taken from the gas cap to establish who put the sugar in my gas tank. Unfortunately, the Constable said the only way they could take fingerprints was if the gas cap had a smooth surface, which mine did not, therefore they would not be able to do this. He did, however, confirm that Larry would indeed be the primary suspect given the circumstances and he asked if I wanted him to go and have a "talk" with Larry about the whole situation. I was feeling very harried after everything that had happened that day and all I could think of was that I did not want to have any more connections with Larry, plus I did not want Larry to be unnecessarily accused as that would only give him an excuse to call me or try to see me again, which I dearly did not want to have to go through. Plus, I simply did not want to accept that this was happening to me. After all, this was not the movies, it was just my normal everyday life.

"No, I don't want you to talk to him yet. I'm not even sure it was Larry who did it." I said.

"Okay, but I want you to keep a record of anything and everything suspicious that happens to you. Constable Morrison will be assigned to your file, so ask for him whenever you call." Then he gave me a file number to quote anytime I needed to call.

I went to lie down for awhile.

As I lay there, I tried to piece everything together…Larry must have been trying to figure out a way to meet me that appeared accidental so that he could talk to me, since he did indeed have a question for me about the Armstrong Fair. He must have put the sugar in my gas tank the night before thinking it would cause my engine to require repairs fairly quickly and since he knew that I always take my car to Canadian Tire, all he would have to do was watch for when my car was in their parking lot and then call to see when it would be ready. After that, all he needed to do was hang around the store until I picked it up so that he could "accidentally" bump into me and talk to me. To make matters even more plausible, he did indeed have a friend that worked at Canadian Tire. But what Larry didn't know, was that I took my car in for a regular oil change, not sugar in the gas tank.

Still, I couldn't believe that the Larry I knew could have devised, and carried out, such a diabolical scheme. He didn't seem the type, especially with how down and out he'd been since the break up. I reasoned that it had all worked too well for Larry to be the one orchestrating the whole thing. It was definitely a possibility, I had to admit, but I couldn't bring myself to truly accept it was Larry, because that would mean my encounters with him weren't over yet, and I wasn't ready for that.

Over supper, I talked to Tom, Billie and Daisy about everything that had happened. We discussed all the possibilities: was it Larry, was it someone else, was it someone from long ago who wanted revenge, was it some of my kids' so called "friends" who wanted revenge, was it someone who had mistaken us for someone else? On the other hand, if it was Larry, what on earth was he up to anyway? Why would he do something like that? They couldn't make sense of it either. It was all too weird. Kids being kids, they mostly wanted to continue on with their lives and hoped, like I did, that the whole thing would just blow over.

Regardless of whether it was Larry who put the sugar in my gas tank or not, there was one thing I knew I had to do the next day, and that was to take steps to protect Daisy from being snatched by Larry after what he'd said at Canadian Tire. Since he felt he had the right to see her without my permission, I could see him trying to do exactly that. Besides waiting at the bus stop with her, I decided to tell all the neighbours what had been going on and ask them to keep an eye out for him. I also explained the situation to her day care and school, and even took them a picture of Larry, so they knew who to look for.

I went to bed early, but at 10 o'clock the phone rang, waking me up. It was from Larry - for me!

"Hi, Sharon. I just wanted to say I'm sorry for getting so worked up at Canadian Tire today. I just want to talk. Can you just give me four good reasons why you want to break up with me? That's all I want to know."

He's becoming a recurring nightmare, I thought. I knew I'd given him these reasons a few times already. He even had them in writing, but for some reason he wasn't acknowledging them. I decided to tell him once more and this time without becoming emotional and hope he'd finally get the message. "First of all Larry, you're not financially stable and you seem to have no real desire to better your situation. Secondly, your attitudes are too old and narrow for me. Thirdly, I don't like the relationship you have with your kids or my kids and fourthly, we just seem to be from two different generations. It's like your stuck in a generation gone by. It's over between us Larry, and *I am not going to change my mind.* When we first broke up, I still respected you, but after everything you've said and done lately, I've lost whatever respect I ever had for you and if I ever meet you anywhere again, I'm going to walk right past you as though I don't even know you...so you should just - *leave - me - alone.*" No more tearful emotions for me. I was angry.

"Yeah, well you have despicable teeth and black gums and..." I didn't want to hear the rest, so I hung up. But the strangeness of what he said, gave me goosebumps.

Monday, October 9

Dieter and Vicki invited Larry over to their house for Thanksgiving supper as they were very concerned about Larry's health. Dieter saw how thin Larry was progressively becoming when they'd meet for their regular tennis lessons and they hoped to get a good meal into him at Thanksgiving, as well as try to help him emotionally. It was not difficult to bring up the subject of the break up as that was all Larry ever talked about anyway.

"You know Larry, it's Sharon's right to break up. This is what can sometimes happen in a relationship," Dieter told him, "but what you have to do now, my friend, is learn how to cope with the situation and concentrate on getting on with your own profession and your own life." Words from the wise, as Dieter had been through many difficult times in his own lifetime and had managed to overcome them and remain a wonderful caring person.

"But Dieter, we had such a good relationship. You saw us. We were happy together. How can I just let something like that go?"

"I'll tell you how to do that. You think about other things. You think about your life, ahead in the future, not in the past. Now, tell me Larry…have you gone to Vancouver to pick up the car I lent you the money for?"

"No, I can't possibly go now Dieter. I'm having too hard of a time with this break up."

"But that is exactly what you need to do to get your mind off Sharon and onto something else."

"No, I can't do it Dieter, not now anyway."

"Okay then, not tomorrow, but soon - soon you should go. And what about apartments. Have you been to look at any apartments?"

"No, I haven't done that either. But I did talk to Ted and he gave me an extension, so I don't have to move out until the middle of November now."

"Good. You go to look at some and when Vicki and I come back from Germany a couple of weeks from now, we will go with you and help you. Agreed?"

"Yes, Dieter, that would be nice. I wish you weren't going away."

Wednesday, October 11

I hadn't heard from Larry since his phone call apologising for his behaviour at Canadian Tire, four days before. I was crossing my fingers that my message actually got through to him. But somehow I knew that would be too easy.

I'd just arrived home from work on Wednesday after lunch, when the phone rang. I answered it, but instead of hearing "hello", I heard the click of someone hanging up. That infamous "click". I held the receiver while fear grew in my gut. I tried to reassure myself that someone had just dialed a wrong number and that I shouldn't jump to conclusions, but I knew better. I "knew" it was Larry. I knew it for certain.

I snapped out of my daze, realising I needed to try and verify where the call had come from. I dialed *69 and got a number, but I didn't recognise it. I called it and let it ring and ring, but there was no answer, so I called my friend who worked for BC Tel and told her what had happened and asked her if she could trace the call. It turned out that it came from a pay phone that was across the street from the same parking lot at the hospital where I always parked my car, and Larry too when he was working at the hospital. Next to the payphone, was the parking lot for a grocery store. From that parking lot Larry could easily watch me getting in or out of my car without being noticed. And then I remembered the binoculars he owned. It started to dawn on me just how easy it was for someone to watch and harass another person without being detected. This was starting to get scary.

I decided to take whatever precautions I could to make my house and kids safe. Using common sense, I went to the hardware store and bought different locks for my entrance doors so I didn't have to worry about Larry using the keys he still had. I also bought the hardware for installing peepholes into both outside doors so that I could see who was on the other side before opening the door, and a motion detector light for my carport. It cost more money than I had to spare, but I didn't feel I could do without them. I came home and installed everything right away. Then I went around to every window in the house and put pieces of wood along the bottom of them, so they could not be slid open from the outside. When the kids came home, I cautioned them once again about watching out for Larry, especially Daisy, who I had to make sure understood that Larry was no longer someone to be trusted. I drilled into them the necessity of keeping all the doors and windows locked at all times, even if they were in the house. I made sure they all had a key and told them they had to take it with them whenever they were out, because it was impossible to get into the house without one. I had made very sure of that.

Even so, sleep didn't come easy anymore.

Thursday, October 12

The next day at work, I had to walk from my office on the fourth floor to the front entrance of the hospital on the main floor, to mail a letter. As I was walking back to my office, I saw Larry coming towards me in the main hallway! I was very surprised to see him all of a sudden, just like that, coming towards me and smiling yet, especially after what I'd said to him on the phone about walking right past him if I ever saw him again. My heart was beating double time, but I managed to stay calm and kept my eyes looking straight ahead. I walked right past him as though he wasn't there.

"Sharon," he called after me. "I discovered I still had your house key and I just wanted to return it to you." I didn't want to tell him it didn't matter because I'd changed my locks, so I felt I had to stop and take the key or he'd figure it out for himself. I stood there, not saying a word, waiting for him to take the key off his chain. He was shaking so badly, this took him awhile to do. As he was working away at trying to get the key off his key chain, he told me that he had come to the hospital to put in his resume at the pharmacy for a job as a pharmacist technician. I still said nothing. I took the key from him and headed back to my office. By the time I got up to my office, I was the one who was shaking badly. Why does he just keep showing up like this? Why can't he just be gone and out of my life? I was worried about him getting hired at the hospital. If he did, my life would have been a living hell as then he would have a legitimate reason to be there. So, I called the hospital pharmacy and spoke to one of the pharmacists that I knew there. "Jordan, I need to speak to you about Larry Scott. Has he just been to see you about a job?" I asked.

"Larry Scott? No, but I did see him sitting in the cafeteria when I went for lunch and I chatted with him briefly. Why? What's up?"

"Please, Jordan. I know I'm overstepping my boundaries here, but please, whatever you do, don't give Larry a job as he's been showing up and pestering me ever since we broke up and if he was to work here, it would make my life impossible."

"Oh, don't worry about that," he said. "I have no intentions of ever hiring Larry."

"Whew...that's a relief." I thanked him and my lucky stars.

That afternoon, I took stock of my situation. This relationship was supposed to be over, not continuing on and on with unexpected appearances and phone calls. What bothered me most was that I seemed to have absolutely no control over the situation. Nothing I had done or said to Larry so far was making any difference. I'd tell him I don't want to see him again and yet he'd keep showing up. I'd tell him it was completely over and yet he'd ask me to be his friend time and time again. And why was it that he never seemed to understand or acknowledge the reasons I gave him for the relationship being over, when I'd told him very clearly several times? Why wasn't he getting it? What else was I supposed to do? My emotions alternated between frustration, confusion and anger, and underlying my every thought was the presence of this growing fear that I couldn't seem to shake or control, no matter what I tried. I'd never experienced anything like it before.

Saturday, October 14

Larry spent his Saturday writing a nine - page letter to me explaining where I'd made my errors in thinking about our relationship. He also took the letter I wrote to him when we first broke up and wrote comments in the margins, also pointing out my misguided thinking. When I came home from work Monday afternoon, I found his letter waiting for me in my mailbox. After all that had transpired between us, I was appalled that he had the audacity to continue to contact me.

His letter reads as follows, *exactly* as he wrote it:

My Dearest Sharon!

I am writing this letter in partial response to your letter, but also to show you how wrong you are on ending our relationship and throwing a fantastic life away.

First of all I <u>did not</u> say I was not going to move in with you and your family. You said to take a few days and think about it, I was doing that and really looking forward to living together as a family. Repairing your house over the winter - what a great

162

project, going skiing, skating, and even trying snow boarding, and just doing everyday family things.

Second, I was taking a couple of days because I did not just want to move in, but to get engaged, I felt it would be good for all of us, it would show our commitment to each other, but also to your children. Instead of Daisy saying Mom's boyfriend is living with us, she would say Mom's fiancé or my #2 Dad is living with us.

Then in April we would have had time to know if we should get married or go our separate ways. You didn't even ask me what I was going to do, you just drew your own conclusions. For two people who said they would never go to bed angry with one another, but sort things out, you certainly fell short on that promise.

I thought we put a lot of money in the bank in our relationship, but I was wrong, as you could not talk to me to solve these problems, but instead came to a rash conclusions that are totally wrong.

Once again you are mistaken, I <u>did not</u> make a decision not to move in with you and your children. I am sorry you told Daisy that I wouldn't be moving in because that was not my feelings. Once again you formed your own conclusion not even discussing this with me.

It makes me laugh when you say from the first time we met, you thought to yourself you don't look my type. As my doctor explained, first impressions nine times out of ten are wrong and do not represent the person.

Sharon you still need help in counselling with your inner feelings. You must tell your partner when something bothers you rather than keep them bottled up inside you as they will never go away but will build up to such a point that they will destroy all your relationships that you get into. You will be in and out of relationships the rest of your life - and you are much too nice a person for that to happen. If you were true to me you would have discussed these problems so we could work them out.

163

I laugh when you tell me that I am too old for you. Believe me you are the <u>oldest</u> woman I had a relationship with. I was holding back because I knew that you can't keep up to me. You spoke about going to bed earlier because you need more sleep than me. You spoke about going dancing. I was the one that suggested we take two step lessons, take various night courses at the rec. centre.

I love to go to partys, Connie and Cliff invited us to many but we never went because we had to get back to Vernon to see your family, but I didn't mind that as <u>you</u> were one of the most important people in my life.

No Sharon we arn't from two different generations, you just kept these inner feelings to yourself and did not communicate with me about these problems.

I would have looked forward to going to party's as a couple and living it up together. Yes I too love to let my hair down and live life to the fullest, it would be really a lot fun doing it together as a team.

I know we didn't go out much, simply for many reasons, two that come to mind are (1) It tore my heart out when we left to go out and Daisy was so upset crying out from her bedroom window "I don't want you to go". (2) Our finances weren't as rich as we would have liked them to be, but things would have only gotten better.

Once again Sharon I never said "It just didn't work out, so goodbye". You are forming your own conclusions without discussing any of this with me. Yes my love for you is true, more than you probably will ever realize, you may have other relationships in your life but, you will <u>never</u> have anyone love you as <u>true</u> and <u>deep</u> as I do.

You say talking to me was difficult and a lot of times I wasn't really interested in what you were saying - this is <u>totally</u> <u>wrong</u>. Again you are drawing your own conclusions - wouldn't it have been nice to have brought this problem up in conversation and say "Larry this is what is troubling me, am I wrong in *thinking this?' or "can we work this out". Yes, it would have taken a lot of strain off you, if you would have only let me know.*

You suggest that you need someone financially stable. I did not take this pharmacy course not to become financially stable, sure since I moved up to the Okanagan I have been a tennis coach, not the strongest financial position in the world but with my pharmacy, tennis coaching it will provide a very stable financial income. Sharon this will probably fall on deaf ears but I must say it anyways "You may find someone that has more to offer financially, but he will fall short in true deep love. One day you will realize that true love is far more important than any financial gains; however, it will probably take you some years down the road before you can come to terms with this".

You say that I can't change because I am the person that I am. Not true. As of next week I am working in construction, coaching at Hedley's and hopefuly very shortly will have a position in a pharmacy in Vernon.

You see a person can change if they want to and I will because having being in a relationship with you and your family I would have had more responsibility and besides its time for me to work hard after moving up from Vancouver and enjoying life.

I'm sorry you felt torn between me and your children. I tried very hard for your children to like me. I cut their hair, never forgot their birthdays, X - mas and graduation. I took them fishing, got up in the early morning so they could catch the bus to go snow boarding and even offered them a beer from time to time. Helped them to buy a belly boat and just tried to be a friend.

I know we could have worked things out as I suggested that we go to counciling and read books about step families. I was prepared to do all of this, but I guess you weren't.

I realize your children are the most important thing to you and I accept that - No problem!! I feel sorry for Daisy, because she accepted me as a second Dad and I was looking so forward to fulfulling that role, we would have real magic times together, all of us.

If moving from your house upsets the children we didn't have to move, we could have reconditioned the entire house and spent the other revenue on holidays and material things, that would have been fine with me - All this could have been discussed.

Sharon we did not have a relationship for 1 1/2 years because we just wanted to have fun. Both of us spoke about different levels of relationships, and we both were working on the marriage level. You love me and I love you, but when we had a conflict the first thing you do is arrive at a hasty conclusion that is not true. Phone your sister who I met only once, speak to your friends who don't know me. You listen to their expertise rather than discuss our relationship between the two of us. It's like being married Sharon, you have to work with a relationship. Just imagine we were married and we had a conflict, instead of working it out, you phone your sister to solve the problem - doesn't make sense!!!

No Sharon, it hadn't crossed my mind to just carry on. I want us to learn from this. The only way I would get back together is if you would receive more counseling in regards to your inner feelings. I would even be prepared to go with you if you feel this would help.

Yes, I have more to offer than just my love. I now can offer you financial stability from a pharmacy tec, tennis coach and numerous other positions as well as a mind with "Mega Memory".

I try not to look at this, but in the future I will be inheriting a substancial amount of money, so down lifes road finances won't ever be a problem.

I have been over to see Joey and Anna and they both have been here with their friends. We have an excellent relationship. I explained to them that it was my fault that I did not see them as often as I should have, they are happy and understand.

I'm sorry for coming around and seeing you when I knew it was upsetting you. I just could not stand to be away from you more than one week at a time. I realize this is wrong and I have driven you further and further away. I even tried just to see you without talking to you, as I thought it would help me but I was only fooling myself. Once again I'm very very sorry. I love you too much.

I'm enclosing a birthday card for Billie with $20.00. I know her birthday is in November but don't know exact date. Although Billie and I are not close, with work this could be overcome.

Sharon my door is always open, I still feel counseling is the only way to go.

Loving you forever,
Larry
P.S. (1) Phone and talk to me
(2) Read this letter 10 or 15 times.
(3) Could you run off a copy or two of the first 2 pages of my resume.

Thanks Sharon - Luv you very, very, very, very Much!!!!!!

This was a difficult letter for me to read. It conveyed a great deal of blame. After reading it, I discovered I still harboured some guilt for not wanting to get back into the relationship, even though I was tremendously angry at Larry for not leaving me alone when I'd asked him to so many times. Our break up was obviously causing him a great deal of emotional distress, for which I still felt partly responsible. Sometimes I felt that perhaps I owed it to him to try again, but in my heart and soul, I didn't want to and I was firm on that. So then, why - why did I still feel guilty after all that had happened since we broke up?

On the day I received Larry's letter, he had been to see Dr. Spelding for his third visit. Either Larry brought a copy of the letter he'd already mailed to me or he brought a completely different version of the letter to show Dr. Spelding, asking him if he thought it was appropriate to send to me. The timing is very strange because I received Larry's letter in the mail the very same day he saw Dr. Spelding. It was postmarked Vernon and Dr. Spelding's office was in Kelowna.

Dr. Spelding read the letter over and told Larry he felt it was appropriate to send as there was nothing threatening in it and it would give me the option of reading it or throwing it away. However, he was concerned that Larry was having enough difficulty with the break up that he was on the verge of having real problems with staying away from my house. Larry confessed that he was finding himself going to Vernon and trying to see me and phone me. Dr. Spelding wanted Larry to go back onto the antidepressants and told him to seek increased counselling, which Larry agreed to do.

At one point during the week, Connie and Larry met for their last visit together before she went to Calgary for the winter. With Connie leaving, Larry was losing a friend he'd been able to count on when things got rough. Connie was very worried about him as he still wasn't eating and was becoming progressively obsessed with the break up, rather than showing signs of getting a handle on the situation. He still hadn't found a place to live and although he'd been trying, he'd been unable to find a job. And now he was having to wave good - bye to Connie too.

"Oh heavens, who am I going to see for emotional support now?" Larry asked her when they were saying their good - bye's.

"Well, there's always Danny and you can see Dieter and you can call me collect anytime you feel like it. Everything's going to be okay, Larry," Connie answered. She said good - bye crossing her fingers that time would take care of things.

Thursday, October 19

Daisy and I decided to go to the Mall to look for a pair of rubber boots for her. We walked from one end of the mall to the other, purchased the boots and were walking back again when I heard Larry's voice calling me from behind.

"Sharon, Sharon," he said. I decided to ignore him and kept walking, but then he started to call out to us louder and louder. People were turning to look at us.

"Sharon, don't walk away...why don't you want to talk to me...I only want to talk to you for a few minutes...can't you even stop and say "hi" to an old friend?"

If I would have been alone, I would have kept on walking, but as it was, I didn't want to make Daisy go through all of the embarrassment she was sure to feel if we continued to walk and Larry getting more and more vocal. We stopped and turned to face him. He came up to us quickly. He talked to Daisy first, asking her how she was doing and how her birthday was. She took safety in hiding behind me and answered him briefly from there, all the while clutching the bag holding her new yellow rubber boots.

He turned to me and said, "Sharon, look...I'm having such a hard time with this break up. Things aren't going well at all for me. Won't you please reconsider being my friend and helping me through this? Even if you could just meet me once a week or so, just to talk things out…I know that would help me…if I could sit down and talk with you instead of someone who doesn't know me, doesn't know you, doesn't know us. It's just that I can't seem to get past our relationship, no matter how hard I try. I even followed you to your bank once, just to see you from a distance. I thought that would help me, but it only made it worse." He was pleading so hard, I'm sure he would have got down on his hands and knees if I'd have asked him to.

"I don't know Larry." I was very, very leery. "There's been some awfully strange things happening to me since we broke up."

"Really! What do you mean? What sort of strange things?" Larry asked.

"Like sugar ending up in my gas tank and…"

"Oh, yeah," he interrupted. "I heard about that when I met you at Canadian Tire. You were talking to those guys about how it got there."

"So, I don't know Larry…" I continued. I really didn't want to agree to what he was suggesting, but I didn't know what else to do. Everything I'd tried up to that point hadn't worked to keep him away from me, so what did I have to lose to try it his way? Who knows…maybe it will work. "I suppose it wouldn't hurt to try," I said slowly. "I could meet with you once a week for awhile to see if it will help you, but it's got to be at a public restaurant and if it looks like we're not making any headway, I'll call the whole thing off. Just remember though, this is to help *end* the relationship, not to start it up again."

As soon as I agreed, I felt a heaviness settle onto my heart. I felt as though I was damned if I did and damned if I didn't. I simply didn't know what else to do.

Larry, on the other hand, almost jumped ten feet in the air. Ecstatic doesn't even begin to describe his happiness. Jubilation was written all over his face—eyes sparkling, an ear to ear grin, just like a little kid that's won a trip to Disneyland. I stood there and watched this transformation in awe, and I made sure I kept my distance. We arranged to meet the following Friday at a Vernon coffee house in public view. He readily agreed to talk only about getting over the relationship.

Daisy and I turned to leave. All the way out I was thinking - What have I done? What have I done?

I lay in bed that night trying to put some sense to everything. And then, out of the blue, it hit me...I hadn't been talking to the guys at Canadian Tire about sugar in my gas tank when Larry was there. We'd been talking about sugar in the inside of my car, not the gas tank. I didn't even know I had sugar in my gas tank when I was at Canadian Tire. So then, how did Larry know about the sugar in my gas tank? I hadn't told him - the guys at Canadian Tire hadn't told him. The only way he could have known about it was if he was the one who put it there! Why didn't I see this before I agreed to meet with him? How could I miss such an obvious implication? Was it emotion, was it fear, was it confusion that made me so blind? Maybe a little of everything, as I was definitely in unfamiliar territory.

Larry's statement should have been proof positive for me that he'd put the sugar in my gas tank, but for some reason, instead of accepting this, my mind was doing everything it could to come up with excuses and dance around the fact. Was I being paranoid and just making things up, I wondered? I somehow could not picture Larry sneaking up to my car in the middle of the night with a bag of sugar hiding under his jacket. No one who knew him could ever imagine him being able to do something like that. He'd always appeared to be too much of a "good guy". Plus, a scene like that was just too dramatic to fit into my ordinary life. And what about seeing him in the Mall? Could it have simply been a coincidence? After all, he'd once contemplated working with the fellow who had a demo set up at the time in the mall. Maybe he just saw me walking by and decided to try one more time to talk to me. On the other hand, why would he drive all the way from the resort to Vernon to see this fellow when they were neighbours at the Resort? My head was spinning from trying to figure out what was true and what wasn't. I wanted to be fair, but I didn't want to be gullible. But most of all, I did not want to be in this situation. Period.

Sleep finally came.

Friday, October 20

In the morning I went out to my car to go to work. As soon as I opened my carport door, chills ran down my spine. My beautiful little car had been badly scratched during the night! Someone had come into my carport and put three rows of scratches the full length of both sides of my car, as well as two deep vertical scratches on the driver's door, like a tic - tac - toe game. It had been done with a very sharp object, as parts of the scratches had cut deep to the metal, with paint curling at their edges. I sensed an enormous anger emanating from the person that made the scratches, just from the way they were placed. This wasn't a prank. This was vandalism directed at my car and my car only as no one else in the neighbourhood had any scratches on their vehicles.

On one hand I was relieved to know it couldn't have been Larry. No one who was as happy as he was in the mall could have ever scratched my car this way. But then, if it wasn't Larry, who on earth was it? I tried to think of every possibility as I drove to work, no matter how bizarre it seemed, but I couldn't come up with anybody.

As soon as I walked into my office, I called the RCMP and asked for Constable Morrison. I told him about the car scratching and the meeting in the mall and how happy Larry had been when I agreed to meet with him once a week for awhile, which ruled out Larry, so what did he think I should do now?

There was a pause. "Sharon...Larry is still your number one suspect...two and two does make four. And you know, sooner or later you're going to have to break it off with him too," he said. "You can't keep agreeing to meet with him. That just drags it out and makes it harder in the end for everybody."

My heart sank. It was amazing how much I didn't want it to be Larry. I was eager to jump at any explanation that excused him. And why? Why was it so difficult for me to see him as the man who'd been stalking me? My fear and confusion had been growing, clouding my mind, but there was more to it than that. At some level I felt that if it was not Larry, there wasn't much to worry about as sooner or later the police would discover the motive behind the vandalism and bring it to an end. It was pretty straightforward, if that was the case. However, if it was Larry, then what he was doing was bizarre. His motives were bizarre. His reasoning was bizarre. And his success rate was frightening. That was not a drama I wanted to be part of. I did not want to be the target of whatever plot his obviously troubled mind cooked up. So, I denied his involvement for as long as I could.

Later that day, I told Suzanne, the research nurse I worked with, about my meeting in the mall with Larry and the scratches on the car and that I had foolishly agreed to meet with him on Friday at a coffee shop.

"Are you nuts?" she said. "This guy is getting dangerous, Sharon. You should not be meeting with him anywhere - ever."

"Yes, I know that now," I said. "But I already told him I would and I don't want to have to call him to tell him that I won't meet with him. Maybe it won't be so bad. Maybe we can actually sort something out."

"Look, if you don't feel you can get out of it, then I'm going to be there too. I'll stay in the parking lot in my car and if he tries anything, you just signal me and I'll be there in a flash to help you," Suzanne offered.

I appreciated Suzanne's concern very much and I could certainly see that she was right about not meeting him. I doubted he would actually try anything, but I was sure glad to know she would be there if he did.

Saturday, October 21

I was working outside in front of my house on the weekend, and I happened to notice my neighbour across the street, a few doors down, doing the same thing. I'd been unable to think about anything else since my car had been scratched the previous morning so I took this opportunity to go over and talk to my neighbour to let him know what had happened and to ask him if he'd noticed any suspicious behaviour around my place lately.

"Come to think of it, my daughter had mentioned that she'd been woken up Thursday night by a loud car that was parked close to your house," he said.

"What do you mean - a loud car?" I asked.

"She said it sounded like the car had no muffler and whoever it was, left it running for over fifteen minutes!"

As soon as I heard the words "no muffler" I knew. It *was* Larry. It had been Larry all along. Finally, I accepted it. No more excuses, no more denial. I was being stalked by this man, this very cunning, very emotional, very distraught, and very determined man. This was not the Larry I had dated. This Larry I had never even met before and he scared me right down to the bone.

I became frantic. I lay awake at night analysing my situation: what should I do, what shouldn't I do, what will he do next? I couldn't make myself relax from the absolute fear I was feeling no matter how hard I tried. Its grip was relentless.

I wanted help. I needed help. I'd been unwillingly dragged into a situation in which I had no previous experience or understanding and I had no idea what needed to happen to make it all stop. Now the police - that was a different story. I was confident they would know how to handle my predicament since they'd probably dealt with many cases similar to mine. They were, after all, the police and certainly would have been trained to deal with people who are harassing you. Up until this point, I'd only called to report what had been done to my car. But now, I felt different. I wanted the police to make sure Larry never bothered me again. I didn't care how they did it, I would leave that up to them. I simply wanted him stopped, and the sooner the better.

I wrote out a detailed diary of *everything* that had happened since we broke up. Then I took this, as well as the letter Larry had sent to me, to the Vernon RCMP station on Monday after work.

<u>Monday, October 23</u>

I parked my car in the RCMP parking lot, got out and looked over my shoulder and all around. I wondered where Larry was watching from. Perhaps he'd followed me from work, parked a block away and now had his binoculars out and was watching my every move and I could hear him wondering why I would be going into the RCMP station. Good, I thought. I hope he's watching and I hope he's worried.

I walked into the station and went directly to the reception window. I asked the clerk there if I could speak to Constable Morrison and gave him my file number. Unfortunately, the desk clerk said that Constable Morrison was not on duty that day. Not on duty! Now what was I supposed to do?

"Look," I said to the receptionist, "I think I'm being stalked and I've written a diary of everything that has been happening to me. Please, take a look at it and tell me what I should do."

He read it over and looked up at me, rather concerned. "I think you should meet with our Watch Commander - Constable O'Riley. He'll be able to discuss your situation with you."

Relief, gratitude, thanks - I felt them all. Things were going to be okay, I thought as I heard the locked door between the outside world and the safe haven of the RCMP station click open, and I was invited in. It was like walking into a secure vault where no harm could possibly follow me. It was the first feeling of relief I'd had from my growing fear and I seriously thought I might be able to convince the police to let me camp in their station for awhile, just for a break from the ever present terror I was experiencing outside their doors.

Constable O'Riley escorted me into his office. He could easily have been nicknamed the "Jolly Green Giant". Not only was he a very large, towering man, but he also had the face and eyes of a good - hearted and understanding man. I liked him right off the bat. Surely, he was the man who could help me, I thought.

I explained my situation to him and handed him my diary. He took his time and carefully read through every word, as I watched him in silence. Then he looked up at me, sighed and leaned back in his chair.

"This has got to be nipped in the bud," he said.

I couldn't have agreed more. "What do you think I should do about meeting Larry this Friday?" I asked.

"You definitely should not go to meet him, that's for sure. It's better to have no contact whatsoever with these kinds of guys. Just let me handle it. I'll give him a call right away and get him to come into the station here and I'll give him a good talking to. That's usually enough to scare them into stopping this silly behaviour."

Yes, I could see where getting a good talking to by this giant of a man would certainly scare me and hopefully it would scare Larry too. I knew Larry had a healthy respect for the police from a hit and run that he had been the victim of a few months before. He would not take a "talking to" by the RCMP lightly.

It was also nice to be taken seriously. So many times in the past weeks I thought that maybe I was making too much of everything and that my paranoia was unfounded. Even my kids told me I was making too big of a deal out of the whole thing. But obviously, judging by Constable O'Riley's reaction, this was indeed serious and I had come to the right place. He was going to take care of it. What a relief!

As I was getting up to leave, Constable O'Riley assured me that he would call me and let me know how things went between him and Larry. I thanked him and went back out, into the land of civilians and crime, scanning for Larry's car as soon as I stepped past the door.

I did, however, sleep quite soundly that night knowing everything was actually going to be alright. I felt much better and wished I hadn't waited so long to go to the police for help to begin with.

Tuesday, October 24

The next day, Constable O'Riley and Constable Morrison discussed my situation. Constable Morrison tried to call Larry's place a few times, but was only able to get the answering machine. He left a message telling Larry it was in his best interest to call the station and sort out the situation he was getting himself into.

Later in the day, I called Constable O'Riley to see if I could bring the rest of Larry's belongings that I'd found around my house to the station so that Constable O'Riley could give them to him when they met. After having sugar put in my gas tank and my car scratched, I found I wanted nothing more in my house that had any connection to Larry. I destroyed all the pictures I had of him and any momentos that reminded me of him. I put the computer disc containing his resume, the tennis racket he gave me, his half of the photographs from our Saskatchewan trip, some old hunting pants and a few other things I'd found around the house into a black plastic garbage bag and took them to the station. I gave the bag to the person at reception and asked him to give it to Constable O'Riley. He looked puzzled as he took it from me, but said he'd make sure Constable O'Riley got it.

It was like housecleaning. The police were doing their part and I wanted to do everything I could to tie off loose ends so that it would truly be over. To this end, I called Dieter and Vicki in the evening - just to let them know what Larry had been doing to me and that the police were now involved. I knew they'd be trying to help Larry as much as they could and would be able to do a better job of this if they knew everything that had been happening, as I was doubtful Larry would willingly tell them he'd put sugar in my gas tank, scratched my car and followed me around Vernon.

Dieter, I discovered, was still in Germany, but was due home soon. I talked to Vicki, however, for quite some time and told her everything. She told me they'd already been trying to help Larry, but were having very little success. Now that they knew the whole story, she said, they would certainly see what more they could do. I asked that they please not tell Larry I had called. This information was for them only. The last thing I wanted was for Larry to turn away from friends who had a chance of helping him, simply because he'd found out I'd talked to them. He needed a friend and I most definitely did not want to disrupt any of his friendships, not because I cared about Larry's well being anymore, I was way beyond that by this point, but I knew that if Larry got better, then he would quit bothering me, which was my ultimate goal. Vicki assured me she would talk to Dieter when he returned home and that they would both keep it to themselves and do their best to help Larry get a grip.

I felt satisfied. I had done all I could. It was out of my hands now.

Wednesday, October 25

Larry had an appointment with Dr. Spelding on this day, but cancelled it without giving a reason.

Thursday, October 26, 1995

It had been two days and I still hadn't heard from Constable O'Riley as to what transpired between Larry and himself. Since I hadn't heard anything, I assumed they would have to be meeting for sure on Thursday, as that was the last possible time for Constable O'Riley to let Larry know I wasn't meeting him for coffee on Friday. When I went to work Thursday morning, I decided to park in a completely different parking lot at the hospital. I was afraid that after talking with the RCMP, Larry would be so angry that he would want revenge and would try to do something to my car again. The hospital has four different patrolled areas for staff to park in. I picked one of them and parked my small blue Nissan between two big trucks, thinking it would be hidden from view, just in case Larry did come looking for it. It was a good try, but it didn't work. I came out to the parking lot after work and noticed some very deep scratches low down on the drivers door. At first I thought that another car door had slammed into it and left the marks, but then I realised the scratches were not in the right place for something like that. I was still trying to sort it out when I picked Daisy up from her daycare.

"Mommy, how'd you get these scratches on the window?" she asked after she buckled up. I looked where she was pointing and sure enough, there were three scratches on my windshield right in front of me. I had been looking right past them into the traffic and hadn't even seen them. That explained the door scratching. Larry had struck again!

As soon as I got home I called the RCMP and spoke to Constable O'Riley. I told him about the scratches and asked how it went with Larry.

"I haven't been able to reach him yet. I've tried several times but have only been able to get his answering machine. I've left messages for him to call me back, but so far, he hasn't. I'm going to keep trying though."

I was confused. I'd thought he scratched my car because he'd met with Constable O'Riley and was angry. But apparently not. He scratched it just to scratch it and only the day before our scheduled meeting. Why, why, why? Was he trying to make me afraid that some unknown maniac was after me so that I would go running back to him as the "man" for protection and safety? Was he trying to show me how powerful he was? Or had he simply lost his marbles? I didn't know. And why did he always attack my car? What sort of warped connection did he have to it? It's true that he was the one who found the add for my car in the paper and told me about it, but I had been the one who had it tested and paid for it and drove it. It was my car and in my name. But for some reason, he must have felt connected to it, but why did that connection make him feel he had the right to scratch it up? None of it made any sense.

And what was I going to do about Friday since it seemed highly unlikely that Constable O'Riley would be able to reach Larry before the meeting. He'd show up at the coffee shop looking for me and when he got tired of waiting for me, he'd be sure to come looking for me. Where was I going to hide for the entire afternoon? This certainly had not been part of the plan.

Friday, October 27

The day of the meeting had come. I was nervous all morning at work. I'd planned to drive directly from work to my massage therapist's office, hoping that Larry hadn't followed me to her place previously and knew nothing about my connection with her. But, what if Larry showed up at my office instead of waiting for our meeting? Or what if he spotted my car while I was driving to the massage therapists and followed me? Or what if he went storming to my house when he realised I wasn't coming and did something to my house? I was paranoid, and rightfully so. I'd become very scared of him and what he was capable of doing.

I drove to the massage clinic right at the time when I knew Larry would most likely be sitting and waiting for me at the coffee shop. I thought this would be my best bet to avoid the possibility of him spotting my car and following me. My therapist was having lunch and invited me to sit down and join her. As we sat there together I told her everything that had been happening to me. She had a very sympathetic ear. I felt safe there and I didn't want to leave. I stayed for over two hours, just sitting on her couch. I wasn't sure how long I needed to stay in hiding and found it very difficult to pull myself away from that safe haven, but I knew I had to. I waited until I knew my kids would all be home from school, hoping that Larry didn't have the nerve to confront me with them around.

I drove into my carport and immediately noticed a box sitting in front of my door. Fortunately, Larry was nowhere in sight. I examined the box. It wasn't ticking and appeared normal, so I picked it up and went inside the house. When I opened it, I saw it was just some more of my belongings Larry was returning.

Saturday, October 28

I phoned Constable O'Riley early in the morning to tell him that Larry had indeed been in Vernon for our meeting as he had left a box of my belongings in front of my door.

"Yes," he said, "he finally called me back and we decided to meet this morning here at the station. I'll call you right after and let you know how it went." Apparently, Larry had offered to meet Constable O'Riley on Friday after the meeting with me, but Constable O'Riley said he couldn't do that as he didn't get on duty until 9 o'clock that night and Larry couldn't wait around that long, so they agreed on the Saturday meeting.

I waited and waited for Constable O'Riley's call, all the time playing out different scenarios in my head about their meeting, but the call never came. So, late in the day I called the station myself and asked to speak to Constable O'Riley.

"What happened between you and Larry today?" I asked.

"He never showed up and he never called. I don't know what happened."

"You're kidding!" This was getting frustrating.

"But don't worry," Constable O'Riley was quick to add. "I'll keep trying to call him and talk to him and I'll let you know what happens."

It was easy for Constable O'Riley to say "don't worry", but to not worry was impossible for me. In fact, my worry, mixed with my growing fear, was affecting my ability to think. I often found myself feeling confused and dumbfounded, unable to think my way through situations that arose. I was too drawn into my situation to be able to gain any type of helpful perspective whatsoever.

In the early evening, Constable Morrison called Larry and left the following message on his answering machine: *"This is Constable Morrison again, from the RCMP in Vernon. This is my second phone call to you. I think it's time that you and I had a talk over here. Your relationship with Sharon is becoming a fine line of being criminal and it's probably in your best interest to give me a holler here or contact me at the Vernon Detachment, either myself, Constable Morrison or Constable O'Riley. It's ten to seven in the evening. I'll be expecting your call. Goodbye."*

Later that night, around 10:00 o'clock, our phone rang and Billie answered it. She didn't say anything, but looked at me with a confused look. She held her hand over the mouthpiece of the phone and whispered to me that a man was calling looking for free sex and that he got our number from the bathroom wall of a local pub saying that if you want free sex, call this number. I listened in on the end of the conversation to see if it sounded like Larry, but it wasn't him. Billie told the man he had the wrong number and hung up. I phoned Constable O'Riley right away to report the call as I was certain Larry was behind it since the pub in question was a strip joint Larry frequented. Constable O'Riley assured me he would go down and have our phone number removed from the bathroom wall so that we would not receive any more disturbing calls.

I went to bed, but not to sleep. My thoughts would not stop. Around and around in circles; was there anything I could do to help myself; could I fight back somehow; could I put a stop to this insanity; could I get some control back in my life? And on and on. One thing I knew for certain. He was not going to stop me from living my life the way I wanted to live it. I wasn't going to hide myself away in fear. I was going to continue on with my life, just as I had before. I'd show him.

Monday, October 30

My bravado lasted one day and ended up turning me into an extremely easy target, as you shall see.

I decided to walk home from work, as I had often done in the past. It was a twenty - minute walk from the hospital to my house. I was two blocks away from my house, when a very large, purple and white Cadillac came up from behind. It slowly crossed over the centre line to the wrong side of the street and pulled up alongside me on the sidewalk. I'd never seen this car before. Keep walking, I told myself, as I quickly glanced at the car. What a shock! Larry was the driver! He looked so tiny sunk down in the interior of this monstrous car. My heart was pounding. I picked up my pace and kept looking straight ahead. The car followed along beside me. Then Larry started to talk.

"Hi Sharon."

Silence from me.

"You like my new car? I just got it. The engine finally blew up in my old Nissan."

I just kept walking.

"Sharon, why won't you be my friend? All I want is for you to be my friend and I don't understand why you won't be my friend."

Why did he keep asking me to be his friend all the time? Can't he get it through his head?

"I will not be your friend, Larry, and I will not tell you why again. I've told you the reasons several times already. I want you to leave me alone and if you don't leave right

185

now, I'm going to go into the closest house here and call 911." I tried to sound as threatening as possible, but that's difficult to do when your heart is in your throat.

"No, no…don't do that. I don't want to cause any trouble," he blurted out. "I just want to know where my stuff is. I need to make some copies of my resume because I've given out all my copies."

"The police have all your stuff and they've been trying to get in touch with you, so if you want your stuff, go to the police station and they'll explain everything to you." And with that I resolved to say no more. I'd been walking fast the whole time. What I really wanted to do though, was run, but I squelched that impulse. I figured running would only make him want to chase me and I knew he was a much faster and stronger runner than I was.

The intersection was a hundred feet ahead. All of a sudden Larry zoomed ahead, did a U - turn and came screeching back to where I was walking. His car was now facing the opposite direction I was walking in.

Oh no. This is it, I thought. He's going to try and grab me and force me into the car and heaven only knows what he'll do after that. I looked around. Where's all the traffic? Where are all the people? The street was deserted, even though it was normally a well - used street.

He got out of his car as I walked past him. My heart was pounding so hard, it ached. But he didn't run after me. Instead, he stood on the street calling out after me, over and over, as I walked away… "I love you, Sharon…No one will ever love you as much as I do…I love you…I hope you have a good life…I'll see you up on the cross country ski trails this winter. I love you…"

I walked quickly and was soon over the slight rise in the road and out of his view. I was only a short block from my house. I picked up my pace even more, glancing around to see if he was following. I went into my carport, key in hand, and quickly unlocked my door and stepped inside and locked the door again. I rushed upstairs to call the RCMP, but I was so shaken up that I couldn't remember the RCMP's number. I grabbed the phone book to look it up, but my fingers were like jelly and couldn't get the pages to turn. Finally, I found the number and called. I reached the receptionist.

"Can you please tell Constable O'Riley and Morrison that Larry Scott is in Vernon right now. He just followed me down the street in a large, purple and white Cadillac. Tell them if they can locate that car, they'll be able to finally talk to him. He may even come to the station to pick up some stuff I gave to Constable O'Riley to give back to him. So if he comes there to pick up his stuff, please don't give it to him, but ask Constable O'Riley to talk to him first." The receptionist couldn't get a word in edgewise, I was talking so fast. She asked me for a few more details about the car and then assured me that she would tell the Constables. She also said I shouldn't worry as they have a standard policy to never give anything to anyone without checking the file first. I thanked her, hung up and collapsed onto a chair.

That was way too close! I couldn't believe how easy it would have been for Larry to have grabbed me, and on a main street in Vernon yet! There was very little traffic all the time he was following me, and no pedestrians on the sidewalk except for one person jogging past, who did not stop to ask if I needed help, even though Larry was driving on the wrong side of the street trying to talk to me while I was walking away, obviously not wanting to stop and chat as though we were friends. My threat of running to the nearest house to call 911 wouldn't have done any good either had I decided to carry it out. The closest house was set at the back of a large piece of property that was completely surrounded by bushes. Even if I would have made a dash for the house, I had no way of knowing if someone was home or not, or if they'd be willing to help if they were.

This whole incident was a tremendous eye opener for me. I realised how vulnerable I'd made myself just because I didn't want to let Larry's behaviour disrupt my life. I'd been very lucky this time and I took the lesson I'd just learned to heart. I *never* walked again and I threw my cocky attitude out the window and replaced it with a more realistic approach to the situation I found myself in. I was being stalked and had to act accordingly...whatever that was.

After talking to me on the sidewalk, Larry drove back to Kelowna. He was to meet with Dieter, who was back from Germany, in the evening.

Dieter saw at once that Larry was in bad shape. He tried to draw him into conversation. "How are you doing? Are you looking for a job? Are you feeling any better now?" Dieter asked.

"No, I am not over it, Dieter, and no, I have not found a job yet." And they discussed for awhile just how Larry was feeling. Then Larry said in a tone that sounded very strange to Dieter, "Well Dieter, I have done things while you've been gone and if you would know what I did you wouldn't want to be my friend anymore."

Dieter knew what these things were from my phone call to Vicki, but he wanted to hear what Larry had to say about it.

"What did you do, what do you mean?" he asked.

"Well," Larry said, "I tried to see Sharon several times, but she didn't want to see me and she acted very badly and she called me names." Dieter knew me fairly well and knew I was not the kind of person to call Larry or anyone names. His concern was not with how I acted, but what he could do to help Larry.

Dieter said to him, "Look, you love Sharon very much, I know that, and your intention is to come back together and do you think following her and doing things which she doesn't like helps you to find your way back to a normal functioning relationship? I tell you what Larry, you give me your word of honour…NOW…HERE…that you are not going to see her for one more year." And he looked straight at Larry to challenge him.

Larry looked at Dieter and then looked at his watch. He looked at the date and said, "Okay, in one year I will contact her again, the next time."

"Yes," Dieter said, "but before you do that you come and see me and we will talk about that. Now, I want your word of honour."

Dieter and Larry shook hands, looking each other straight in the eye and of course at that very moment Dieter believed Larry completely. Who wouldn't?

The same evening Dieter and Larry were making pacts, I was down at the RCMP station talking to Constable O'Riley trying to come up with another plan of action - something more than the RCMP trying to reach Larry by phone. I told Constable O'Riley about Larry following me along the sidewalk that day and asked if he had shown up to pick up his stuff. Unfortunately, he hadn't. I wasn't surprised. I felt tired and worn to a frazzle as I slumped back in the chair.

"This has gone far enough," Constable O'Riley said. "Larry has to be stopped. Tomorrow morning I'm going to drive out to the resort really early and catch him before he gets out of bed and bring him back to the station and give him a good talking to."

"You're going to drive all the way out there that early in the morning? You'd really do that?" I asked, somewhat surprised that a policeman would go that far out of his way to help me, especially at what would have to be five or six o'clock in the morning.

"Yes, I will. We need to put an end to this!"

No argument from me on that point. I could envision Constable O'Riley's plan working quite well. Larry would be awoken from his sleep by a knock on the door and when he opened it, there would be a stone - faced, giant RCMP officer staring at him. He wouldn't be able to get out of that situation too easily.

"Okay," I said, "but you'll have to be early to catch him. I'll give you the name and number of the manager of the resort so you can call him first and he'll be able to tell you if Larry's car is there or not, so you don't make the long drive for nothing."

Constable O'Riley took the number and stood up to show me out. I was feeling positive about his plan. The combination of drama, spontaneity, and sneakiness would be enough to scare the dickens out of Larry, which, I was hoping, was all that was needed to get him to stop harassing me. I had a lot of confidence in Constable O'Riley's resolve as well, so when he told me he'd be sure to call me to let me know how it went, I believed him, even though he hadn't called me back in the past.

I went home and fell into bed exhausted, only to be startled awake at midnight by the phone ringing. Half asleep, I answered and heard music playing - no hello, no talking - just music. I hung up and traced the call back to the resort using *69. I recorded the phone call in the diary I was keeping for the police. Eventually, I fell back asleep, but not until I'd pictured many satisfying ways that Larry's morning meeting with Constable O'Riley could go.

Tuesday, October 31

I woke early thinking that right about now Constable O'Riley would be at the resort, knocking on the door. I was dying to know what had happened, but I thought I'd give Constable O'Riley the morning to get back to me. But, the morning came and went with no call from Constable O'Riley. Most of the afternoon went by as well and still no call. Finally, I couldn't take the suspense any longer. I called the RCMP station and asked for Constable O'Riley.

"So what happened? Did you talk to him?" I asked quickly.

"Ah…actually, I didn't go out to the resort because I called Larry's number first and all I got was his answering machine, so I didn't think he was home. I'll keep trying to call him, though."

I was too shocked to answer. Wasn't it Constable O'Riley who said this had gone on long enough and had to be stopped… "nipped in the bud?" Wasn't it Constable O'Riley who said he'd been frustrated with Larry never returning the messages left on his answering machine? Surely it must have occurred to him that Larry had been screening his calls ever since the police started leaving messages on his phone, just to avoid talking to them. And why didn't Constable O'Riley try calling the resort manager to find out if Larry was at home or not? It had been such a good plan, and a timely one too as, unknown to the police and me, Larry had an appointment to see a lawyer for later that very day.

It was a long, hard fall from the hope I had to the disappointment I felt - an enormous let down. I realised then, that being stalked was basically my problem. It had become obvious to me that I couldn't expect any serious help from the RCMP. Either they didn't know what to do, or they knew, but didn't really want to do it. What a terrible feeling that was. How was I supposed to know what to do? I'd never been involved with stalking before on any level, except for perhaps some movie clips I'd seen once or twice, and from what I recalled, they never turned out very well for the victim. How was I ever going to shake Larry by myself? He was like a monkey that clung to my back...my own personal terrorist.

Larry went to his first appointment with a lawyer named John Clark. He'd made the appointment to seek legal advice about a message that had been left on his answering machine by Constable Morrison. As a defence lawyer, John did not like the way the police used the statement "It's probably in your best interests" and told Larry so. He explained to Larry that this statement implied the RCMP didn't have much to go on and were probably hoping to induce Larry into making some sort of admission or statement. He also pointed out that statements have to be obtained voluntarily or they could be considered inadmissible in court. John got out Section 264 (the criminal code section on criminal harassment) and read it to Larry. He told Larry this had been in place for a few years already and had put a whole new gloss on the battle of the sexes, as at one point in time, persistently pursuing the love of your life was appropriate conduct, whereas now it had become a criminal offence, if it truly is harassing the woman. John also explained the intimidation section of the Code as well, saying to Larry that it is an offence to try to persuade someone to do something that they're lawfully entitled not to do, or to try and make somebody do something that they're not lawfully required to do.

In the first hour of their meeting it became evident to John that Larry was having a very difficult time with the break up of the relationship. Larry described to John in euphoric terms, how our relationship had been very close and that he was very much in love with me, how we'd been on picnics together, going on holidays and how everything was going along extremely well and then, all of a sudden, I ended the relationship. Larry broke down and started to cry in John's office. He seemed bewildered, as though he was grieving someone's death. He couldn't understand why the police wanted to talk to him or what kind of trouble he could possibly be in. Larry seemed so disturbed that John decided to give him the phone number of a counsellor, Shirley Rumpel, whom he knew had experience in handling men's emotional trauma. He also asked Larry to do a written statement of what had taken place from Larry's point of view, and include some history about himself, as well as a resume. This was a common practice for John as it helped him get a feel for his clients personality and where they were coming from.

At the end of their visit, John advised Larry that he should not go to the police station, because he did not *have* to go. "If the police are going to arrest you Larry, they will come out and arrest you at which time you have a long standing right not to say anything, a right not to incriminate yourself." John continued to try and impress upon Larry the importance of him not talking to the police as, even though John felt Larry hadn't done anything, he did feel that Larry might express himself to the police in such a manner that they would be able to jump on his words and use them as evidence of an intent to criminally harass me, when all he seemed to be trying to do was something lawful, which was to continue a relationship with me.

That evening, Larry was visited by Luke Penner. Luke had recently moved to Blue Lake Resort and had only met Larry a few times, but he'd heard from neighbours that Larry had been asked to move out of his place by mid November and thought he'd do the neighbourly thing and tell him if he needs a place to stay, he was welcome to move in with him for awhile. They talked for a bit and in the end, Larry agreed that when the middle of November came he would indeed move in with Luke and thanked him for his offer. Then he voluntarily told Luke that the police had been trying to contact him because of the break up, but it was all okay now because he had a lawyer who was taking care of things. Luke was surprised that Larry was telling him this, instead of trying to hide this sort of problem. He was still willing to help Larry out, however. They parted and Larry sat down at his desk to compose the letter the lawyer had asked him to write.

Wednesday, November 1

I was at work at my afternoon job. Every morning I worked for Dr. Robson and twice a week in the afternoons, I worked for Dr. Schnieder. Normally, I worked Tuesday and Thursday afternoon, but there was a filing backlog that needed to be dealt with so I was at work on a Wednesday afternoon. The job was repetitious and did not require my full attention. My mind kept wandering to all my problems with Larry, and I started feeling worse and worse, to the point where I couldn't seem to function very well at all. I decided to take a break and go for a short walk outside to clear my head. I walked out to the parking lot where my car was parked. By this point in time I never got into my car without walking around it, sometimes twice, to see if it had been damaged in any way. When I approached my car, I saw something under my back tire. As I got closer, I could see that it was a square of quarter inch plywood, 1" x 1" with an ardox nail sticking right up through the middle of it. It had been put right up tight to my tire. If I'd have moved the car even one inch, the nail would have punctured my tire. This time, my heart did not start beating faster. Instead, it seemed to slow down. I felt stiff and numb.

I took the nail back to the office and showed it to Dr. Robson. He was also becoming very concerned as he watched his normal, optimistic receptionist turn into an emotional basket case as the days went by. He took it upon himself to call the RCMP. He spoke to Constable Morrison and asked why nothing was being done. After their conversation, he came and told me that Constable Morrison seemed well intended, but it seemed there wasn't much the RCMP could do. Constable Morrison had told him they were doing everything within their power, but their hands were tied. It was frustrating for everyone involved.

Well, my hands weren't tied. After I got over the initial shock, I knew I had to take some sort of action, or go crazy. I went to see the hospital administrator for the first time. I explained what Larry had been doing to my car in the hospital parking lot and how he had unexpectedly appeared twice in the hospital already, plus all the things he had done besides. I asked if there was any way I could get some sort of protection in place at the hospital as I was getting no where with the police. The administrator was very concerned and said that first thing in the morning he would have someone come by to see me to set up hospital security for me.

After work, I went directly to the RCMP station to talk to Constable Morrison myself. This was the first time I'd actually met him in person. To my surprise, he was a much smaller man than Constable O'Riley and his face looked hard and tough. One look at him and I knew I'd never feel understanding or empathy coming from him. Instead, he had an air of coldness and indifference about him. I would have much rather spoken to Constable O'Riley, but he wasn't on duty and since Constable Morrison was assigned to my case, he was the one I had to see.

I carefully handed him the nail I'd found under my car tire, hoping he could get fingerprints from it, thinking this would finally give the police the evidence they needed to implicate Larry. Constable Morrison took the nail from me, looked it over and said he wouldn't be able to take fingerprints from it. Because it was an ardox nail, the surface was too rough for fingerprints. The same with the plywood.

"Do you need this nail for anything?" he asked me.

"Me?" I replied. "I have no need for it." With that he pushed the nail back out of the plywood and threw both pieces in the garbage, along with all my hopes. Back to square one again. I was getting very tired of never getting past square one.

I told Constable Morrison about Constable O'Riley's failed plans to go out to the resort early in the morning, but he said I must have been mistaken as Constable O'Riley did not have the right to bring Larry from the resort to the Vernon station. I knew I wasn't mistaken, but Constable Morrison seemed very sure of himself and I was in no shape to stand up for myself and argue.

"So what can be done now?" I asked him.

"Unfortunately, I can't do much at the moment because I can't find your file. Constable O'Riley must have mis - filed it or taken it home with him, so I'll have to get in touch with him before I can find out what's happening with it," was his reply. "But, I think it's high time that some hospital security was set up for you and that's something you should look into as soon as possible." I told him I'd already been to see hospital security and I was meeting with them the next morning.

He went on to describe to me what a peace bond is and what a restraining order is and the difference between them. Because the restraining order really carried very little impact, he felt the peace bond would be more suitable for me and I agreed, although my brain did not seem to be registering much of what was said, no matter how hard I tried to concentrate.

What I needed to do to get a peace bond in place, according to him, was to write a statement showing my genuine fear of Larry and the reasons why I was so afraid. He emphasised that it was my genuine fear that was the key to having a peace bond granted, therefore I must make sure to bring this message across in my statement. When they had my statement, an application would be made before a judge. The police, Larry and myself would have to be present for the judge to make his decision. Once a peace bond was issued, however, if Larry did bother me in any way, he could be made to pay a fine. Because the peace bond was harder to get and carried a stiffer penalty, I also agreed to choose it over a restraining order.

Constable Morrison also explained to me about something called Victim's Assistance. Apparently they would be able to help me with some of the emotional problems I was experiencing because of the stalking.

Their office was right in the police station. He told me to make an appointment to see them - the sooner the better. I made it for two days later.

I went home to my children, all wanting supper and to share their day with me, but there was not a single part of me that I could make available to them. I was drained, empty and plain old worn out. I closed myself in my room and started to write my statement for the peace bond. I asked myself - did I really have a genuine fear of Larry? Damn right I did. I was afraid to the core, and having to put it down on paper made me feel it even more.

This was the day I hit rock bottom. My fear was at its greatest level. I'd never felt more powerless than I did on this day.

After Larry put the nail under my tire, he drove back to Kelowna to drop off his letter to John Clark. John accepted the statement, but did not have time to talk to him other than to explain once again to Larry that he must stay away from me and that he does not need to contact the police.

The following is a portion of Larry's letter and was read at the Inquest by John Clark:

"One and a half years ago I placed an ad in the personals of the Daily Courier. Sharon Velisek of Vernon, BC replied to my ad. From the first date we really enjoyed each others company and found something magical to be with one another. We immediately started seeing one another at least three times a week. From the first date we became lovers - right up to the end of our relationship, approximately 15 September, 1995. Many times we told each other that we were both in a very true deep love. In the last six months we had looked at property to buy with the idea of building our own home. Although Sharon did not have much self confidence in herself, I constantly kept praising her and helping

her raise her self esteem. I was the first person she had dated since she left her husband of seventeen years. She had been living with her five children in a house in Vernon when I met her. We spoke of marriage many times and both said that we wanted to spend the rest of our lives together. We spent the third weekend of August in Saskatchewan, Moosejaw, Avonlea, Regina and Southey, meeting my parents, her parents and all her relatives in Southey. At that time she said to me that all her relatives approved of me and felt that I am a very nice person. And in turn, I felt the feeling was mutual. A week later we returned back to the Okanagan. On the 9th and 10th of September we went to Nakusp. Sharon's two oldest boys, Jake and Matt had decided to live with their father in Nelson. Jake picked Matt up on the 9th and left for Nelson. Sharon and I tented at the Hot Springs on the 9th and on the 10th on the Arrow Lake. On the morning of the 10th it was Sharon's birthday. We made breakfast in the outdoors and sat under an apple tree to enjoy this magic moment. I had bought her a birthday present - a watch and silk panties - approximately $150.00. It was at this time that Sharon said to me that there is nobody in the whole world that she wanted to be with more than me. We felt deeply bonded together. Later on that day we returned to Vernon. Sharon's three children remaining at home had prepared a surprise birthday party for her. The following week I had phoned Sharon to discuss moving in with her as she had indicated two to three weeks earlier that would be fantastic. It was at this stage that she said that Tom, the fourteen year old boy said it was okay with him. Billie, the twelve year old, felt that she would like Sharon and my relationship to remain as it is. And Daisy, the seven year old, felt that I should not come, because then she could not climb into bed with her mother. I did not say too much other than that I did not want to move into a "hornets nest". Sharon said she would give me a couple of days to think about it. The following day she left a message on my answering machine saying "Larry, we'd love to have you move in *with us, that's great. Also, if you decide not to that's okay too. Whatever you decide". The following day, Friday, she phoned and said we must talk and wanted to see me Saturday or Sunday. I indicated to her that I had to go to Salmon Arm and could not see her. There was silence on the phone. Then she started crying and said she could no longer talk and hung up the phone. On Sunday, returning from Salmon Arm at approximately two p.m. there was a message on my answering machine from Sharon saying "Larry, this is Sharon. As far as I'm concerned our relationship is through. Goodbye and good luck. I immediately phoned her to try and get to the bottom of this, but to no avail. Her personality had changed. She sounded very condescending and angry. She indicated that I would be getting a letter in the mail. I immediately met her on the following day in the parking lot of the hospital. We exchanged personal belongings but there was no way I could talk her out of ending our relationship - and she said she talked it over with her divorced sister and some friends. And that it is final. I (Larry) have not a decision in the matter. The more I tried to reason with her, the more distant she became. I found myself in complete shock with the break up of our relationship. How Sharon could throw this all away I could not understand. I could not eat for eight days and even now pick at food. I have lost twenty two pounds. Dr. Spelding had given me medication to get over the depression feeling and we've had several counseling sessions on how to cope with the break up of the relationship. I was in the Vernon Mall the last week of October and ran into Sharon and Daisy, the seven year old. I spoke to Sharon briefly about seeing one another for one hour each week for the month of November. She agreed we would meet the following Friday at a cafe. She did not show up. In the meantime I had dropped off some more of her property at her house. On Thursday, the day before we were to meet, a Constable O'Riley left a message on my machine saying he would like to speak to me. I had told him that I was meeting Sharon on Friday at 12:45*

*p.m. He said that he started work at 9:00 p.m. I indicated I
could not wait this long to see him, but I would try to see him
Saturday or Sunday. However, I forgot on Friday evening I had
to pick my daughter Anna and her friend up from Penticton as
they were spending the weekend with me. It is the following week
that I have received two messages from a Constable Morrison,
Vernon RCMP detachment that say "It is in my best interest to
contact him, as my relationship with Sharon is becoming a fine
line of becoming criminal (?), and to contact him or Constable
O'Riley and he will be expecting my call".*

After John read Larry's statement, he called Larry to
discuss the situation further. He found it difficult to
believe the police would be wanting to talk to Larry for the
type of conduct mentioned in his statement. There was
nothing there that could be considered harassment, no
assault, no uttering of threats, no threat of violence in the
facts Larry had given, nor had Larry ever expressed any
anger toward me in their discussions.

"Have you been doing anything else to Sharon, Larry?
Something that you might have neglected to put on your
statement?" John asked.

"Well, the police might think I put something in the
gas tank of her car," Larry offered.

"Well, did you?"

"No, I didn't, but I was in the vicinity at the time it was
discovered."

"Look, you've got to stay away from the police and
you've got to stay away from Sharon!" John explained in
no uncertain terms. "I'm going to read you Section 264 of
the Criminal Code again. It points out very clearly, Larry,
that attending someone's place of work, making persistent
phone calls and trying to persuade someone to continue a

relationship when they clearly do not want to continue could be considered criminal harassment."

"But why…why…why is she doing this? Why is it over?" Larry asked John. And then he started to cry and collapsed into feelings of grief and self - pity.

John didn't know what to say. He found Larry's state to be pathetic.

"Look Larry…you're in no state to be calling the police. Your emotions are just too volatile. I'll call the RCMP for you and explain to them that I've advised you not to go to the RCMP station, therefore you won't be coming in and if they want to arrest you, they can come to the resort and arrest you." At least this way John knew the RCMP would have a response and maybe would quite calling Larry. Larry was greatly relieved at hearing this.

However, that same evening the RCMP left another message on Larry's answering machine asking Larry to contact them.

Thursday, November 2

Larry went to his first appointment with Shirley Rumpel, the counsellor John had told him about. First, they discussed Shirley's fees and that they would have to be paid by Larry himself, as counselling fees are not paid by the medical plan. They had a long discussion about the difficulties Larry was experiencing in letting go of the relationship. She found Larry's presentation of his difficulties to be no different than numerous other men she'd seen that were in similar emotional states. She ended the hour - long appointment by giving Larry some ways to help him cope with stress. When he felt emotion taking over, he was to stop and breathe deeply ten times or more and this was to clear his immediate rush of emotion. She also asked him to write a letter telling something about himself, such as where he'd come from or whatever else he felt he would like her to know. At the end of their meeting, Larry told Shirley about the police trying to call him because he had been trying to talk to me so often. This, however, did not alarm her, as she felt it was not uncommon to have a fellow calling his wife or girlfriend after a break up and being told not to call. She felt it was just part of Larry's upset.

When Larry got home that evening, he called John at his house asking if he'd phoned the RCMP yet because another message had been left on his answering machine. John apologised for not having done it yet. He'd been very busy after their talk the day before, but promised he would do it first thing the next morning at his office when he had Larry's file with him. Once again, John reiterated, that it was unlikely the police would come out to arrest Larry as there didn't seem to be reasonable and probable grounds for that.

"But if they do come out and pick you up - so be it, but remember, you've got the right to remain silent."

While Shirley and John were trying to help Larry, hospital security and I were wondering over the hospital grounds searching for ways to make me as safe as possible at work. We decided upon a well - lit parking spot at the back of the hospital where there was a lot of activity during the day, and in full view of the shipping department. I was given a code to dial if Larry showed up in my office, which would send everyone running to help. It was also decided that Larry would only be allowed on hospital property as far as the emergency room, which is at the very front of the hospital. If he was found any other place in the hospital, or on hospital grounds, he would be escorted out, as there would be no possible reason for him to be anywhere else in the hospital, other than the emergency room. My office was on the fourth floor and about as far away as you can get from the emergency room. I took some comfort in these safety measures - everything that could be done had been done. But I knew Larry had enough knowledge of the hospital from the time he worked there to easily gain access to any part of the hospital he wanted to without being noticed. I remember saying to the man from hospital security that he'd done everything he could, but Larry could still walk into my office and shoot me dead before I'd even have time to lift my head to see who'd come in. And that was exactly how I felt. How could anyone, after all, truly protect someone from a crazy man?

Next, I met with the hospital's night watchman. He was a retired RCMP officer, who gave me advice on how to stay safe no matter where I was. He told me to always carry a strong flashlight in working order in my car and not to put it in my trunk, but somewhere that I could grab it easily from the driver's seat. That way I'd never be stranded in the dark, plus I could use it to blind someone by shining it into their eyes. And he told me to make sure I always drove up as close as I could to my house door and not to open my car door to get out until I have the key to the house in my hand, ready to insert into the house lock.

"Don't worry," he said to me after I'd given him a photograph of Larry, "I'll keep a close watch out for this guy. Boy, I'd love to catch him and beat the stuffin' out of him."

Photographs of Larry were distributed to the people on lookout for me. I felt a modicum of safety and wondered why I hadn't asked for help from the hospital earlier.

Friday, November 3

True to his word, John Clark did indeed call the Vernon RCMP in the morning. He asked to speak to Constable Morrison or O'Riley, but was told neither was on duty at the time. He ended up leaving a voice message for one of them.

"Please call John Clark in Kelowna. I'm the counsel for Larry Scott. I'm calling in response to your telephone message." He left his Kelowna phone number for the police to call. When John did not hear back from the RCMP by mid afternoon, he left another message for Constable Morrison stating: "This is John Clark calling again. I left a message earlier this morning. I've spoken with Mr. Scott. I've advised him, as you might expect of a criminal lawyer, that he doesn't have to attend the police station. If you have grounds to arrest him, then arrest him but I'm advising him not to come in. I've advised him of his right to remain silent. He has also been advised to stay away from Sharon Velisek."

Then John called Larry and left a message that he had contacted the police and once again he stated emphatically that Larry *must* stay away from me as his behaviour was indeed coming close to being considered criminal harassment.

Somehow Connie had found out about Luke Penner offering Larry a place to stay when it was time for him to move out. She didn't think Luke could possibly know what he was getting himself in the middle of, since he'd just moved into the resort and didn't really know anybody very well. She called Luke from Calgary and told him that it might not be such a good idea for Larry to move in with him right now because Larry was going through a bad time and seemed fairly unstable. "He's seeing a doctor and taking medication and everything, but he's still having a hard time of it and it might be best for you to just leave Larry go his own way," she told him.

Luke thought this was a strange thing for Connie to be telling him, since he'd thought Connie and Larry were good friends. He didn't understand why she'd be trying to cut off avenues of help for Larry instead of trying to encourage them. But then again, he realised that he didn't know Connie any better than he knew Larry. He decided to call the RCMP and see for himself what was up with Larry. When he called he was put on hold. When the receptionist came back again, Luke told her he was phoning regarding a Larry Scott and was there anyone there he could talk to about him? The receptionist told him there were two officers he could speak to, Constable Morrison or O'Riley, but neither were on duty at the time and perhaps the best thing would be if he called back the next morning when they would be there. It seemed to Luke that Larry's name didn't start bells and whistles ringing at the police station, so he couldn't be in that much trouble. Luke decided to call the resort manager instead and ask for a character reference on Larry. The manager told him that Larry was a good employee and was a stable sort of person from a business point of view, but he wasn't able to comment about Larry on a personal level. He did say, however, that he knew Larry had been very upset about the break up with me.

This report satisfied Luke well enough and he decided he did not need to follow it up with the RCMP the next morning. Larry could still move in with him mid November, never mind what Connie said.

I went to the RCMP station for the appointment I'd made with Norman Mayer of Victim's Assistance. I'd brought along the peace bond statement Constable

Morrison had asked me to write. Norman was in the middle of reading this statement when Constable O'Riley walked by the office. Norman excused himself and went out into the hallway to talk to him about my case. Then instead of Norman coming back in, Constable O'Riley came in and sat down. He read my statement. It took him quite awhile to read through all six pages, but once he did, he had that same concerned look on his face he'd had the first time I'd met with him.

"We've got to get this stopped," he said, shaking his head. "I'll talk to Constable Morrison and we'll keep trying to make contact with Larry. He's going to need to stand in front of a judge in order to get a peace bond in place anyway, so we'll have to just keep trying."

I talked a bit more to Norman Mayer. He asked if it was okay with me if he sent someone around to my place with some pamphlets. He also suggested the police do a safety check on my house, just to see if there were any ways my house could be made safer. This was all more than fine with me and I gave Norman my permission.

Then Constable O'Riley asked if I had my car in the parking lot. According to him, if we hurried the sun would be just right and he could get some photographs of the scratches on my car. So we went outside and he took several photographs of the scratches that had been made two weeks before.

I wanted to protect myself as much as I could. With this in mind, I went to check out the possibility of purchasing a cell phone. I wanted to have a way to call for help at all times. I tried several places, but nothing was within a price range I could afford. I was telling a friend about this and she suggested I talk to her friend who bought a personal alarm a while back when someone was harassing her. I went to see this friend to ask her where to get such a device and how it worked, when she offered to lend me hers. The guy who had been bugging her had quit, so I gladly accepted. In the evening, my kids and I tried it out. The sound this alarm made was absolutely deafening. Perfect, I thought. I carried it with me whenever I left the house from then on, fully intent on using it when Larry showed up again.

My next step was to try to catch Larry in the act of vandalising my car so that I could give the RCMP the proof they seemed to be waiting for. I decided to keep my dog tied at night in my carport so that when Larry came around, she would bark and I would know he was there. However, George, my little Sheltie, who'd been a faithful companion for 7 years, was not used to sleeping outside and I was afraid she'd either freeze or run away to find shelter. So I nailed some plywood together under my workbench in my carport to shield her from the wind and from view and laid out some blankets on the cement for her in preparation for the evening.

After supper the volunteers from Victim's Assistance came to my house to see how I was doing. They brought some brochures they thought might be helpful and they offered me their ear if I wanted to talk. It was kind of them, but I needed action - not brochures. I thanked them for the material they brought, but after they left I still felt like I was in a pit so deep that no rope was long enough to reach me.

Before I went to bed, I led poor, reluctant George out to her new quarters and tied her leash onto a door handle I'd attached to the plywood.

"Now you bark up a storm when Larry comes, George, and then hopefully this whole thing will be over with soon and you can stay inside again." I closed the door to the house and felt awful. I should have been hiding out there - not my dog, I thought.

All night I barely slept. I kept listening for barking or any sound, however slight. My bedroom was right on top of the carport and I figured I'd hear Larry for sure as long as I didn't fall asleep. But all night, nothing happened.

Saturday, November 4

Constable O'Riley made two more attempts to reach Larry by phone with no luck.

Somewhere between Friday, November 3rd and Sunday, November 5th Larry made a quick trip to Vancouver, and left the following message on his friend Steve's answering machine: "Hi Steve, I'm here in Vancouver and it looks like we're going to miss each other again. I hope you have enough strength to carry on the next day."

Steve was surprised to hear this message when he got home from his two - week holiday. He didn't know Larry was planning to come to Vancouver. They hadn't spoken for a long time. He wondered about the strange message though. It just didn't sound like Larry. Steve's friends had often asked him why he associated with someone like Larry. They'd always thought of him as being odd. Maybe, he thought, they were right.

On Saturday, I was feeling a tremendous amount of nervous energy. I was sure Larry was close to striking again. So far, his pattern had been to do something every three to four days, which meant it was high time for him to make a move. I looked around the outside of my house. How could I make it safer? My shrubs! Of course. Why hadn't I thought of them earlier? I had three shrubs that grew right outside the front of my house. Two of them stood sentry on either side of my front door and were eight feet tall and three feet wide. Either one would have hidden Larry easily, undetected by neighbours or passersby. It would not be difficult for him to hide there, ring the doorbell and when someone answered, muscle his way into the house in broad daylight. The shrubs had to go, I decided. I put on my gloves, took my saw and pruners, and went at it. I worked furiously, cutting and sawing non - stop and even though it was a cold November day, I was soon sweating. In a few short hours all three shrubs were no more than three feet tall with all their clippings stuffed into several black garbage bags.

That night I decided to try something different with George too. I re - thought my plan of leaving George outside, realising it would never have worked anyway, because all Larry needed to do was talk to George and she'd be wagging her tail instead of barking. They knew each other too well. Plus, if he had shown up, then what was I going to do - run outside and take a picture of him at night, with no flash? No, for this night I had a better plan. I would tie George up inside the basement door so that Larry could not see her and speak to her. This way, George would hear someone in the carport and would start barking, which would wake me up. I planned to switch bedrooms with Daisy as her bedroom window faced the street and overlooked my carport entrance. This way, when Larry came running out of my carport, I'd be able to see him. Then, I'd call 911 and tell them Larry was at my place and hopefully they would be able to catch him. I knew it was a long shot, but that was all I had, plus it felt much better to be doing something rather than just waiting and worrying. When night came, I tied George up downstairs and went to sleep in Daisy's room. Once again,

I couldn't sleep. I waited for the slightest sound. Many times during the night I'd get up just to look out the window, thinking how perfect it would be if I'd catch him sneaking up to my place. But the night came and went and not a trace of Larry. I wondered if perhaps he was watching me setting a trap for him, or did he have a sixth sense that warned him? Whatever the reason, it left me feeling frustrated once again. I went back to sleeping in my own bed with George protecting me in my room. I needed to get some sleep.

Sunday, November 5

Larry returned from Vancouver late Sunday. I received a hang up phone call at 2:30 in the morning, which I traced back to the resort using *69. After I hung up the phone, I called the RCMP and told the receptionist to tell either Constable O'Riley or Constable Morrison that Larry was at the resort right now as he'd just done a hang up phone call to me from there, so if they really wanted to talk to him, now was the time to do it. I was going through the motions, even though I knew this hot tip was useless…the police hadn't done anything so far, so why would they jump in their car now, especially in the middle of the night, and drive out there?

I tried to go back to sleep, but that's impossible after a hang up phone call. I took some comfort, at least, in knowing that he was at the resort and not in Vernon skulking around my house in the middle of the night.

Monday, November 6

I received another hang up phone call after work. I was by now a bundle of nerves and the simple 'click' on the end of the line was as frightening as anything he'd ever done to me.

I traced this call to a payphone from the Village Green Mall in Vernon and I immediately reported it to the RCMP detachment.

Later that afternoon, Constable O'Riley called me to inform me of a turn of events. Apparently, a lawyer representing Larry had left a message saying that Larry would only talk to the police through a lawyer.

"A lawyer!" I said. "What on earth has a lawyer got to do with this?"

"I'm not sure. Larry must have hired one. Anyway, I'm going off duty so it'll be Constable Morrison that will contact this lawyer to find out what's going on and then he'll give you a call and let you know what's up."

I was not about to wait for Constable Morrison's call. That evening, when I knew he'd be on duty, I called the station and asked to speak to him. "Constable O'Riley told me this afternoon about a lawyer that had called the station about Larry. He said you'd be calling the lawyer and I wondered if you had?" I asked.

"No, I haven't done that yet. I've been looking for your file and I can't seem to find it. I'm going to have to get in touch with Constable O'Riley to find the phone number of that lawyer so I can call him back. I'll keep in touch."

Lost my file! Again! I should have ranted and raved and shouted obscenities into the phone…demanded action instead of excuses for once, but I'm just not that type of person. I don't rant and rave well.

"I'll be waiting anxiously for your call," was all I said.

On the same day, Larry dropped a letter off at John Clark's office that said: *Sharon stated to me that Constable O'Riley has these items but there's no way I'm going down to collect these items.* Apparently Larry wanted John to find a way of getting his stuff back from the RCMP. He also gave John my address, my residence phone number and the phone numbers of both my employers and the time of day when I would be at each job to help John do this.

Tuesday, November 7

Large, wet snowflakes fell all afternoon in Vernon and by evening, Vernon was covered in a healthy foot of fresh snow. Because it was our first snowfall of the season and an early one for Vernonites, cars were slipping and sliding all over the place, even with winter tires.

Constable Morrison did not call with news from the lawyer and I could easily understand why. The RCMP had their hands full with accidents from the large snowfall. I didn't think Larry would chance the drive to Vernon either, so I had a day of relative calm, thanks to the weather, until I received a call from the high school saying that my son Tom had been in an accident and had been taken to the emergency room. Apparently, there'd been a snowball fight, which escalated into a rather nasty affair of a car been driven out of control into the crowd of kids that had gathered. Tom had tried to stop the driver of the car by punching his arm through the car window. He was cut badly enough to require stitches and was sent to the emergency department. On top of everything, I was informed that he was one of the students that would be facing a permanent suspension, since there was zero tolerance for violence at his school.

Another sleepless night, but this time out of concern for Tom and what would happen to him.

<u>Wednesday, November 8</u>

Constable Morrison called me at home in the early afternoon.

"Hello, Sharon. I just finished talking with this lawyer and, according to him, he's made it very clear to Larry that he has to leave you alone."

"Okay…but what happens if he doesn't? What if he still calls or comes around? Then what?" I asked.

"Well, he's told Larry that if he has any contact with you whatsoever, he will no longer be willing to represent Larry."

"Really? That doesn't sound too threatening."

"No, but I let the lawyer know what Larry has been doing to you and he said he'd talk to him again and make very certain that Larry understood he was to stay completely away from you."

"God, I hope the lawyer actually does get through to him. So, what do we do now?" I asked.

"We wait and see. Just make sure you record any further contacts Larry has with you."

Okay, I can do that, I thought to myself, and I agreed to let Constable Morrison know if anything further happened.

I wished and I hoped it was truly over. I longed for an end to the fear so that I could lead a normal life again. I knew Larry would have to be spending time and energy packing his stuff right about then, since he only had another week before he had to move out of his place. Maybe being busy moving and the excitement of a new place, along with the lawyers admonishment would catapult him over his devastation of the break up and back into his own life again. I hadn't heard from him since the hang up phone call a few days previous. I crossed my fingers that it had been our last contact.

After speaking with Constable Morrison, John called Larry and challenged him regarding the two hang up phone calls Constable Morrison told him I'd recently reported. Larry said he couldn't have done the call during the day because he was walking on a beach with another woman at the very time the call was reported. He did not, however, have an alibi for the one during the night that was traced back to the resort. John was upset and he made it very clear to Larry what his terms were: "Look Larry…you stay away from Vernon and you stay away from Sharon or you find yourself a new lawyer!"

My mother called. One of her regular check up calls to see how I was doing. There was lots to talk about between Tom's school problems and the involvement of the lawyer now. At the end of the conversation, she asked me if I really thought it was over with Larry. I thought for awhile, and then answered, "No, he may not show up for awhile, but I know it's not over. It's just a matter of time before he does something to me again." I felt a terrible dread as I said this, because I knew for certain it was true. For it to have been truly over would have been too easy.

Thursday, November 9

Larry had his second meeting with Shirley Rumpel. He came into her office rather upset because the police had told John about two hang up phone calls they assumed he'd made. He told Shirley that he knew he couldn't have done one of them and he couldn't remember about the other one. Mostly, he was afraid he was going to be charged with stalking because of the calls.

215

He also reported that he'd tried to focus on the here and now and to do the deep breathing. He had some success with it, he told Shirley, but often felt like his spirit was drifting out of his body, so he would only take three breaths in a row instead of ten, as she'd asked him to. He said he also called up an old girlfriend and they had a good, long talk as well.

Shirley went over the letter he had written and noticed that in each relationship he mentioned, the women had left him, yet he always presented himself as being supportive and considerate. Something was amiss, she thought. She explored this avenue with him. Close to the end of their meeting she asked Larry if he'd ever had a head injury.

"Actually, yes, I did. About two years ago I fell on some wet grass while I was playing golf. I ended up with a mild concussion. I was sick for four or five days but then I was fine."

"Maybe we'll have time to explore your head injury more at the next appointment." They were running out of time. "In the meantime, keep writing for me and try to stay focused on the here and now as much as possible. I'll see you next week."

Not once did Larry make any threats toward me or show anger in any other way while talking to Shirley. Even though she knew the police were involved and that Larry was having trouble staying away from me, she felt there was absolutely no hint of violence in Larry's demeanour and therefore no need to call the police. He was simply acting like the hundreds and hundreds of other men she had counselled in a similar emotional state since the 70's. Quite simply, he was heartbroken.

<u>Wednesday, November 15</u>

Larry had reached his deadline for staying at the resort, but the day he'd set to move in with Luke was not until the 17th. He needed to go somewhere for a few days, so he called his old tennis buddy, Danny Fisher, and asked if he could crash at his place for a few days. He brought his gym bag only, everything else was left at the resort.

Instead of eating at Hedley's gym, Danny brought food home with him that night to share with Larry. Neither of them had been eating well; Danny because he was sick with the flu and Larry because he was still distraught from the break up. Danny had heard that Larry was quite depressed, but he was surprised at how bad Larry really was.

"Have you been taking your antidepressant medication?" Danny asked him.

"No, Danny. I haven't."

"Well, if you take one, then I'll take one…because you're making me depressed, man!" Larry went and got the bottle from his gym bag, gave one to Danny and took one himself. Shortly after that Larry became very anxious and started to shake more than usual, which really worried Danny.

"How long are you planning to stay, buddy?" he asked Larry.

"Well, I should be moving on soon, so three or four days should be enough."

By 'moving on' Danny thought Larry had found another job or another place to live.

"Great," he said. "Did you get a job?"

"No, I didn't get a job, Danny. I've just had enough of this life and I've decided to move on. I'm going to take a lot of my stuff to Penticton to give to my kids so moving will be easier, wherever I end up moving to."

Danny did not like the sound of this at all and decided that in the morning he would call Dr. Spelding and get another appointment for Larry A.S.A.P. as something was definitely not right with his friend.

They sat up until two o'clock in the morning talking and watching T.V. But Larry didn't seem to be able to talk about anything else besides the break up and how he couldn't seem to get a handle on it. "I think about our break up from morning till night and as hard as I try, I just can't seem to shake it," he told Danny. "I'm completely devastated."

Danny consoled him with typical replies - life goes on, let it pass, there's more fish in the sea, time will take care of it...but Larry wasn't hearing any of it.

"You want to know how bad it is, Danny? I've even gone to Vancouver to see if I could hire a hitman. But I couldn't. They were too expensive."

Danny thought Larry was just talking nonsense as he didn't see where Larry would have had the time to go to Vancouver, plus it seemed too far out of character for him.

"Yeah, right," Danny retorted as though he'd just been told the impossible.

But Larry continued, "She's made my life miserable, Danny. I could just go to Vernon and shoot her."

Danny figured Larry was just spouting off the top of his head, letting some of his anger out. Danny's flu symptoms had been getting worse as the night wore on, so he said to Larry, "Shoot me instead, I'm the one who's feeling miserable here."

"Oh, I could never do that," Larry said.

"I know you couldn't," Danny answered. "You couldn't shoot anyone." And that was all that was said about shooting and hitmen for the rest of the night. They continued to watch T.V. together. Sometimes Larry would mumble something, and then he'd talk coherently, only to start mumbling again. Sometimes he'd stop talking and just stare for awhile. As the night carried on, Danny grew increasingly worried.

Thursday, November 16

Danny had no phone, so the first thing he did when he got to the gym in the morning was to call Dr. Spelding and tell him what Larry had said about moving on with no place in mind to go to and the fact that he was planning to give his things away to his kids. He also told Dr. Spelding about the severe shaking and depression. He decided not to mention the remarks about hitmen and shooting, though, since he really didn't believe Larry was capable of such a thing anyway. Larry was given an appointment to see the doctor that day.

Next, Danny phoned Connie in Calgary to discuss Larry's emotional state with her. He told her everything from Larry's suicidal comments to his comments about shooting me and hiring hitmen. He also told Connie that he'd made another appointment for Larry to see Dr. Spelding and felt the doctor would be able to take care of things.

Connie was alarmed. "Danny! If you think Larry could really shoot Sharon, then you've got to call the police!"

"If I thought he would do that Connie, I would call the cops. Honestly, I would. But I just don't think he

219

could do it. You know Larry…he's just too passive to do something like that."

"Yeah, you're right. He's pretty gentle. But if you ever get the feeling that he could, you have to call the police."

"Don't worry…if I thought he'd do it, I'd call the police right away."

Now Connie was extremely worried. She knew that Larry was supposed to be moving in with Luke any day and wondered if anyone had told him where Larry's head was at. She decided to call and warn him. She told him Larry mentioned to Danny something about going to Vernon to shoot Sharon.

"What!" Luke exclaimed. "Did Danny call the police?"

"No…he called me instead, but don't worry. Danny said he'd call the police if he thought it was necessary."

"What do you mean, if he thought it was necessary? That's not good enough," Luke insisted. "The police should be called…I'll call them…Sharon should be called too…someone's got to warn her. I'd call her, but I don't even know her last name and I don't know her phone number."

"No, no, no…Listen, I know Larry Scott very well. I've known him for years. He's a non - violent person. He wouldn't hurt a fly. We don't need to call the police about this yet. He hasn't been taking his medication and that's why he's acting like this. Just leave everything to me, Luke. I'm going to contact Larry and see if I can straighten him out, even if I have to fly from Calgary to sit down and talk to him."

"I don't know Connie," Luke said. "This sounds pretty serious to me."

"Don't worry. I'll take care of it. Besides, what would we tell the police anyway? That a friend said Larry had mumbled something about shooting his girlfriend while they were watching crazy T.V. shows? They'd just laugh it off. Lots of people say 'I could just kill my girlfriend' or 'Boy, I could just kill my husband.' It's just a figure of speech - something blurted out when tensions get high. He'd never really *do* anything like that."

Luke finally agreed to let Connie handle it, but he still felt very uncomfortable about the entire situation. He really felt he should be doing something. He called Larry and left a message on his answering machine to call back as soon as he received the message. When Larry did call back, Luke told him that he could still move in with him on the seventeenth, but only with his clothes at first and if things didn't work out between them, he would have to be prepared to move out on one day's notice.

Larry was quiet for awhile, but then said "Okay".

Later that day, Larry went to see Dr. Spelding. They had another very prolonged discussion about his difficulties in dealing with the break up. Larry said he was still very depressed and angry about the break up of the relationship. He was frustrated that he didn't have it under control yet and felt that he had to get this relationship sorted out and back together again as he just couldn't seem to let it go. He told Dr. Spelding he hadn't been taking the medication but had been to private counselling sessions on two separate occasions. He thought it had done him some good, but he would not be able to continue due to the cost. He confessed he was still having difficulty staying away from Vernon and in fact would find excuses to go there, such as checking up on potential job applications.

Dr. Spelding's recommendations were that Larry restart the antidepressant. Also, to avoid putting himself into a frustrating situation, he should *not* go to Vernon for any reason whatsoever. He referred Larry to the Intake Unit for further counselling sessions that would be free and told Larry he could expect a call from them very soon. It was obvious to Dr. Spelding that Larry was not getting better, but was actually getting much worse.

They made an appointment to meet in one weeks time.

Dr. Spelding wrote to the Intake Unit stating that Larry was in a crisis situation, that police were involved possibly in regards to a restraining order, as his girlfriend had contacted the police, and that he needed to be assessed A.S.A.P.

During the following week, the Intake Unit phoned Larry to do a telephone assessment to determine what would be the best course of action to take with him. From the phone interview, they decided Larry would best be followed up by the psychiatric ambulatory care department and set the process in motion for an appointment to be set up.

Friday, November 17

Connie called Hedley's gym early in the morning and asked what time Larry was scheduled to come in to teach tennis. They said he'd be there at 1 o'clock, so Connie asked them to pass the message along to Larry that she'd call him at 2 o'clock, and he should wait for her call.

As promised, Connie called right at two and Larry was paged. She started off by telling him that she'd heard he had been going to Vernon still.

"Yes, I have. I've done some terrible things, Connie. I've been going to Vernon too much, trying to follow Sharon...and I've done some things to her car and I wrote some bad things about her on a bathroom wall in a pub in

Vernon." Connie was shocked that Larry was actually telling her what he'd done. She thought he would have been too embarrassed to tell anyone or that he would be trying to hide it instead of blurting it out.

"I know...I've heard that," Connie said, "Now you listen to me, Larry. I want you to stay away from Vernon."

"I have to Connie. I'm not allowed to go there anymore. My lawyer said I could be charged if I go there again."

"That's good...then you make sure you stay away from there." It seemed Larry understood his situation, so Connie thought she'd change the subject. "How's your tennis going?"

"I'm giving it up - I'm getting out of tennis, Connie."

Connie was alarmed. This sounded suicidal. "Well, are you seeing any other women?" She thought maybe another relationship would rid Larry of any suicidal thoughts.

"Yes. Actually, I'm meeting a 21 year old tonight."

"That's great," Connie said.

"But no one can replace Sharon."

"No one can replace anybody Larry," Connie said, "but you have got to get on with your life. Look Larry, I'm going to be going overseas in a few weeks time, but you know that if you ever need to call me you can call me collect here in Calgary or even when I'm overseas. I'll give you my number and I want you to keep in touch with me. Okay?"

"Okay, Connie. It's been nice talking to you."

That night Connie did not sleep well. She had a feeling that things were very bad with Larry and she was really bothered by all she had found out in the last couple of days. In the middle of the night, she said to her husband: "I've got to call somebody. I've got to call Dr. Spelding. I have to do something here because it's just not right. It doesn't feel good to me. Maybe I should call Sharon."

"You can't do that, Connie," her husband said. "You can't call someone up and say that someone told you that someone's going to shoot you, because then she's going to live in fear for the rest of her life, and maybe that's not necessary."

She closed her eyes again. Maybe Cliff was right. Or maybe she was going crazy. How could Larry, who was so even - tempered and mild ever develop enough anger and guts to plan a shooting, or hire a hitman for that matter? He just wasn't that type of guy. But, on the other hand, if he wasn't that type of guy, why was he even talking about it? No, it couldn't be…it just couldn't be…this is ordinary life we're talking about…ordinary people - not Hollywood and high drama, with guns and shoot 'em ups. People you know don't go out and shoot other people. Or do they? No…no, he'll be okay. It'll be okay. It will all blow over - it's just a matter of time. And with that, she attempted to fall asleep again.

This was the day Larry was supposed to move in with Luke. But instead of moving in, Larry called Luke and told him he would move in the next day, Saturday.

Saturday, November 18

Larry phoned Luke once again and told him he'd move in on Sunday instead of Saturday.

Sunday, November 19

When Sunday arrived, however, Larry phoned Luke again, and said he would not be moving in at all as he was moving in with Danny Fisher instead. Luke was relieved. He felt his obligations to Larry were now over.

Larry spent Sunday morning packing some of his belongings into his car. He then drove to Penticton to see his ex - wife, Theresa, and his children. Theresa's fiancé was at her place when Larry arrived. Larry came into the house carrying some of his things, and Theresa asked why he was bringing his things into her house.

"I was hoping you would mind some of my stuff for me. Some of it can be divided up amongst the kids."

"What do you mean?" Theresa asked. "What's going on Larry?"

There was a slight pause as Larry took a deep breath. "I no longer have the will to live, Theresa."

She was alarmed. "Let me pray for you Larry," she said. "Let me take you to see the pastor. I'm sure he'd be able to help you."

"No, I don't want to see your pastor. You know how I feel about religion. You may as well pray for me, though. I've tried everything else and nothing seems to work. I just can't seem to get Sharon out of my head."

"What about going to see a doctor?" she asked.

"I'm already under the care of a doctor."

"What about seeing a counsellor?"

"I'm already seeing a counsellor too," he said. They talked a bit further and then Larry left.

Theresa thought perhaps she should call the police and even tried to get the license plate on Larry's new car to give to them, but she couldn't get it before he drove away. She decided not to call after all. She figured the doctor and the counsellor would already be doing everything they could to help Larry in the situation he was in, so a call to the police really wasn't necessary. It was obvious to her that Larry was considering suicide, but she didn't know what more she could do for him, but pray. So she worried and she prayed.

Monday, November 20, 1995

Theresa phoned the resort early in the morning to see if Larry was okay. He'd spent the night in his old place, instead of Danny Fishers. One minute they were talking, and the next minute, the phone went dead. She called back.

"What's going on Larry?" she asked.

"I'm going to be leaving the resort. They've asked me to move out."

"Well, give me a number where I can contact you."

"I don't know where that will be. I don't know where I'm going."

"Okay...so then call me as soon as you find a place. Let me know where you are. I want to keep in touch with you."

He agreed to call her as soon as he found another place and they said good - bye to each other.

It had been two weeks since I last spoke with Constable Morrison. Since that time, Larry made no contact with me whatsoever. No hang up phone calls, no letters, no vandalism, no unexpected appearances. My fear was starting to loosen its grip on me. I felt like I was in remission, which was fortunate, as Tom needed my help working out his school problem. We'd already met with the Principal and the Superintendent, all to no avail. An appointment for an appeal had been set for November 23rd.

Wednesday, November 22

At 6:15 in the morning, Larry was at Hedley's gym to teach tennis for Danny, who was still sick with the flu and couldn't make it for his early appointment. He taught until 7:45 and then met with Dieter on the court for a scheduled 8:00 a.m. lesson.

Dieter found Larry to be in very bad shape during the lesson. He seemed disturbed and was shivering and trembling so much that he could hardly play tennis. Halfway through, Dieter said, "It appears to me Larry, that you have made very little headway in getting over the break up. You are too distracted to play tennis. Let's go upstairs and have a coffee and talk instead."

Gladly, Larry agreed.

"Tell me how you are, my friend. How are you feeling today?" Dieter asked Larry after they sat down.

Larry looked straight at Dieter and in a relatively firm and calm voice, he said, "I'm alright."

Larry's composure surprised Dieter after what he'd seen on the tennis court. He hoped that maybe, somehow, in that instant, something had happened in Larry's mind to rid him of his problems.

"What is it? You say you are okay, what do you mean by this? What are you planning? What is it you are going to do?"

"I need a good rest, Dieter."

"What do you mean? Are you going away? Where are you going?"

"Well, never mind. I need a good and a long rest, and I will have that!" Larry explained. Dieter became very concerned at this statement, taking it to mean that Larry did not have travel plans, but suicide plans instead.

"Larry, if you are talking about what I think you're talking about, then don't do it. It's not worth it."

"No, no. Don't you worry, don't you worry," was all Larry would say about his plans for a rest. Dieter pushed for answers, but Larry would tell him no more so Dieter decided to leave it at that for now and try again the next day after their tennis lessons. They confirmed their plans to meet the next day for lessons and parted.

After having coffee with Dieter, Larry ordered a big lunch at Hedleys. It was common knowledge amongst the regulars at the gym that Larry had not been eating well for quite some time, so it was a welcome relief for everyone to see Larry finally eating a good lunch. They all hoped this was a sign that he'd turned the corner and was going to be alright now.

As Larry was finishing his lunch, Danny showed up. "Glad to see you eatin' buddy," he said. "I was surprised when they said I'd find you in the lunch room. Way to go."

Larry smiled. "I've got to pick up my Nissan from the mechanics around 2 o'clock. Do you think you could go with me and drive the purple beater back here for me?"

"Sure," Danny said. "I'll meet you back here at 2 o'clock."

Then Larry drove to Dr. Spelding's for his 12 o'clock appointment. They had another prolonged discussion about where Larry's head was at the moment. Larry told Dr. Spelding that he was not happy with receiving only a phone call from the Intake Unit as he didn't feel a phone call was adequate at all in terms of helping him. He wanted and needed one on one counselling. Dr. Spelding explained that this would be coming very soon because the Intake Unit had recommended he be seen by the psychiatric ambulatory care department in the outpatients department of the hospital.

Dr. Spelding's main concern, however, was Larry's plan to give his stuff away to his kids. He asked Larry point blank if he had indeed been doing this.

"Yes, I have been to Penticton and I've given some of my stuff to my kids," Larry answered.

"Why have you done that?" Dr. Spelding asked.

"Because I can't stay with Danny that much longer. Pretty soon I'm going to need a place of my own. So I took certain things to my kids, the kind of things that could be given to my family - things I might otherwise not be able to take along with me when I move to a new location."

They discussed fully and frankly whether or not Larry had any suicidal intentions at this point. Larry said he was definitely not making any plans about suicide, but he did feel depressed and had briefly contemplated it in the past week or so.

Dr. Spelding suggested very firmly to Larry, that he be admitted to the Psychiatric Short Stay Unit in the Hospital as this is where he would receive the type of one on one counselling he needed. But Larry stated that he did not wish to go there at that time and since he was not obviously suicidal and was not psychotic, Dr. Spelding could not commit him. So he did the next best thing. He made a pact with Larry: "Either you will contact me, or you will get yourself to the hospital if you feel desperate over the next 24 hours, and you will continue taking the Luvox® and you will call me tomorrow with your decision about the Psychiatric Short Stay Unit. Agreed?"

"Agreed," Larry said.

Dr. Spelding explained further that he would leave instructions at the emergency department that if Larry came to the emergency room at the hospital, any time of the day or night, the psych unit would be made available to him and he would be taken care of.

"Yes," Larry said. "I understand." He left the office to go back to Hedleys to meet Danny.

They drove together to the insurance agent to insure his Nissan. Larry chose the twelve month package and set up automatic monthly deductions from his account. Then they drove to the mechanics to pick up the Nissan with its newly rebuilt engine. While they were driving, Larry asked Danny, "How'd you like to go out for a few drinks with me this evening and maybe even go two - stepping?"

"If I didn't already have plans made for the evening, I would go with you for sure, buddy. Maybe we can do it another night soon." What a relief, Danny thought - he's eating again and he's got his car all fixed up and insured, and now he's even planning on going out and having some fun. He's definitely on the road to recovery.

Larry paid the mechanic cash, then drove his Nissan back to Hedley's gym and Danny drove the old, purple and white Cadillac back. They parked both cars in the parking lot behind Hedleys Gym. Larry thanked Danny for his help and they went their separate ways.

When Danny got back into Hedleys, Connie was on the phone from Calgary.

"How's Larry doing, Danny? I just heard that he's eating again."

"Yeah, that's right. He's doing great! He's the best I've ever seen him. He ate a big meal here today and he got his car all fixed up and then he even asked me to go out two - steppin' with him tonight. I think he's going to be okay, Connie. I think he's turned the corner."

"What a relief! I've been worried sick about him," Connie said.

"Yeah, me too!"

I'd been out at my usual Wednesday night volleyball game with the girls. We'd gone to the bar afterwards, but I was too preoccupied with the schoolboard meeting I had the next day to be able to relax and enjoy everyone's company. Plus, I was still nervous enough about Larry to be constantly looking over my shoulder everywhere I went. It was only 10 o'clock, but I decided to go home early to get a good nights sleep for the next day.

On my way home I was thinking about how important it had been for me to take Wednesday evenings off just for myself, going out with the girls and getting some exercise as well. It certainly had helped me somewhat to deal with the stress I'd had the past few months, between Larry stalking me and now Tom's problems. Soon, I thought, I'll be able to take some time on the weekends too and start cross country skiing again - maybe I'd even enter a loppet or two. I was looking forward to the freedom of doing whatever I felt like doing and not being held back by someone else.

I pulled my car up into the carport as far as it could go. I'd been doing this regularly since talking to the security guard at the hospital. My car door was no more than three feet away from my house door. I got out, closed the car door and turned to go to my house door with the key ready in my hand, when a motion at the corner of the carport caught my eye. I turned and what I saw froze my blood. Larry was standing there - with a gun - and it was pointing straight at me! He *never* said a word. He just stared at me with this crazy, wild look in his eyes.

This can't be happening, I thought. It's too bizarre…it's too violent. He can't really be planning to *kill* me! It took a second to realise I wasn't hallucinating. No, he was really there, and he really did have a gun and, Oh my God, he's coming towards me.

"Larry, don't do this," was all I could say. I started to back up as he came closer, his gun still pointing at me. I turned and started to run to the other side of the car with him chasing me. We ran around the car once. Then he stopped and rested the gun on top of the car to get a better aim as I came by. I knew I was going to hear the sound of that gun go off any second and I knew the only part of me he could see was my head and I kept thinking that I don't want to be shot in the head - I didn't want him to blow my head off. I didn't want to die that way. But there was no blast. Instead, he came after me again and we ran around my car again. Once more he stopped and tried to aim at me over the top of the car. Still no blast. Every time I got around to the carport entrance I yelled for help as loud as I could.

Seconds became eternity while thought after erratic thought bounced around in my head: This is it - I'm actually going to die, right here, right now, I won't see tomorrow...So this is what it feels like to face death...Oh no, what if he's going to shoot me and then go and shoot my kids...Oh my God - what if he's already been in the house and shot my kids...Why's he doing this...I've got to run...I've got to run as fast as I can...Why is no one coming to help me...I'm screaming and screaming for help, but no one's coming. Please...please...somebody help me.

But Billie had heard me. She'd been getting ready for bed. She rushed downstairs to come into the carport to help me, but as she got close to the door she realised she should call 911 instead. She ran back upstairs into my bedroom, where Daisy was sleeping, to call. Daisy woke up to find Billie crying into the phone.

I came running around the car one more time. I was so frantic by now that I hadn't noticed that Larry had quit running and stood waiting for me, gun raised and ready. I knew I'd had it then. All I could do was turn and run. A few more steps and I heard the blast. It sounded like a huge explosion. The shot hit my left arm and I collapsed onto the driveway. I closed my eyes. I didn't want to see the rest.

I was in shock as I lay helpless on the driveway. I wasn't thinking about Larry anymore. I was thinking about dying. I knew my end was very close and I started to think about the life I'd led. Time ceased to exist as I went through a simple life review. I had no regrets, none whatsoever. I was satisfied with my life in every aspect, knowing it had gone exactly as it was meant to. I thought of my children and saw that each and every one of them was a wonderful human being that would do very well in life, without me. I saw no worries for them at all. I was at peace with myself, except for one thing...I was just too young to die.

That's when I felt the next shot. Larry had walked up to me, placed the gun on my back and pulled the trigger. It was a pump action, 12 gauge, sawed off shotgun. Amazingly, that shot didn't kill me, but it did do a lot of internal damage.

Truly now, my time was up. I felt an incredibly warm feeling of absolute peace flow into me and surround me. It was energising, yet calming at the same time. It felt like complete love and acceptance on a scale much larger than humans are capable of. And I just "knew" everything was going to be okay. I became *very* relaxed. Then I heard a voice talking to me. It seemed to be coming from inside my chest. It said a couple of times: "Roll over and play dead, or he's going to shoot you 'til you are dead!" Those are the exact words. I didn't question this voice, nor did I hesitate. I simply did as it said. I'd been on my side, laying on my left arm, the one that had been shot. I rolled over onto my back and as I did so, I let my right arm flop down lifelessly, away from my body. I groaned as I let my head fall to the side, opening my eyes briefly and then shutting them again, just like I'd seen on T.V. I didn't move a muscle and I dared not breath.

There was a few seconds of complete quiet, and then - another shot! Before I could open my eyes to see what had happened, I felt something land on my outstretched arm with a dull thud. I opened my eyes and saw Larry lying beside me, his head resting on my outstretched arm. He groaned and closed his eyes as his head turned toward me. I could feel the life leaving him as he died...right there on my arm, thinking that we had died together. What he didn't know was that I was still breathing.

Everything was so quiet now. Not a sound to be heard.

It was over. It was *all* over.

How I loathed this man, lying quietly, so close beside me, as though we were a couple. I was full of hatred and anger and I wanted to push his body off of me. I wanted him out of my sight. I wanted absolutely nothing more to do with him, ever again. But I was trapped. I couldn't move - not even a muscle. He'd blasted my left arm to pieces and his dead weight lay on my right arm. I could do nothing on my own to free myself from this awful, awful man. The only thing I could do was wait for what seemed an eternity, for someone to come.

Tom, came out of the house, crying. Over and over he told me, "You're going to be okay, Mom. You're going to be alright." And then he ran back into the house to get blankets to put over me to keep me warm. Matt, who'd come back to visit for a few days, went to the back porch and threw up. Billie and Daisy were still in my bedroom. They didn't know everything was over and that Larry was dead, and when Tom came running back into the house to get the blankets, they thought it was Larry coming in to shoot them. Daisy made herself as flat as she could under the covers and pulled the blankets right over top of her. Billie lay huddled in a corner, crying.

Tom came back out and covered me up, still assuring me that I was going to be okay. The neighbours were there now too and I heard the welcome sound of the police and ambulance sirens. I tried to lay still and to keep myself relaxed. Larry was dead, I was alive, so were my kids, and help had arrived.

All the weeks of stalking, the fear, the worry - it was done with, it was truly over. The relief and the release I felt was tremendous, and I simply *knew* that I was going to be okay.

Except...it was getting rather hard to breathe.

The police took Larry's body carefully off my arm. Finally, I thought. One of the policemen knelt down beside me and looked at me. I saw in his eyes a genuine look of care and concern and I knew he would take care of everything. The ambulance attendants were busy all around me. There was a problem, apparently, of getting me onto the stretcher due to the fact that when I rolled over to play dead, my left arm became stuck underneath me. Hurry guys, I thought, and I concentrated on keeping calm and breathing shallow and slow.

"Call Grandma, Tom," was all I could say. They lifted me onto the stretcher and then into the ambulance and started to cut off my jacket as they drove quickly to the hospital, sirens blaring.

Tom went in to call Grandma, along with my neighbours from across the street looking for the rest of the kids. They found Billie and Daisy still in my bedroom and told them everything was over now, that I was alive and had been taken to the hospital and that Larry was dead. They took both Billie and Daisy to their place for the night, and the RCMP came later to give them special teddy bears.

Tom and Matt went to the hospital and spent the night in the intensive care waiting room, worrying and wondering. They thought I had only been shot in the arm and figured I would be okay, until a doctor came in and explained all my injuries to them and said it would be touch and go, but they would do their best.

Four doctors, two anaesthetists and several nurses orchestrated the operation that lasted for six and a half hours.

"Who is this we're working on anyway?" one of the doctors asked halfway through the operation.

When someone said, "Her name is Sharon Velisek," a hush fell over the operating room. I was a long time friend of one of the anaesthetists and had become acquainted over the previous two years with the doctor who had his hands in my lungs.

I was transfused with 14 units of blood during the operation. The doctors amputated the top half of my right lung and stapled up the remaining portion. The gunshot wound on my back was very large, approximately 5 x 4 cm with a surrounding flare of pellet holes and was full of pellets, fabric pieces, shards of bone and a large piece of plastic wadding of some sort, which was given to the police along with several of the pellets. The wound was cleaned as well as possible and muscles and skin were stitched back together in the best fashion possible.

Attention was then given to my left arm. There was a question of whether or not it would need to be amputated. But further investigation revealed that my arteries and veins were not blocked - just twisted up and when these were carefully straightened out, the blood to my hand started to flow again. Amputation would not be needed. However, my humerus had been completely shattered and much of it lost…the muscles ripped apart due to the blast. A device called a Hoffmann was used to hold the two sections of my arm together until I was stable enough to be transferred to the Vancouver hospital for reconstructive surgery, if I survived the next few days.

It didn't look good. No one knew if I would live or die. One of the doctors gave me a 30% chance of living. My family were told to prepare for the worst and the RCMP were also notified of my critical condition.

While I was being operated on, the RCMP were contacting next of kin. Tom had already called my mother and she in turn called my brother Doug in Saskatchewan and my sister Jennette in Victoria. They all caught the first flights out. The RCMP in Nelson were contacted to notify my ex - husband. He picked up my oldest son Jake, and they drove to Vernon. The Penticton RCMP were contacted to notify Theresa about Larry's death. The RCMP in Moose Jaw, Saskatchewan were notified to let Larry's parents know about his death. The Coroner and a funeral home were contacted to deal with Larry's body. Victim's Assistance was called to the scene. A Constable was sent to the hospital, while others checked out my carport. They found two expended shells on the driveway near me and upon further inspection discovered another one in the carport. The gun itself had one expended shell in the chamber and a live round ready in the magazine.

Constable Gordon was one of the RCMP officers who attended the crime scene. He was very disconcerted by what had taken place. So much so that he went back to his office in the wee hours of the morning, after everything was taken care of and cleaned up, found my file and reviewed it. How could this have happened, he wondered? Everything was there. My complaints, my diary, my statement for a peace bond, documented vandalism and my requests for help from the RCMP. Even Section 264 had been mentioned in my file. Why wasn't it more fully investigated? The results of the autopsy toxicology results a few days later showed drugs or alcohol were not behind Larry's actions: *Ethyl Alcohol not detected. Morphine not detected. Cocaine not detected.* So then, why did he do it? And why wasn't he stopped?

The RCMP issued the following press release the next day:

Vernon RCMP are currently investigating a shooting incident which occurred shortly after 10:00 p.m. on 95 - 11 - 22 in Vernon's East Hill area. A 51 year old man shot his estranged girlfriend with a shotgun before turning the weapon on himself.

The woman was returning home when confronted. She is in the hospital in critical condition. The man was dead at the scene.

No names are being released pending the notification of next of kin. Police are continuing to investigate.

Thursday, November 23

Danny Fisher was at home listening to the early news while getting ready for work. He stopped dead in his tracks when he heard the report. He couldn't believe what he was hearing. No names were given, just ages, but he knew it had to be Larry…who else could it be?

As soon as he got to work, he called Connie: "Connie, how old is Larry?" And then he told her what he'd heard on the news. She was in shock. She immediately called the RCMP in Vernon. "Is it true? Is Larry Scott dead?" she asked.

"I'm sorry, I can't release that information. Who am I speaking to?"

"My name is Connie. I'm in Calgary now, but I also live at the resort. I'm one of Larry's best friends and I've been helping him with the whole break up," she said. Because she was so upset, the constable told her that Larry was indeed dead. Then he took her phone number and address and told her that she may have to be a witness at some point in the future.

When Connie got off the phone, she was beside herself. She called Luke right away, but only got his answering machine. In tears, she left a message for him to call her back right away.

In the afternoon, Constable O'Riley called Connie back to discuss the case with her. "You know, it's amazing that this happened because there was no history of abuse whatsoever, with Larry and his ex - wife or with Larry and Sharon," he told Connie. "He'd been tampering with her car, writing obscenities on bathroom walls, but even Sharon herself did not believe it was Larry who was doing these things and stalking her!"

"Yeah, I know. I knew Larry so well, too. I never would have thought he could possibly do something like this." They talked for some time, repeatedly assuring each other that there had been no warning signs of violence from Larry that they could have seen.

Luke Penner also heard the news in the morning and was stunned. He listened to Connie's message and called back right away, but there was no answer. He felt awful.

He was upset with Connie that she hadn't done anything and he was upset with himself for listening to her. In the evening, Connie called Luke back.

"We should have phoned, Connie. I shouldn't have listened to you. We should have phoned! We could have helped her."

"I can see that Luke," Connie answered. "I can see that we should have, but we didn't, and now it's too late."

The local TV station managed to obtain a video of everything that happened in my carport after the ambulance and police arrived. They'd interviewed the RCMP, and along with clips from the video, they were ready for the 6 o'clock news. It was their headline story. Their newscast included the following comments by the RCMP:

> *"Some strange things had happened, some suspicious things, after the woman had broken up with this individual. The paint on her car had been scratched a few times. I think she found a board with a nail under her tire. She had every reason to believe this individual was responsible, but we couldn't tie him into it."*

Then a reporter goes on to say:

> *"The RCMP say Velisek did not feel she was in any danger because her relationship with Scott had not been abusive. He didn't have a criminal record or a history of violence. When Velisek did call the police, it was only to say that she suspected her estranged boyfriend was the person responsible for damaging her vehicle. Ironically, while RCMP were trying to locate Scott so they could talk to him about the vandalism, he was waiting outside Velisek's house."*

Friday, November 24

The RCMP called Doug, Jennette, and my mother to the station, offering to answer any questions they had. My family's attention was piqued when the RCMP told them I had asked for no further action in the end. This was not what they remembered from my last conversations with each of them. They all knew I'd been told by the RCMP to "wait and see" and report any further contact, which is exactly what I was doing. However, none of us could have ever guessed that the very next contact to report would be an attempted murder and successful suicide.

Sharon Velisek

Part III

Sharon Velisek

The Aftermath

I slowly came to. There was a nurse by my side telling me the doctors had paralysed me so the breathing machine could breath for me for awhile, and that was why I couldn't move anything. What a relief. I thought I'd been permanently paralysed from the shotgun blast. I was intubated so I couldn't talk, which felt strange, but I knew I was in good hands. It was good to be back.

I stayed in the intensive care unit for six days and during that time I had daily visits from my family and my children. At first I didn't understand why everyone had come from so far away to see me. I had no idea just how serious my injuries were. What I did know was that I was alive and I was going to be okay. It simply never occurred to me that it could turn out any other way once I saw that Larry was dead.

My sister had been to see the school officials on my behalf and Tom had been pardoned because the school officials did not want to add additional stress to what was already a stressful situation for my family. My employers both told me they would hold my job until I was feeling ready to return, so I wasn't to worry about that. And the nurses helped make a birthday gift for Billie from me, who was turning thirteen in a few days, of a blown up surgical glove. So I wasn't to worry about anything. Everything was under control. The doctors visited me regularly, checking and re - checking. Pulling tubes out, hooking up wires, monitoring machines, asking questions, can you move this, can you feel that? And the nurses were absolutely wonderful. I loved them all.

I was a mess, I've been told, with everything that was hooked to my body, not to mention my ballooned up face.

When Billie first saw me, she had to leave the room to throw up. Daisy started crying when she saw a monitor's zigzag line go flat until the doctor explained it didn't mean I had died.

I still couldn't talk. I tried, but couldn't seem to get the sound to come out. I had to answer everyone's questions by writing the answer on a piece of paper held up for me. Often, they couldn't read my writing either.

"What can I do for you Sharon? Is there anything at all I can get you?" one doctor asked.

"I scribbled 'cup of coffee'," and he laughed. But I got my cup of coffee.

Constable Gordon came to see me to ask questions about what had taken place in my carport. I nodded as he asked away. He seemed to have the facts straight, but what puzzled me was why there were four empty cartridges found and only three shots fired. Did I miss hearing one of the shots, he asked? No, there were definitely only three shots fired. I was certain of that. They had been burned into my memory.

"Did you know there was another shot ready to go in the gun's chamber?" he asked.

No, I shook my head. And that's when I saw just how important playing dead had been. If I hadn't, Larry would have shot me again as he had another shot ready to go for that very purpose. I'd come so close to death - far too close. People tell me I'm lucky, but I don't think so. It was that voice that saved me - not luck.

As for the extra shell - it was only years later that a good friend suggested to me that perhaps Larry had tried the gun out by firing it once before he drove to Vernon, just to see how well it worked, and when he cocked the gun in my carport that empty shell fell out, leaving four cartridges in my driveway and just three shots fired. To me, that seemed like the most plausible answer I'd heard so far.

At the end of six days I was stable enough to be transferred to a Vancouver hospital via air ambulance. I was glad to go as I desperately wanted my arm fixed. Every day the dressings had to be changed, which was excruciatingly painful. When the bandages were off I couldn't stop myself from looking at the wound. It didn't look like an arm at all; more like hamburger meat surrounded by bolts screwed through pale skin. It made me cringe.

I was first taken to the trauma unit in a Vancouver Hospital where I spent one week and was then transferred to an ordinary ward for two more weeks. I had a total of three operations: one to clean the wound, one to pin and screw my remaining bones together and one to do a skin graft to cover the wound. I had a partial radial nerve palsy as well, which meant I couldn't lift my left hand up from the wrist, nor could I get my fingers to respond. A brace was devised to hold my hand up, complete with elastics to hold my fingers up.

It was a long three weeks. I tried to read, but couldn't focus. I tried to write letters, but couldn't seem to control my writing very well. I tried to think about what had happened and what had gone wrong, but I couldn't get past the night in the carport. I relived it hundreds of times. Why didn't I run to the back of my house and try to hide? Why didn't I scream louder? Why didn't I run down the street? Why didn't I set off the personal alarm in my pocket? Why, why, why? I was beating myself up as though it was my fault. I should have acted differently - I should have been braver, more cunning. I should have tried harder, I shouldn't have been so afraid. The only comfort I found was when I turned on my walkman and listened to music.

Jennette came across on the ferry from Victoria to visit often. She'd give me updates on how my kids were doing. My mother was staying with them in Vernon and taking excellent care of them, with the help of neighbours and many other generous people in Vernon who would bring boxes and boxes of groceries. People were giving so much, my mother was running out of places to put everything. A trust fund had been set up for me with many people and companies generously donating money. Daisy's school had a hotdog sale and all the proceeds went to the trust fund. Other agencies had raffles in my name and on and on. The media was constantly reporting on my progress. I realised then that Vernon is an amazing city - definitely the most caring community I had ever come across.

One day as I lay in my hospital bed, surrounded by flowers sent to me by so many people, a man walked in carrying more flowers, and came over to my bed.

"You don't know me Sharon. My name is Don Parker. I'm Theresa's fiancé," he said.

Strange men scared me. And why would Larry's ex - wife's fiancé, who I don't know from a hole in the ground, drive for six hours in the dead of winter over treacherous roads to visit me in the hospital, I wondered?

"Theresa couldn't come herself," he explained, "so she asked me to come for her. These flowers are from her." He put them on the windowsill with the others.

"They're very nice. You'll have to thank her for me."

Don stood by the side of my bed and told me how terrible Theresa felt about what had happened and how her kids hoped I would be okay. He said they were planning to get married, but they knew it would be a tough go because of all the abuse Larry had dished out over the years.

"Did you just say 'abuse'? Are you telling me that Larry abused Theresa?" I asked. This was news to me.

"Yes, he did, physically and emotionally for many years. That's why she finally left him. I thought you knew."

"No, I didn't know. I had no idea. Larry told me that she left because she was mentally unstable…that she had become an alcoholic and an emotional basket case after a car accident that wrecked her back so that she couldn't play tennis professionally anymore. He said it was because of her emotional instability that he fought so hard in the courts to get custody of the kids."

"No, that's not how it was at all." Don went on to explain that Larry had started to abuse Theresa not long after they were married and settled in Vancouver, both teaching tennis. As the years went on the abuse became greater and greater and Theresa was having a hard time coping with it. She ended up seeing a lawyer who gave her no help whatsoever, and she even went to the police. Larry knew she was thinking of leaving and started threatening her as to what he would do if she did. She had a nervous breakdown and ended up in the hospital, due to Larry's terrorising, and that's where she got the help she needed to get enough courage to leave him." Listening to this, I was feeling sick to my stomach.

"And what about his kids? Did he abuse them too?"

"Well, I don't think I should be speaking for Theresa on that. I will say though, that things were not right between Larry and his kids and that's one of the reasons why our marriage is going to take a lot of work and patience."

I wanted to know more, but I was already physically exhausted and needed to rest. I had to say good - bye to Don, but I told him that when I'm better, I would like to get together with him and Theresa and talk more, to which he readily agreed.

After Don left, I lay there and wondered. How did I miss it? How could I have gone out with Larry for eighteen months and not have seen any signs of him being abusive? Was he just exceptionally good at hiding it or had I been too accepting and forgiving to pick it up? I couldn't remember him ever being abusive to me or the kids or to anyone. I was horrified and sickened by the realisation that if I had continued on with this relationship, it would only have been a matter of time before he started to abuse me and who knows, maybe even Daisy as well! I was equally horrified that I had been unable to detect any signs of abuse in an eighteen month relationship. My mistake, I reasoned, was in assuming that abusive traits are obvious and easily recognisable. I could see now how wrong that assumption had been.

It slowly dawned on me that being alive in a hospital bed was actually the best possible outcome from my relationship with Larry. What a terrible thought; to think that in the end, my only alternatives with this man, this man that I had so much fun with in the beginning, were to be either abused or murdered!

Three weeks after the shooting, I had my last operation in Vancouver and was transported via air ambulance back to the Vernon hospital, where hospital staff had reserved a private room for me. I was so glad to be back and to see everyone again, especially my kids. They couldn't quit talking about the mountain of presents under the Christmas tree. People just kept bringing more and more stuff, and although my kids missed me, they were pretty pleased with the way their Christmas tree was shaping up.

My mother was doing fine with my children and my finances were being taken care of by Criminal Injuries Compensation, which is similar to Worker's Compensation, but is for people who have been injured due to a criminal act, through no fault of their own. I had little to worry about, other than my health.

On one of their visits to the hospital, my family brought some of the newspaper clippings they'd saved, to show me. I was surprised at how many there were. I read through them and was quite surprised to see statements like "…but there was never any threat made or violence that we're aware of," or "He had been stalking her for about a month and a half and we had a restraining order in place," or "Velisek returned to the police detachment Nov. 8 saying she wanted no further police action as she thought the matter had been resolved." Who, I wondered, was coming up with such outright lies? It bothered me that the situation had not been reported correctly, but I put that aside. My task at hand was to get healthy, and all my energy had to go towards that if I was to succeed. I would look into the newspapers later…maybe.

I started to cry a lot. Sometimes I would start crying just out of the blue and I would cry for hours on end. Sometimes I would wake up crying and often I cried myself to sleep. My emotions rode a roller coaster. I was often tremendously angry at Larry for what he'd done, but the worst of it was, there was no way to tell him that. No chance of justice, no retribution, no possibility of meeting him face to face and punching his lights out. All I could do was lie there in the bed and try to accept that my life was never going to be the same again, all because of Larry. I didn't want to accept it...I wanted to fight it...but there simply was no one to fight.

The weeks dragged on in the hospital until I thought I could no longer bear it. Nothing but day after day and night after night, just lying in a bed, no energy to do anything but sit up once in a while and go for a walk in the corridors. My body was fighting off a pseudomonas infection it had picked up during my last operation. I had become very thin and every part of me was weak. My legs could barely support me. I forced myself to concentrate in my mind on getting better, and ever so slowly my body and the antibiotics eradicated the pseudomonas. January 6th, six weeks after the shooting, I was allowed to go home.

To be in my own house again was the most wonderful feeling. What was even better was to be in my own house and not have to do any of the work! My mother cooked and cleaned and took care of the children, including their arguments, and all I had to do was sit back and relax. I was able, for the first time in my life, to find time for reading and just relaxing or listening to music and not feel guilty about it. I was on holidays in my own house. I still cried a lot though. I was told this would continue in spurts for some time to come yet. My left arm was in a sling and my hand was still in its fancy elastic finger brace. My ribs and back ached *all* the time and I constantly felt like there was a 300 pound sumo wrestler standing on my chest. I was numb in many places on my body due to permanent nerve damage. But...I was home...alive...and not in a coffin. I had a lot to be thankful for, and I was.

Physio started immediately and soon became the focus of my life. I soon discovered the difficulties involved in having only one arm. Everyday occurrences like putting clothes on and off, doing up buttons, and tying shoelaces became a test of endurance and ingenuity. I wanted my left arm to work again and I knew physio was my only ticket, so I did everything my physiotherapist told me to do. The stronger I became, the more I could do - and the more I could do, the stronger I became.

The press would call occasionally to talk to me about what had happened and how I was doing, but I didn't want to talk to them. Not yet anyway. I was still so confused about the whole situation, I didn't know what I could say. Plus I couldn't understand why they said I never asked for help. The healthier I got, however, the more I was bothered by that statement. Finally, I got up enough nerve to call the RCMP station and find out for myself. My knees went weak and my heart started to pound, as I asked to speak to Constable Morrison. We chit chatted for a little while, I asked him if he found my car keys yet (the police had taken them from my carport the night of the shooting and had not returned them). He said he would look into the matter. Then, I asked him if he knew where the press would have got the idea that I wanted no further action taken from the police.

"Oh, I don't know," he said, adding rather nonchalantly, "but you know the press, they're always putting words into people's mouths."

I started to say something when he interrupted me to say he had to go - there was another call coming through that he had to take. He promised he would try and get my keys back to me and then he hung up before I could even say anything. I looked at the phone still in my hand, bewildered. Why the sudden brush off?

A few days later, Constable Gordon dropped by my house to give me back my keys. He was very friendly, very concerned and wanted to know just how I was doing and how everyone was coping with the situation. I liked his supportive manner. Just before he left, I told him that I had been thinking about writing a letter of complaint to the RCMP about the way they handled my case and I wanted to know what he thought about it. Was it worthwhile - would it do any good, I asked him? He was quiet for awhile. It seemed to me he was looking for the right words. Yes, he finally said…he would encourage me to write such a letter because something had gone very wrong in my case and it would be better to bring it out in the open and have it investigated so it wouldn't happen again. I thanked him for his honesty.

Over the next few weeks my health returned slowly but steadily. I was able to do most of the cooking with the help of my children and they were capable of doing the cleaning. I was even back to driving my own car, carefully and slowly, but I could do it. After being with us and helping for over three months, my Mom was finally free to go back home to Saskatchewan, leaving us truly on our own, which I found a little scary at first.

I still hadn't written my complaint letter to the RCMP. I was stalling. I wasn't sure I was ready for a confrontation with the police. Then one day, as I was lying on my bed doing exercises with my arm, I heard a man on the TV talking about me. I flew off the bed to see what was going on. Daisy had been looking around for a certain video and had accidentally put in the video that had been recorded of the newscast the night after I was shot. I listened incredulously, hearing for the first time what was said…

"The RCMP say Velisek did not feel she was in any danger because her relationship with Scott had not been abusive. He didn't have a criminal record or a history of violence. When Velisek did call the police, it was only to say that she suspected her estranged boyfriend was

the person responsible for damaging her vehicle. Ironically, while RCMP were trying to locate Scott so they could talk to him about the vandalism, he was waiting outside Velisek's house." How dare they? How dare they say I didn't feel I was in any danger and only called to report vandalism? How dare they lie by saying they were trying to locate Larry to talk to him about the vandalism at the very time he was waiting outside my house when they were doing nothing of the sort? I was incensed. I was infuriated. I was absolutely beside myself. I had Daisy play the video over and over until I could write down every word that was said.

I went back to my bedroom and lay down again. No wonder everyone thought I hadn't asked for any action. It was the police that were telling them I hadn't, right from day one. They must have been sure I was going to die to think they could make statements that were simply not true and get away with it. After all, what are the chances of anyone living through a shotgun blast in the back? "Sorry guys," I quietly said to myself, "I'm very much alive and rather upset that you misrepresented me." It was definitely time to write that letter.

The next day, as I was doing errands around town, I happened to turn the radio on just in time to hear an expert on stalking being introduced as the guest for the days talk show. His name was Phil Moriarity. I felt validated just listening to him. It seems I wasn't the only one who had been stalked. I wanted to listen to the whole program, but couldn't because of my errands. I ended up missing his contact number at the end of his show. That night, however, my sister called me and said she'd heard the end of the program, but not the beginning, and took down Phil's name and number to give to me. I called him right away. I desperately needed to talk to someone who was familiar with what I was going through. We talked for a long time. I found our conversation very comforting and supportive. I told him about the letter of complaint I was in the middle of writing and asked if he had any suggestions. He said the RCMP would be sure to call me in to talk to me in person after they received it, and when they did, to make sure that I did not agree to anything they proposed, but to tell them I needed time to think about it. He also said I should ask to see my file, and write down everything that's in it, that is if they let me.

After a few days of writing and rewriting, I was satisfied with my letter. I simply wrote about everything that had happened while I was being stalked, what the police had and hadn't done and how I felt about it. And at the end of four pages, I added:

> *Most women in my situation have not been so fortunate as to live through this type of experience. The odds are really stacked against women in these situations. Because I have lived through it, I feel it is tremendously important to let the police know how I felt in dealing with them so that in future cases they come across (and I'm sure there will be some) they may be able to handle the situation more effectively.*
>
> *When I first came to the police station I was very much in need of help. I had no idea what I was up against and I felt sure that the police would know how to handle this type of case. Unfortunately people who have never really had much to do with police before in their lives tend to have this view of the police in that they will save and protect you from the "bad guy" and that they know what to do. I was at a total loss as to knowing what a stalkers way of thinking is. It was something I had never dealt with before. I was confused and scared and I assumed the police would know what to do and that they would do it. I didn't think I would have to take the squeaky wheel approach or question their actions. Looking back at it now, I have the feeling that the*

police aren't very informed about a stalkers way of thinking at all. Either that or they don't take it too seriously and develop a "wait and see attitude". This attitude can never be appropriate in a stalking case. You can't just wait and see what happens while the stalker methodically destroys someone's life. It shouldn't have to end in tragedy if it is taken seriously from the beginning. If I would have known then what I know now, I would have been much more demanding with the police as to just what they're going to do about my case and why weren't things getting done? It's important for the police to realise that many women coming into the police station for help are feeling the same way I did…they're counting on the police to know, to take them seriously and help them out and they believe the police will do something when they say they're going to. If the constable is waiting for the victim to give him instructions as to what she wants done, then he should tell her that. It's very frustrating and extremely frightening when you find out that nothing is being done as this leaves you all alone at the mercy of the stalker.

I was very disappointed when I was told that my ex - boyfriend was going to be brought in and then nothing was done about it. This is inexcusable. It could have prevented the shooting entirely. I am sure the police I was dealing with know this and that is why there was such a rush to come up with an excuse for inaction after I was shot. Someone told the press that I had told Constable Morrison not to take any further action during our last conversation. THIS WAS NEVER SAID BY ME. I was going on his instructions of "wait and see" when I asked Constable Morrison what do we do now.

I would like something positive to come out of what I went through. I strongly feel more training is needed for the constables in the area of stalking. They need to get much more aggressive with stalkers right from the beginning and they need to do what they say they are going to do. When you are in the position of being the victim you count on this. Something also needs to be done about the filing system. So many times I heard "I can't seem to locate your file. I'm not sure what the other constable did with it"! This is not acceptable at all, especially if it is used as an excuse for lack of action.

If you would like to talk to me further regarding this letter you can reach me at home."

On March 25, 1996, I hand delivered my letter to the RCMP station and asked that it be given to the Inspector. I went home wondering if anything would ever come of it. I was quite surprised when the very next day the Inspector called me at home and said he and the Sergeant would like to talk to me soon. We arranged a meeting time for the very next day at the station.

I was so nervous. I didn't know what to expect from the meeting. I knew I'd be dealing with strong authoritative men, which had me worried. My physical health was getting better, but emotionally, I was still very vulnerable and mixed up. Frankly, I wasn't sure if I could keep myself together, or if I'd just break down in the middle of it all. But I knew it was something I needed to do, no matter how it ended. As I parked my car at the RCMP station, I went over what Phil had told me. I sat calmly for a few minutes, took a few deep breaths and then walked into the station. While I was walking, I couldn't help thinking how nice it was to not be looking over my shoulder to see where Larry was this time.

Sergeant Doyle came to greet me. He seemed likeable enough with a broad, friendly smile and warm handshake. He was not the large, imposing man I had imagined he would be, so I started to relax a little. We went to his office and after preliminary small talk, Sergeant Doyle started to talk about my case. He felt there had definitely been errors in the handling of my case that should not have gone unnoticed and that he regretted that someone other than him had handled the case at the time of the shooting, due to the fact that he had been out of town. I agreed, there had been many errors. He wanted to know what I wanted from the RCMP now…what would make me feel better about the situation. I wasn't sure how to answer that. I really didn't want anything, except that the mistakes made would be corrected and never happen again in the future to anyone else. Sergeant Doyle proposed that I meet face to face with Constable's O'Riley and Morrison so that I could discuss my disappointments with them and ask them whatever questions I had.

"No, no - I could never do that. I would find that much too intimidating," I said.

"I can be in the room with you if you'd like, or you could meet with them one at a time. Whatever makes you feel comfortable," Sergeant Doyle said. He seemed to be pushing, ever so slightly.

"I'll think about it and let you know," I said, "but I really don't feel comfortable with meeting them face to face and asking them questions. I'm still trying to sort out what hit me and why. I would appreciate though, if you could photocopy my file for me to help me with this."

He didn't see where this would be a problem and he took me to meet with Inspector Dunn while he went to photocopy my file. Inspector Dunn looked very solid in his uniform. He towered over me as he shook my hand with a strong grip and welcomed me. Throughout our meeting I was surprised to see how quickly and completely his facial expressions switched from soft to hard. I was never sure what he was thinking. At first, he told me that I had raised some very serious points. He said he could offer me no excuse except for laziness on the part of the constables involved, but of course he wanted me to understand the difficulties police often face when dealing with domestic abuse and violence - such as a woman, who after placing a complaint, decides to go back to the abuser and does not want charges laid. And then there was the other problem of the courts throwing cases back at them for a number of reasons. And then, of course, I was not to forget that the RCMP detachment is just a reflection of what is going on in society and that there are also police officers who abuse their spouses and every policeman brings his own set of baggage to a case sometimes. I just kept listening and nodding. I hadn't thought about any of the points he was bringing up. I was quite surprised at what I was being told, as though I'd just discovered there were 150 pieces to the puzzle instead of 100. Inspector Dunn's main concern, however, was with the checking system that was in place. It was an expensive system, according to him, and for some reason, it didn't work in my case and he wondered just how many other cases it hadn't worked for as well. When I asked him just how this checking system worked, he explained that when a file is started, whenever there is any action on it, it goes to a file checker who checks to see if proper policy procedure had been carried out by the Constable attending to the file. If it hadn't, the file should be given back to the Constable telling him to do whatever it was he hadn't done. This system had been put in place to double check on the actions of all Constables so that policy was always adhered to, and to catch something a Constable might not be aware he had missed due to changing policy. But somehow this system failed to pick up the errors in my case, and that's what he wanted to investigate.

The meeting had lasted close to two hours already and I could feel my energy draining away. Sergeant Doyle brought back my photocopied file, explaining that he could only photocopy what I had put into my file - nothing that anyone else had added. This won't do me any good, I thought. I already have all of that. So, ever so innocently, I asked the Inspector if he would mind if I copied, by hand, the rest of my file.

I could sense his deliberation as he looked over at Sergeant Doyle, saying, "Yes, that would be okay." Then he looked directly at me and said, "We have nothing to hide."

I started in, copying everything word for word, exactly as it was written. I was immediately struck by the brevity of what had been written by the Constables and by how much of my case hadn't been written up at all. There were abbreviations I did not understand, but rather than ask their meaning, I simply copied them down, knowing I could ask Phil to interpret everything. But when I got to the November 17th entry, I was dumbfounded. Constable O'Riley had made the entry...*Turned items over to Scott!* This, I had to ask about. "What happened here? Does this entry mean that Larry actually came to the police station and Constable O'Riley gave him his stuff?"

Inspector Dunn took a look and said yes, that appears to be what happened. I couldn't believe it. Constable O'Riley and Morrison had continually told me they were trying to reach Larry, to no avail, and then when he actually walks right into the station to ask for his belongings - they simply hand it over to him and he's free to go. How, I wondered, did they ever find the nerve to tell the media then, that they were still out looking for him? They didn't even try to catch him when he walked right into their own station! I knew I'd caught them red - handed.

When I was done Inspector Dunn asked me what questions I wanted answered. He told me that he most definitely wanted to do an investigation into my case and when I let him know what I wanted, by way of a formal letter, he would decide whether it would be an informal or a formal investigation. I asked what the difference was and he said there were some differences, but in both cases he would be the one that picked the investigating officer. Thanks to Phil, I agreed to nothing. I told him I would have to think about it for a few days and that I'd get back to him with my answer. I stood up to go and found my legs had turned soft. Somehow, I made it out of the station and into my car. Thank God that was over.

Phil called that night to find out how the meeting went and we spent the next hour discussing what was in my file and the options open to me. He pointed out that both the formal and informal investigations would only be the RCMP investigating themselves and it was doubtful much good would come from that to help other stalking victims. My other option, he said, was to go public with my story and then ask BC's Attorney General for an independent investigation into the case. That way, he explained, it won't be the RCMP investigating themselves.

"Go public…you mean tell my story to reporters? I can't do that Phil. I don't have the energy for that. Just a few hours with the police and I'm completely wiped out. I've been lying down ever since," I said. "Plus I don't think someone as high up as the Attorney General is going to have any interest in me. No, I think I'll stick to having Inspector Dunn do an investigation and just leave it in their hands." I couldn't imagine doing anything more than what I'd already done. But…on the other hand, Inspector Dunn had pointed out some serious problems in the system that I didn't even know existed before I met with him. I wasn't at all convinced that an internal investigation orchestrated by him would fix any of them. I spent the next while sitting on the fence.

Theresa called one evening and asked if I felt healthy enough to meet with her and Don for lunch in Vernon. I was more than willing as I thought this would be an opportune time for me to get her opinion of the investigation choices that lay ahead of me. Plus, if I did decide to go public, she would no doubt be brought into the overall picture, not to mention how tough it would be for her kids to have to go through more media coverage of their dad. I wanted to warn her about this possibility.

Theresa and Don were already seated when I walked into the restaurant. I sat down and we started to talk immediately. We had to force ourselves to quit talking just so we could order. Theresa wanted to know how I had fared through everything and I wanted to know more about the abuse Don had mentioned while I was in the Vancouver hospital.

What Theresa then divulged to me was nothing short of a horror story. There had been physical abuse, emotional abuse, and sexual abuse. Larry had, on separate occasions, grabbed Theresa by her hair and thrown her across the room onto the floor, held her head in a toilet to make her quit smoking, thrown her on their bed after pulling her out of the bathroom where she was trying to hide, held her down and with fist clenched, posed to strike, told her and their horrified children, who happened to be watching, that there would be no separation agreement. On another occasion he told Theresa that if she ever left, he would take their son away from her and once he told their daughter that she should warn her mother that if she tried to stay in the house, the big tree in the yard would end up falling on the house.

Emotionally, he constantly belittled her and often threatened he would have her committed to the psychiatric ward. There were some signs of abuse before they were married, she said, but she thought it would get better with time. Instead, it escalated.

Theresa also told me of a time when Larry had been thrown out of a Vancouver tennis club where he was an instructor because he assaulted a woman he was coaching. Apparently, he had grabbed her breasts during a lesson. The woman wanted to press charges, but when Theresa found out, she asked the woman not to because it would make living with Larry even more difficult. The woman acquiesced.

Eventually Theresa did indeed end up in a psychiatric ward and that is where she got the strength and support to finally leave Larry. She took the kids and went to Penticton where she had family to help her as well as the Penticton transition house, who helped her remain sane through Larry's use of fear tactics and continual belittling after she left. He often threatened to take her back to court to take her children away from her, which he assured her would be a nightmare for her. Both Larry and Theresa knew that if she had another breakdown it would mean Larry would most likely get the kids in a court battle. Eventually he did indeed go through a court battle with Theresa, where she had to defend herself and her sanity so that she could keep her kids. He tried to wear her down, but in the end, she won and was allowed to keep her children.

I didn't want to hear any more - it was all too sickening. I told Theresa the story that Larry had told me and all his friends about her...that she'd had a mental breakdown because of a car accident which did not allow her to teach or play tennis anymore, and that because of this frustration, she had become an alcoholic, a drug addict and then turned religious to the point where she had "lost it" and ran away with the kids, and that, sadly, we all believed him. After all…why wouldn't we? The way he told the story, it sounded so authentic.

We also discussed the various types of investigation possibilities. I asked how she felt about my going public with the story. Her largest concern was how it would affect her kids. They'd had a rough go of it with their classmates and friends knowing their father had tried to kill someone and then committed suicide. But I pointed out to Theresa that she should think about the future and supposing her daughter became the victim of a stalking case as she got older. Wouldn't she be glad that we had contributed to making some changes now, when we had the chance? After some deliberation, Theresa agreed that it would be a good idea and she told me that whatever route I decided to take, she would be okay with it.

I was curious what had happened to Larry's place and belongings since his death. I had hoped his kids would have at least got something from him, but Theresa said that Larry's father had the body flown back to Saskatchewan, where he was cremated. As far as she knew his father had taken care of everything and she wasn't sure what was going to come to the kids. His place at the resort, she had heard, was so filthy it had to be fumigated. As for the watch Deiter had given Larry, Theresa had no idea what had happened to it. I was glad to hear though, that her kids were doing fairly well, all things considered.

We parted company. It had been a most informative luncheon and I needed to go home and digest much more than my food. I obviously had been fooled, along with everyone else who had nothing but good things to say about Larry.

The following week a flu bug took over my body with a vengeance. I hadn't been sick in the four months since the shooting and I wasn't sure how well my body was going to be able to fight, especially since I was missing a large portion of my lung. I lay in bed most days and nights, which gave me a lot of time to think about what direction to take with the RCMP, but I still couldn't make up my mind. On one hand I would have liked nothing more than to simply hand the investigation over to Inspector Dunn and wash my hands of it, so that I could get back to concentrating on my health. But on the other hand, what good would that really do? After my meeting with the RCMP and talking to Phil, who was an ex - cop himself, I knew much more about how the RCMP was supposed to handle a stalking case and it troubled me that there had been many more mistakes made in my case than I originally knew of. I would make up my mind one day, only to change it the next.

And that's when I heard about it. The Gakhal shootings. April 5th, 1996, I was lying on my bed stuffed up and achy with the flu when Billie came in to tell me that her friend's Dad had just called to say that they should not go out anywhere because he'd just heard on the news that some crazy man was running around Vernon shooting people. We listened to the news and the more I heard, the more horrified I became. A man had come to the Gakhal's house at the time when everyone there was preparing for a wedding. He started shooting, first the father outside who was washing the car, and then inside - going through room after room, eventually leaving nine people dead. He then went back to his motel and shot himself. I could just feel the absolute terror - I knew what it was like to have someone running after you with a gun, knowing you were going to die at any moment, just waiting to hear the blast.

But what I couldn't imagine was the absolute panic of knowing it was going to happen to everyone in the house and not being able to do anything about it. Shot after shot and body after body left dead. An unspeakable horror!

I read in the newspapers that this man had been married shortly and then separated from Rajwar Gakhal, one of the occupants of the house. He had been harassing her and she had complained to the RCMP. But when I read that the RCMP said Rajwar had complained three times to the Vernon RCMP, but had not wanted them to take any action - my decision was made. It sounded all too familiar. Unfortunately, Rajwar hadn't lived to check what the RCMP were saying, but I had. In that moment I knew for certain I had to go for an independent investigation, especially since the RCMP operational policy at that time clearly stated that the RCMP are to "conduct a complete investigation even where the victim may not agree to co - operate." This was built into the policy simply because so many women who are in fear for their lives come to the police for help, but then are afraid to pursue the help offered to them because they know the man in question will make their lives even more difficult for going to the police in the first place. This clause was to take the responsibility off the victim and give it to the police where it rightfully belongs. No matter what the victim says, the police are to carry on with a *complete* investigation. The RCMP should have known that, especially after all of the red flags my case had raised with the people in charge of the Vernon detachment. Yet, here they were still trying to excuse themselves to an unsuspecting public, by suggesting there was nothing they could do because "she" didn't want them to take any action. The RCMP's behaviour had been inexcusable in my estimation. I knew what I had to do.

I called Phil and told him I had decided to proceed with going public. He would see what he could do, he said, and it wasn't long before he called back that a reporter from *The Province* would be calling me for a telephone interview, which she did. I told her my story.

The next day Phil called to say he had arranged for a reporter from the *Vancouver Sun* to meet with me here in Vernon, around the time of the Gakhal's funeral, which he was covering. Phil was also coming to Vernon and we decided all three of us would meet and do the interview together.

Hours of one - handed typing at my computer left me tired, but certain. My letter to the BC Attorney General was done. I included all the pertinent information I could think of; my diary, the statement of my relationship with Larry, the RCMP notes I had copied, some newspaper clippings and my transcript of the TV newscast. I bundled the package up and sent it off by courier just before I met with Phil and the *Vancouver Sun* reporter.

We spent over three hours talking. The reporter covered every aspect, every angle. It was much more in - depth than my previous telephone interview with *The Province*. He wanted to take all my documents with him to review, and he wanted my guarantee that I had indeed written to the Attorney General. In return I wanted his assurance that he would point out the problem areas and not just go for sensationalism. He agreed he would do his best and with some hesitation, I handed him everything I had. I felt as though I was signing over my life; agreeing to have myself exposed, knowing I had no control over what was going to be said.

I went home, utterly exhausted, and lay on my bed wondering and worrying about what I had started. It was as though I had been caught up in a whirlwind - some sort of force other than my own that was in charge, using me and everyone else like a pawn for its own end.

On April 15th of 1996 both the *Vancouver Sun* and *The Province* had my story on their front pages. Both reporters had written excellent articles, which was a great relief to me. The very next day Phil faxed me a copy of the press release the BC Attorney General's office had just released: *"Attorney General Says RCMP Will Review Velisek Case."* I had no idea the media could be that powerful and that fast! However, this was still not an independent investigation. An inspector from another detachment would review my case and make a recommendation from his findings. I wanted to talk to him - to tell him my side of what had happened, but I was told that he did not have a mandate to talk to me! Fortunately, he saw enough to concern him without my input. His recommendation was for further investigation.

On May 8th, Inspector Dunn rang my doorbell. He had been instructed by his superiors to come and tell me in person that there was a press release ready to go stating that an independent investigation, headed by Josiah Wood, had been ordered into my case. Mr. Wood was the same person who was heading the investigation into the Gakhal murders. Inspector Dunn and I spoke for awhile standing in my driveway, very close to the spot where I'd been shot. I knew having his detachment investigated was no fun, but I was surprised at how upset he was. "I know what you're trying to do," he said, pointing his finger straight at me, eyes narrowed in a face turned to stone. "You want something good to come out of this, but it never will. Nothing will ever come of it!" What could I say...I certainly didn't want a confrontation. But as I said good - bye, I thanked my lucky stars I'd chosen the route I had. Obviously, all was not well at the Vernon RCMP station.

It was time to find myself a good lawyer. I knew an Inquest had been ordered to look into the Gakhal murders, for which I was glad, but the problem as I saw it, was that Rajwar was dead taking the truth with her. Neither were there any family members left alive who knew enough about her situation to speak for her. I was concerned that because of this, too many important issues, not to mention the truth, would be left undisclosed. There was simply no one left to challenge the authorities. I also knew the independent investigation would not be made public, but an Inquest would be. Having witnessed the power of the press, I realised the importance of involving the public if changes were ever going to be made. And changes were definitely what I was after. Changes to the RCMP's knowledge of stalking and changes to their policy, as well as a better understanding of what's truly involved in stalking cases by the public.

But I was just little 'ol me - one person who managed to survive the attempt made on her life and even though my story was full of tragedy and drama, one story and one person was not enough to move the powers that would grant an Inquest into my case, and I knew it. I definitely needed a top notch lawyer - one who wasn't afraid to step on toes or speak out, one who's very appearance spoke of authority, and most importantly, one who was willing to represent me pro bono as I had no funds with which to pay anyone. I choose Jack Steeple of Steeple & Associates, who turned out to be an excellent choice.

After Jack's many letters requesting an Inquest, we did indeed succeed. An Inquest was granted by the BC Attorney General into the death of Larry Scott and was to be held in Vernon in September of '96. So now there was to be two separate types of investigations into both my case and the Gakhal case: an independent investigation by Josiah Wood and a Coroner's Inquest.

A great deal of work and planning went into the preparation for the Inquest. As well, I met with Josiah Wood for questioning and to discuss my concerns. The investigations ran in tandem, but they never crossed.

September finally came. My knees were shaking as I walked up the steps of the court house. TV cameras and reporters with microphones ready to stick in my face were everywhere, but Jack had advised me not to say anything. He did the talking for me, for which I will be eternally grateful. I'd always been a very private person. I was definitely not looking forward to speaking in public and facing the media.

Jack showed me where I'd be sitting, along with all the other witnesses, and although Phil was not a witness, he was allowed to sit with me for moral and emotional support. The inquest was held in the Supreme Courtroom, which was lavish and spacious with a high ceiling to accommodate the steep viewing galleries that looked down upon us from above. This was where the press had gathered. The coroner sat in the judge's chair, behind an extremely long, dark mahogany desk that was raised just enough so that everyone had to look up at him. Behind him were several long stained glass windows. It was an impressive sight. Opposite us, was where the jury sat. In the very centre of the courtroom sat the lawyers. There were five of them! One represented the Coroner, one represented the RCMP, one represented the Attorney General, one represented Constable Morrison and one represented me. The entire proceedings were taped. I'd never been in court before, let alone take part in an Inquest. I was apprehensive, that's for sure. I had no idea what to expect.

As witnesses were called up and questioned by the lawyers and sometimes the jury and coroner, I discovered more and more new information. It felt as though the blurry parts of the picture were slowly coming into focus. Every time I found out a new bit of information, I had to add it to the bits I already knew and do some adjusting. It was also nerve wracking wondering what everyone was going to say. This was not a rehearsal—it was live.

For the first time I heard what Larry's lawyer, doctor, counsellor and friends had said and done to help him. And for the first time since the shooting, I actually felt some pity for Larry. It became increasingly obvious to me, as the Inquest progressed, that his life after our break up must have been a living hell. His reaction to what he saw as my rejection of him had been extreme. But why, I wondered? Why did it gain such a strong hold on him? Why couldn't he get past it and on with his life as others do? Was it because he had so many other major stressors in his life at the same time and it was all just too much for him, or was it because he'd become too attached to his own personal tragedy? Was it the "poor me" and "look what she's done to me" attitude that sucked him in and held him, forever the helpless victim? Whatever the reason, I could see that he definitely had a tough time of it at the end as he became completely and utterly obsessed.

I was especially interested in what Constable's O'Riley and Morrison had to say. Constable O'Riley was put on the stand first. His posture had changed in the year since I'd last seen him. His shoulders were slouched and he looked much older and somehow very sad. I'd heard that he had been one of the first to arrive at the Gakhal's house after the shooting and that shortly after, he resigned from the force after being with them for over 24 years. I was surprised at how few details he remembered about my case, but I didn't get the feeling he was trying to hide anything.

Constable Morrison, on the other hand, took my breath away. The leather of his polished gun holster and shoes squeaked in the hush of the courtroom as he walked to the witness stand. He sat down in the witness chair, throwing both arms back on the wooden armrests on either side of the cubicle, looking ever so smug. My lawyer questioned him the same way he did all the other witnesses, trying to bring to light information the other lawyers seemed bent on trying to avoid. Mostly, Jack wanted to know Constable Morrison's opinion as to why more action had not been taken on my case by the RCMP. Jack quickly became frustrated with Constable Morrison's evasive answers. Finally he glared at him and said, "What did it need - what further information or evidence did it need to move it then into that category of being a violence in relationship file in your perspective?"

Without any hesitation, Constable Morrison answered, as if it should be completely obvious to everyone there. "Some violence," he said!

I gasped. He could have just as well knocked the wind out of me. All that time I'd been asking for help and waiting for the RCMP to do something to protect me, thinking they knew what to do, trusting them, only to find out they were actually sitting back waiting for something violent to happen to me before they took my case seriously enough to take action? I was outraged at Constable Morrison's insensitive attitude. Did he realise that the violence he was waiting for would have been at *my* expense and pain - the one he was supposed to be protecting!

Another point I had been completely unaware of until the Inquest, was the role of Victim's Services. It was revealed to me for the first time that there are actually two types of Victim's Services: Police Based Victim's Services and Specialised Victim's Services. The mandate for the Police Based Victim's Services is to offer counselling and emotional support to victims of a crime. However, if the case in question has anything to do with domestic violence or violence against women, child abuse, stalking, etc., then that case must be immediately referred by the Police Based Victim's Services to the Specialised Victim's Services, whose mandate is to help women and children in these situations to receive support, counselling, and education. They also advocate on behalf of the client with the police, to make sure police are taking appropriate action to ensure the safety of the client. I was never referred to them. It seemed like such a pity. That simple referral could have made all the difference, as I would have been given the support, the advice and the advocacy I so desperately needed while I was being stalked and basically on my own.

The Inquest into Larry's death was interrupted to make way for the Gakhal inquest, and resumed again in November of '96. Finally, on the 20th of November, it was over - with the jury handing in their recommendations after several hours of deliberation. Their main recommendations were that the RCMP in Vernon have an officer that dealt solely with domestic violence, that there be further violence in relationship education for police officers followed by periodic examinations, that there be crisis centres set up for men in emotional upheaval, that there be increased public awareness as to the meaning of stalking, that stalking is a criminal offence in and of itself, that children be taught anger management and appropriate relationship behaviour, and that physicians should possibly be allowed to communicate to the police when concerned about a patient contemplating violence to himself or to others. All excellent recommendations.

As to why Larry had tried to kill me and then himself - that question was never answered. Everyone had their own idea, their own interpretation of the events, but the truth lay with Larry and he'd taken the reasons with him.

The Inquest was over. Finally, I could breathe easy. No more public attention and reporters to deal with. No more meetings and phone calls about the Inquest. I was able to settle back into a more relaxing routine and concentrate on regaining my health again. I was physically very weak, with lack of air being my biggest problem. My left arm still had limited movement and even though I knew it would never be normal again, I wanted to work at getting it to do the most it could possibly do. I relaxed into a regular routine, waiting to hear how the Inquest results would be implemented.

I waited and waited, but nothing seemed to be happening. Whenever I asked if there was any decisions forthcoming, I was told the Attorney General's office was still waiting for the results of Josiah Wood's independent investigation before it made any announcements. This seemed fair to me, but little did I know at that time that Josiah Wood's report would not be completed for two more years! It was a long, long time to wait during which I often wondered if I had perhaps imagined the Inquest and Josiah Wood's report, as life's ordinary day to day events started to overtake and heal the drama I had been previously living. Every now and again I would call Josiah Wood's office just to make sure the report was really and truly coming. Always I was told it was still being worked on. Every now and again a reporter would call me and ask if I'd heard anything, and I'd have to say, "No, have you?"

Then they'd call Josiah Wood's office as well, only to be told it was still being worked on.

In the fall of '98, three years after the shooting, the report was finally released. A copy was sent to me in advance of the press release to give me time to read through its 106 pages so I could formulate my opinion, in case I was asked for it by the media.

I was close to tears as I turned the pages, especially when I read: *"The first* [difficulty the RCMP and police have in providing adequate responses to violence against women] *is determining the appropriate police response to a complaint from a reluctant victim of relationship violence where there is no recent or ongoing violence, no physical evidence, no witnesses and a request from the victim that the complaint be kept confidential. The second is changing the outdated attitudes which some police officers have to complaints of relationship violence. particularly when that violence takes the form of criminal harassment, and ensuring that those officers are provided with adequate education, training and information to permit them to appreciate the dynamics of relationship violence, to recognise the indicia of violent or abusive relationships and to appreciate that, as a serious criminal offence, relationship violence must be fully investigated."* (pg. 9 of Josiah Wood's report). When I finished reading the entire report, I wanted more than anything else, to go to Vancouver and hug the man.

To make matters even better, the RCMP's new operational policy was also included at the back of the report. What I hadn't realised until the Inquest, was that the RCMP generally follow their own policy - not the policy given to them by the Attorney General's office. So to have the RCMP themselves introduce their own new provincial policy at the same time as the report, was the icing on the cake as far as I was concerned. In the RCMP's previous policy, criminal harassment had been grouped in as part of the Violence Against Women in Relationship policy and was rarely mentioned on its own. I had always found this disturbing as my own experience of being stalked left me with the feeling that stalking was unique unto itself and needed its own definitions and set of rules as opposed to trying to lump it in under the broad category of domestic violence. Fortunately, the policy makers agreed and included criminal harassment in a separate section stating the following:

Criminal harassment is, without lawful authority and knowing that another person is harassed or recklessly as to whether the other person is harassed, engaging in conduct that causes that other person to fear for his/her safety or the safety of anyone known to them.

1. *Criminal harassment includes following or watching a victim, communicating with a victim or someone known to the victim, or threatening a victim or the victim's family or friends. Criminal harassment does not include vandalism or other minor criminal offences, however such offences, combined with the above may indicate the severity of the situation (i.e.: degree of risk to the victim).*
2. *Victims may feel powerless, overwhelmed, confused and unable to concentrate. They may find themselves isolated and afraid to leave their home.*
3. *A stalker can be anyone: a spouse/partner, a person who lived with the victim, someone the victim dated, a client, a former employee, co - worker, a fellow student, a peer or a total stranger.*

(A member of the RCMP must):

In suspected cases of criminal harassment or stalking, ensure literature from the Ministry of Women's Equality entitled "Are you being stalked…" is obtained and thoroughly discussed with the victim/complainant.

1. *Pay particular attention to the intensity of the emotions displayed by the suspect. Refer the case, immediately upon consent, to Victim Services.*
2. *Complete a Criminal Harassment Guidelines Check Sheet, Form "E" Div. 566 (Appendix IV - 1 - 8) in <u>every</u> case and forward it to your supervisor.*
3. *Ask the victim to prepare a log of all past suspicious occurrences and to maintain a log on an on - going basis of all future events.*

Members are cautioned that there is a very narrow discretion for not conducting a complete investigation. A member may decide not to contact or interview the suspect or anyone likely to inform the suspect that a complaint has been made. However, all other components of a complete investigation must be completed.

And for the first time in history - a Criminal Harassment Checklist that is separate from the Violence in Relationship checklist:

<u>Criminal Harassment</u>

To be completed on both attended and unattended cases when it is determined that an investigation may indict an offence of Criminal Harassment.

– CONDUCT A COMPLETE AND THOROUGH INVESTIGATION.
– DO NOT ATTEMPT TO RATIONALIZE EVENTS

- *Inform the victim of the nature of the offence. Be honest with the victim regarding the potential threat.*
- *Record all occurrences related to the victim; both criminal and non criminal, including details of conversations, threats and unusual events. Collate all occurrences into a history of events.*
- *Advise the victim to maintain a log of all unusual events, no matter how trivial; and to retain any notes, gifts, telephone answering machine tapes or any other evidence related to the investigation.*
- *Advise the victim not to initiate or agree to any contact with the offender but to record any attempted contact in a log.*
- *Provide the victim with an Occurrence Report number and advise the victim to quote that number when making future complaints.*
- *Request the victim to inform relatives, neighbours, friends, co - workers and employer of the Criminal Harassment and include a photograph of the offender, if known.*
- *Contact Victims Services with the victim's consent and arrange for a meeting:*
  - *during the initial interview.*
  - *immediately after the initial interview.*
- *Conduct PIRS / CPIC and Protection Order Registry queries of the victim and offender (if known) to establish a pattern of current and history complaints and activity.*
- *Determine offender's psychiatric history and all access to firearms.*
- *Place the information regarding the investigation on the Watch Briefing.*
- *Interview relatives, neighbours, friends, co - workers and other persons identified by the victim.*

THREAT ASSESSMENT:

- *Determination:*
  - *Risk is slight (no immediate danger).*

- □ *Moderate (psychological or property)*
- □ *Extreme (physical harm)*
□ *Recommended level of intervention - include rationale on investigative report:*
  - □ *No intervention*
  - □ *Face to face deterrence*
  - □ *Peace Bond (Section 810 Recognizance)*
  - □ *Arrest*
□ *Distribute mandatory VOC Act and Criminal Harassment literature from the Ministry of Women's Equality*
□ *Ensure statements are on file for the victim and all witnesses*
□ *Refer file to GIS for assistance.*
□ *Date completed: _____*
  Member: _____

SUPERVISOR:

- □ *Document complete investigation, verbal and written statements.*
- □ *Witnesses (i.e. friends, neighbours, children) statements on file.*
- □ *Document previous complaints by accused or victim.*
- □ *Document victim assistance provided.*
- □ *Document victim's reasons for requesting a complete investigation not be conducted.*
- □ *Document why case not referred to Crown.*
  Supervisor: _____
  Diary Date: _____

I couldn't have been more pleased. Both Josiah Wood's report and the new RCMP policy were well worth waiting for since, in my view, as far as policies went, a more airtight policy couldn't have been devised. It left very little room for a stalking case to slip through the cracks, virtually no way a Constable could justify not taking appropriate action, clear guidelines in the use of discretion, and an understanding of who was accountable for what, in case something went wrong.

It remained to be seen how well this new policy would be implemented and followed, however, which is where the real difference by the general public would be felt, but I felt the mere fact the RCMP was making their policy public meant they were not trying to cover up or hide their mistakes. To me, it was indeed the breath of fresh air, the honesty and integrity, I had long ago hoped for in my letter to the Attorney General. I was satisfied.

For the first time since I wrote my letter of complaint to the Inspector, several years before, I felt released from a large burden I had been carrying. It was as though a giant snowball that had been barrelling downhill, carrying me with it, had come quietly to rest on flat land, releasing me from it's grip. I felt lighter than air and content in my heart and mind.

"THE END"

Sharon Velisek

Afterword

For five years after the shooting, I worked away on this book. My soul searching, at times, seemed endless. The dynamics behind relationships and criminal harassment are by no means easy to sort out. Writing this book, however, has helped me understand what used to be jumbled up thoughts roaming around my brain - making sense of what seemed to be so senseless in the beginning. Hopefully it will help others sort themselves out too.

Both I and my children are doing fine. We have all survived the ordeal and life is back to as close to normal as we can get. I have even managed to jump across the protective barriers of fear I'd raised for years, to being able to date again. More importantly, I have been able to end relationships when they don't feel right to me. Anyone who was been stalked knows how truly frightening this can be.

I received excellent counselling paid for by Criminal Injuries Compensation, which was a tremendous help, but unfortunately my children were not eligible for counselling because they had not been injured. My children say they are okay because I am okay and so far this seems to be holding true. Knowing them the way I do, I am sure they will continue to be okay. But I do think it important to point out that if children witness a horrendous crime to their parents, they will need counselling to come to a positive understanding of the event. They may not have been physically damaged, but psychologically they cannot escape some form of damage.

There have been many events since the shooting, that have triggered extreme and sudden emotion in me. It's as though my body itself had been re - wired from the trauma of the stalking and shooting and reacts on its own, no matter how much my brain tries to control my reactions. I remember the first time this happened...I was sitting in the grandstand watching a local rodeo. The clown came out to do his act. It was obvious that he would eventually be shooting off the explosives that were part of his act. Everyone was forewarned, but regardless, when the explosives went off, tears started rolling down my cheeks and try as I might, I could not stop them. They sounded exactly like the shotgun. Daisy, who was with me, was worried about what was happening to her mommy and didn't know what to do. Neither did I. There wasn't anything else I could do, but let those tears keep falling, which they did for about half an hour. For years I'd jump whenever I heard a loud bang, but slowly my nerves lost some of their rawness and I was able to bring my mind into play a little more, telling myself it's okay, it's just another one of those physical reactions and it'll end soon. I know that as time goes on, I will feel less and less of an effect, but I also know that some of the triggers I will most likely have for the rest of my life, for which I am actually glad. They are my friendly reminder to be very careful with my choices.

I've learned so much from the entire trauma. It's caused me to examine and discover pieces of myself and the world that I would have found no other way. Rather than seeing trauma as negative, as we mostly assume it must be, I see it as a unique opportunity that opens us up to some very grand possibilities, if we look for them. For me, I would never have believed I was a strong person before...I believe it now; I loved life before, but now my love for life is overflowing with gratitude and amazement no matter what direction I look in; I knew people affected each other before, but now I know the effect one person has in the world is absolutely limitless and more powerful than I would have ever dreamed. So I try to keep myself positive; I still go to the same job every day, have the same house, the same kids - I simply "perceive" everything differently. It is the difference between living with my eyes closed and my eyes open.

So, if you have been in a traumatic experience - if you've been stalked and injured - if you sadly think to yourself, "My life will never be the same again!", you're right...it won't be the same again. It could be even better. You do have the power to make it that way.

Sharon Velisek

My Discoveries

Author's Note

Because of my personal experience, the experiences others have shared with me, and my research into the subject of criminal harassment, I have developed some tips and insights I would like to share with you in this section. Every stalking case is different and therefore you may find some advice relevant, and some irrelevant. Take whatever fits. It is my hope that it will be to your advantage.

20/20 Hindsight

It took awhile, but eventually I was able to admit to myself that I had made many mistakes throughout my relationship with Larry, and it was those mistakes that played a part in my being stalked and shot. It was far easier to blame and hate Larry, which I was more than happy to do for quite some time, but when I stopped blaming and took responsibility for where I was, I learned valuable insights into my character, plus it turned me into a survivor instead of a victim. And since it was me who made the mistakes in the first place, it was also me who could choose to avoid making the same ones in the future. I could change. I had some power afterall! But before I could avoid the same mistakes in the future, I had to learn exactly what they were in the first place. This book is a result of some of my soul searching and just in case you didn't catch some of my mistakes while reading through the book, I would like to point them out now in a more point blank form. Perhaps you will recognise some of them in yourself.

The primary mistake, of course, was not listening to my intuition when Larry and I first met. If I would have, our relationship would never have happened...I would not have been stalked...I would not have been shot...and this book would not have come into being. I didn't listen to my intuition, for two reasons. Firstly, I'd been married for seventeen years, which left me totally inexperienced when it came to dating. I was curious, I was eager and I couldn't see where playing a bit of tennis could hurt anyone. I didn't want to listen to my intuition and snuff out a bit of fun that I naively thought I had under control. Secondly, I had physical and emotional desires that were far more powerful than I would have thought possible. Meeting Larry brought them out from where I had them safely tucked away. Nothing smothers the willingness to listen to intuition faster than weakness, desires and need.

Another big mistake was acting according to some misguided beliefs I had. These beliefs were so basic and at such a deep level, I didn't even realise I had them. One of my beliefs was that I (and everyone else for that matter) had to have a partner, a man in particular, in order to be having 'real' fun. It did not occur to me that I could have fun that was fulfilling doing what I wanted to on my own, without a man. I never even spent time trying to sort out what it was that "I" wanted to do. Instead I was trying to fix what society had trained me to believe was broken - I was a woman without a man and I would not be complete in any area of my life until I had one, which explains why I wasn't overly particular in my choices and why I was so bent on hanging on to the relationship.

I also was of the belief that you have to "find" a man, so I spent countless hours and energy searching for one.

So many times I asked myself, "How am I ever going to find a nice man?" However, a more appropriate question would have been, "Why am I looking in the first place?" When you're searching for someone and do not find them, or are constantly disappointed with what you do find, you'll be left with a sense of loneliness and as time goes on, an increasing desperation, which creates a vicious cycle. Your loneliness leads to more desperation and your desperation leads to more loneliness, until "finding" a man becomes the focus of your life. In my opinion, love comes when love comes...but it can never be hunted down. So why was I looking? Because I was lonely and because it never occurred to me that I could find the happiness I hoped someone else could give me, right inside myself, from myself and with myself. I didn't need to find a man - I needed to find my own self.

Adding sex to the picture far too soon was also a big mistake on my part. Just getting to know someone without sex raises enough emotions and questions to contend with, but if you add sex to the picture as well it becomes more than a mind can handle. It's like a pot that's on too high of a heat. It has no choice but to boil over. I am guilty as charged. I was so overcome by emotions that I hadn't any hope whatsoever of telling what was right and what was wrong the next day. The worst of it was that I thought Larry and I had truly embarked on a meaningful relationship because we had sex! Sex is just sex - it is *not* a relationship. If I had kept an appropriate distance from the beginning, I may have been able to see that dating Larry was not a direction I wanted to go, but once sex was involved I lost any opportunity I might have had to see that.

I discovered time and time again that I was the queen of denial. If something wasn't right in our relationship, I would simply work the problem out in my own mind until it was no longer a problem for me. I manipulated myself simply to avoid confrontation of any sort with Larry. But by not being upfront with my concerns, the relationship often went in directions I was not happy with, taking me along with it.

It's difficult to know what a good relationship is if you've never had one. I didn't know what I wanted in the way of a relationship - but I did know what I didn't want, and that was abuse and disrespect. I was sure I'd be able to recognise them. But that's not always the case. The negative behaviour you've been exposed to, and perhaps accepted, in your past relationships will seem familiar to you and therefore you may not even notice it. Your body will not give you the warning signals you think it will, because your body quit having them in your past relationship when you quit listening to them. I'd lived for years doubting myself and eradicating my boundaries - losing a sense of respect and caring for myself, along with the warning responses a body normally elicits. "Danger, Danger" should have been flashing in florescent lights in my mind, trying to warn and protect me when Larry asked me if I wanted to look at the horses in the corral at the end of a secluded path, but it wasn't. Instead I felt a dulled sensation of concern, which I didn't pay too much attention to anyway. The clincher, however, is that I didn't even realise until years later, and with much reflection, that if Larry had respected me, he would never have even asked! It's taken me a long time to build up a healthy sense of self - respect again. It doesn't bounce back automatically simply because you've ended a relationship.

Hindsight is a wonderful thing and used properly, you may never have to learn the same lesson twice. My so called "mistakes" were not so much mistakes as a lack of awareness and some misguided beliefs on my part. I have spent a great deal of time trying to sort out where I went wrong. I am satisfied with what I have discovered about myself and hope you can learn from my mistakes rather than having to repeat them yourself.

Who Will Stalk and Who Won't?

You meet someone who seems very nice and everything seems to be so good in the beginning of the relationship. Sometimes the relationship carries on to become very satisfying and fulfilling for both parties. But sometimes the relationship takes a turn for the worse and ends. In these cases, for some the end is truly the end, but for others the end becomes the beginning of criminal harassment. The problem is that the people who become stalkers often seem okay, or even exceptionally wonderful, in the beginning stages of the relationship. How then, can we tell early on who has the potential to stalk and who doesn't? There are no cut and dry rules or specific characteristics that will work for everybody. Everyone's different and every situation is different, however I have compiled some characteristics which you may want to take note of. The qualities may seem rather generalised, but that is one of the problems inherent in criminal harassment dynamics. Often, it's the qualities that attract us in the beginning that cause us the most trouble in the end - namely interest, caring, concern, attentiveness and persistence. When the relationship ends and love turns to hate, the attractive qualities can turn into obsessive qualities, and criminal harassment begins.

Qualities To Be Aware Of In The Very Beginning of the Relationship:

Basically, a potential stalker has a very low sense of self - esteem and an obsessive tendency. Over the years they have learned to cover up their lack of self worth by creating an acceptable exterior of themselves to present to the world. They hide their obsessiveness by expressing it as attentiveness when first meeting other people. They *do not* stick out like sore thumbs in the crowd.

The key to the following characteristics is not so much *what* they are doing, but the *intensity* with which they're doing it.

A Potential Stalker May:

* be very intent on creating a *very* good first impression of themselves during your first times together. If you think this person is too good to be true - they probably are. Some of the ways used to create good impressions are tipping excessively, giving you expensive presents in the beginning of the relationship, name dropping, telling you intimate stories that reflect how good they are, being *overly* romantic from the very beginning.

* hide any financial debts they have by creating the perception from the beginning that they are financially well off, and have the potential to become even more financially successful. Even if it's obvious their finances are not as good as they say they are, they will be completely convinced that they are on the verge of success (once such and such happens) and they will try to sell you on this idea.

* find it *very* important to be well dressed for all occasions. The reason for this is they are very concerned about the impression they give other people. They gain their sense of self - worth by fitting in, being acknowledged and admired by others. To them, their surface image *is* who they are, so they take good care of their outer appearance.

* seem *very* intent on listening to your every word and have a great ability to empathise with your past hurts and problems. They may seem very caring, concerned and interested in your past relationships and interests and ask you many questions about yourself, always listening carefully for your answers. This may make you feel as though they are very interested in you as a person, but really, they are trying to find out as much as they can about you as quickly as possible, so that they can discover the way you need to be treated to accept them with open arms.

* claim you as their property in public. It doesn't take much in the way of body language; constantly holding your hand, their arm around your shoulder 99% of the time, never leaving you talk to others by yourself, suddenly wanting to leave a party or social event, expecting you to leave as well. These gestures may be seen as an endearing sign of love and affection, but they can become smothering as time goes on.

* not be able to respect your "No" as meaning NO, or they may not be able to respect your decision if it is contrary to their own. To them "no" means you're playing hard to get and they must try harder to persuade you to change your mind. They may think they know what's best for you and they may try to point out to you that you are wrong or misguided, while they are right.

*   need to win at whatever they do - i.e. games, conversations, arguments, etc. Losing or not getting their way can create various mood swings, such as silence, pouting, sudden anger, blaming others, defensiveness. Losing is not something they easily laugh off. Neither is criticism.

*   have dreams or goals that do not fit with the reality of the situation they are in, but they are unable to see the difficulty of getting from where they are to where they want to go. They sometimes seem out of touch with reality.

*   be of above average intelligence. They know how systems work and just how far they can go to use them for their own advantage. They are often known to others as "good" people whose credibility is not questioned. They are definitely thinkers and planners and are often born manipulators.

Don't think you needn't be concerned because there isn't any physical violence, as violence is only one of the many ways abuse and disrespect shows itself. You should be concerned if your partner shows a definite lack of respect for you, your intelligence, your belongings, your beliefs, your attitudes, and your decisions.

Behaviours To Watch For In Yourself:

*   If you find yourself making excuses to yourself and others for your partner's behaviour, stop and ask yourself why you'd need to do that.

* If you're trying to convince yourself that your partner is right, better, smarter, or stronger, while you are not, stop and ask yourself why you'd think so much more of your partner than you do of yourself.

* If you feel your partner needs you to be "less than" the person you know you are, ask yourself if you are happy to continue on that way.

* If most of your friends do not like your partner, perhaps it's time to take their insights into consideration. Don't minimise or deny what an ex - girlfriend or ex - wife has to say about your partner.

* If your gut instinct or intuition is trying to get through to you, but you haven't been listening, take the time to truly listen and believe what it is telling you. Remember, that since the beginning of time people have been saying that "love is blind" for a reason.

If you've decided to end a relationship you are concerned about, you must end it with certainty. You cannot change your mind. If you do, it only shows your partner that your "no" doesn't really mean "no". Once the relationship is definitely over, be aware that the intensities of emotion will increase dramatically for a potential stalker. They are people who do not like to lose and do not like to be seen by others as having lost. They do not like to take no for an answer and they have no intentions of accepting your decision - why should they? They've never respected you before, why would they start now? The potential stalker feels they have every right to continue the relationship, to continue contacting you, and to show you how wrong you were to end the relationship. Don't underestimate their seriousness. They want you back and they do not intend to lose!

What To Do If You Are Being Stalked

For me, being stalked was the most frightening experience of my life. I only wish I had known then what I know now. I hope my own insights will help to alleviate your sense of helplessness and fear and allow you to take some control of your life again.

The stages I found myself going through were:

1. Guilt for being adamant that the relationship was over.
2. Not wanting to accept or believe that I was actually being stalked.
3. Feeling constantly uneasy. Always looking over my shoulder.
4. Minimising events. Denying the seriousness of my situation.
5. Acceptance, finally, that I was being stalked and my situation was serious.
6. Debilitating fear that slowly paralysed my thinking processes.
7. Frustration with lack of police action.
8. Helplessness due to feeling I had no control over police action or the stalker's actions.
9. Inability to concentrate.
10. Inability to sleep.

<u>Important Steps That You Can Take:</u>

1. Get A Handle On Your Fear:

The fear you feel from being stalked is incapacitating. It has the ability to paralyse you by seeping slowly into every aspect of your life, altering your sense of reality. It doesn't matter how intelligent, how strong or how brave you are…this fear will have its effect on you. You may become quietly numb, or angry and abrasive, or an erratic, frantic worrier. Everyone reacts differently. But no matter what your fear has done to you, you *must* get a handle on it if you really want to help yourself. If you give in to your fear and do nothing, you will be giving the stalker a very useful tool to manipulate you with.

In my opinion, the best way to handle your fear is to find out everything you can about criminal harassment. Find out what the police should be doing for you, and if they're not doing it, tell them. You have the right to ask for a different constable if you are not happy with the one assigned to your case. If you have complaints, ask to see the Supervisor and if you are still not happy, ask to see the Inspector of the Detachment. Ultimately, complaints can be made to the Public Complaints Commission for investigation and also the Attorney General's Department.

Read everything you can find on criminal harassment. Take the responsibility upon yourself to become as informed as you possibly can, as knowledge can be a very powerful tool and when you feel powerful, you will feel like you have some control, which will lessen your sense of fear. Even though the fear cannot be eradicated, it can be kept at an appropriate level. Your nearest Women's

Centre, Transition House, Victim's Services, library, and internet are good places to start to look for information.

Find out which agencies in your community can help you with emotional support and advocacy regarding criminal harassment and establish a connection with them.

Develop a plan of action for several worst case scenarios. That way, if the stalker does try something, you will be mentally prepared and fear will not be your first and only reaction.

Do not wait for others to help you. Help yourself by taking some action. Do whatever you think is necessary around your property to make it safer. Demand the police do a safety check on your house, today - not next week sometime as next week may be too late.

Make your situation as public as possible. Talk to neighbours, teachers, employers, friends and anyone else you can think of. Don't hide what is happening to you. Be open about it - you need as much help as you can get.

2. Throw Your Guilt Out The Window:

If you terminated the relationship - you have no reason whatsoever to feel guilty about it. Your intuition told you to sever the relationship and since you are now being stalked by this person, your intuition was correct, so forget about the guilt. You have nothing to feel guilty about. He/she is not stalking you because of something you did or did not do, even though that is what they may say. They are stalking you because of their own lifelong problems and their inability to handle their problems, not because you have created these problems for them. You just happen to be an easy target for them to blame, rather than coming face to face with themselves.

Guilt has no place in a stalking case. If you are not able to get rid of your guilt, it will play right into the hands of the stalker. If, at some level, you feel you deserve to be treated poorly because "look what you've done to the poor guy" you will be too accepting, rather than being outraged. The stalker relies on being able to make you feel guilty and knows, after having a relationship with you, exactly which buttons to push for a guilty response.

Remember, you have nothing to feel guilty about. This person is stalking you and stalking is against the law. You are not making the stalker break the law. That's the stalker's choice, not yours.

3. The Denial Must Go:

Denial in a stalking case is equivalent to living in a thick fog yet saying you see everything clearly, while all the people around you can see you are actually stuck in a thick fog. And when they tell you what they see, you will not believe them.

Denial is the most difficult emotion to come to terms with. It is difficult to hear yourself being in denial. You don't want to be as scared as others tell you you should be. You don't want to give up the way you live, your pets, your job, your routines, everything you've worked for. You don't want to accept the seriousness of your situation, even though you're constantly looking over your shoulder. You agree that others have serious problems, but yours is just minimal and will stop on its own eventually, because the person stalking you isn't really *all* that bad!

This attitude is very frustrating for the police and anyone else trying to help you. Your situation is bad enough that you go and ask for help from the police, but because you are in denial you accept little action or no action from them because your denial says it's really not that bad anyway. The truth, however, is that *every* stalking case should be considered as a potential homicide right from the beginning! The police are the wheel that starts the investigation in motion. If they don't get the investigation rolling, nothing's going to happen anywhere down the line. Even though they should do this without any prompting from you - your attitude can make a big difference to the police. Don't deny the seriousness of the situation. Demand action and plenty of it right from the beginning. The best chance of stopping criminal harassment is in the very beginning before the stalker starts to enjoy the sense of power that comes from the thrill of harassing and getting away with it.

If you want to continue with your denial, that's your choice, but at least make sure your will is up to date.

If fear, guilt and denial continue to be the basis for your reactions, you will continue to play into the hands of the stalker. Even if you are fortunate enough to have well - intentioned police trained in criminal harassment helping you, the best help you can get is going to come from yourself. You are in this situation for a reason. There are lessons for you to learn here and they are not lessons someone else can teach you, so don't collapse in on yourself. You will discover a part of you that you never knew you had. Take a deep breath and dive in. There is no other way out.

4. If You Decide to Disappear Temporarily or Permanently:

Disappearing is something to consider seriously. When the stalker no longer has a target, it suddenly puts an end to the possibility of playing the game. Your disappearance can give the stalker a chance to get out of his obsessive "stalking" frame of mind and back to a more normal sense of reality.

To disappear effectively, you must do so without leaving a trace behind. This is a very complicated matter in our computerised society. If you are serious about disappearing to escape a stalker, you need to contact your police station, Transition House, or the Attorney General's Department for further direction. There are agencies that deal specifically in this area.

It is not the solution for everyone as many of us have ties that we cannot simply "disappear" from. But looking at it with hindsight, I can definitely say that it would probably have worked in my own case, had I thought of it *and* realised my situation was serious enough to try it.

The Stalking Mindset

The mind of the stalker is very dangerous indeed. Every stalker is different and every stalking case is different - there are even different types of stalking, however, there is one thing you can be sure of: the stalker's thoughts and actions make perfect sense to them, no matter how bizarre they may seem to everyone else. Their actions are often based on their refusal to accept your rejection of them - "I'll show her"... "She can't do this to me and get away with it"... "She made my life miserable, so now I'm making hers miserable"... "I gave her everything. She's going to pay for leaving me and so is her new boyfriend"...and on and on. All are forms of retaliation at being rejected. The stalker becomes a victim of their own bitterness and self - pity and because of this, they can't seem to get a grip on themselves. Don't wait for them to "come around" in time, as the chances of that happening are extremely slim. As far as they are concerned, they are not the ones who need to "come around" - you are. To them, you're the one with the problem - not them and it doesn't matter how much you try to tell them they are the ones out to lunch, they simply can't, won't and aren't able to see it that way. Stalking is a very closed and narrow mindset.

The stalker's goal is to establish a connection with you - any connection. It doesn't matter to them if your reactions to their contacts are angry, threatening, or teary. All they want is a reaction - that is their connection to you. That gives them their fuel. If they call and just breath into the phone without saying anything, and you yell out, "Who is this? I told you to leave me alone!" and slam down the phone, then you have given them what they want - a reaction. They hang up the phone feeling they have succeeded, as they start to plan their next way of making contact with you. Remember, no matter what the stalker says, he is not looking for love - he is looking for control and a special kind of "high" he gets from being able to control you and continuously get away with it. It's like an addiction.

The stalker devotes an incredible amount of time to thinking and planning what to do to you. Often, they have an uncanny sense of knowing what they can get away with and what is going too far in the eyes of the public and the police force. They often have a great deal of credibility amongst the people who know them. Enough credibility in fact, to diminish your credibility by spreading believable, but untrue rumours about you to others. Never underestimate a stalker's intelligence or their ability to concoct elaborate schemes, no matter what their personality was like before they became consumed with stalking.

As they continue harassing you, the stalker develops what Dr. Don Dutton calls "tunnel vision" where the stalker's interests become narrower and narrower and increasingly focused on one objective - what they are going to do to you, all the reasons why they should, and all the when's, where's, and how - to's needed to pull it off. Whatever else is in their life loses importance as they become totally focused on you. Do not count on life's everyday problems to jolt the stalker back to reality, as their reality has become stalking you. Everything else is on the periphery and of no major importance to them. Once they are in this tunnel, there is very little that will snap them out of it. This is when disappearing may be the only thing that can save the victim.

The stalker becomes addicted to the power and control they feel when they are successful in their harassing tactics. Don't make the mistake of waiting them out. The most opportune time to help a stalker come to their senses, is in the very beginning, before they have made too many contacts with the victim. Swift and strong action by the police in the very early stages of a stalking case, followed by swift and strong action by the courts offers the best chance of putting an end to the stalking.

What To Expect From The Police

Don't assume, as I did, that the police have all the answers and will take appropriate action. There is always the possibility that the police officer you are dealing with has not been adequately trained in criminal harassment and therefore does not understand what is meant by a complete and proper investigation, or that the police officer's own belief system is built around power and control - the very issues at the heart of stalking cases, making it difficult for these police officers to register the events in a stalking case as being criminal and of an urgent nature. For your own good, become as informed as you can about criminal harassment and then make sure the police are doing everything they should be doing.

<u>The Police Should Generally:</u> (according to former Sgt. D. LePard of the Vancouver Criminal Harassment Unit and the Dep't. Of Justice Canada's handbook: "Guidelines For Police and Crown Prosecutors: Investigating Criminal Harassment")

* *not* advise you to meet with the stalker to ask them to stop.
* refer you to a Victim's Service worker for help and advocacy at your first complaint.
* be willing and able to recognise and identify stalking behaviour and develop a strategy to manage and ideally resolve the problem.
* not minimise the seriousness of stalking and should advise the victim to not minimise or keep secrets. Be clear with the victim regarding the potential threat.

* enlist the victim's support by keeping a log of all incidents.

* advise the victim that although it is not fair, the victim may be required to alter her/his lifestyle and usual routines, schedules, transportation routes, and places regularly frequented by victim.

* seize and hold any physical evidence, such as answering machine tapes, gifts, letters.

* most definitely conduct a *thorough, independent* interview of victim and suspect obtaining as much background info as possible.

* deal with the stalker face to face. A phone call is not sufficient.

* identify suspect to victim's friends, neighbours, etc. (preferably by photo).

* use whatever phone technology is available to them.

* consider using surveillance.

* consider using search warrants.

* consider arrest as often the only relief for the victim is when the offender is incarcerated.

* know applicable criminal codes sections: S.264 - criminal harassment, S.264.1 - threatening, S423 - intimidation, S - 372 - harassing phone calls, S.524(2) - breach of process, S.810 - peace bonds.

* discuss and implement safety precautions with the victim.

* continually be assessing the amount of risk and threat involved.

For a detailed description of the above, see the *"Guidelines For Police and Crown Prosecutors: Investigating Criminal Harassment"* @

http://www.canada.justice.gc.ca/en/dept/pub/hp cp/annexea.html

Police play an extremely important role in the proceedings of a criminal harassment situation. They are the ones who get the ball rolling. Their actions, or lack of them, from the beginning will determine the success or failure of the case and the degree of the victim's safety. If police fail to carry out a proper investigation, fail to heed and act on the warning signals, fail to document all incidents, fail to gather evidence - how then can Crown Counsel properly defend the victim, and how then can a judge be expected to make an appropriate decision if the case reaches the level of the courts? If the judge is not shown sufficient evidence, he can hand out no more than a slap on the hand, which leaves the police frustrated, the stalker laughing, the victim feeling even more victimised and the public questioning what's become of our legal system.

Proper police action is a *must* from the very beginning of every case. As the person being stalked you have the right to demand that appropriate action is being taken. After all, it's your neck on the line.

Sharon Velisek

Appendix

My RCMP File:

Note: NFAR stands for "No Further Action Required" and CH stands for "Concluded Here". "CPIC" and "PIRS" are police computerized identification systems. If anyone has ever had a record or been charged, they will show up on one of these systems. The problem is that not all detachments throughout the province of BC use this system. Some of the municipal police departments use their own identification system. To do a thorough check, therefore, all systems in all detachments in the province must be accessed.

October 6:

Someone has put sugar in frnt seat and dash of veh. Took veh to Canadian Tire for plugged fuel filter & it was determined someone put sugar in gas tank. Rpt for info.

October 20: Vandalism to vehicle.

Details: Vehicle keyed. Request members call. Has had a few other susp. occurrences and suspects ex - boyfriend.

Details: Com. (complainant) rept. (reports) mischief to vehicle. Suspects x - boyfriend. Doesn't want him contacted. Rept. for info in the event she feels that further action be taken. ie. restraining order. NFAR CH Detailed statement on file.

<u>October?? [no date given]:</u>

CIN's [complainants] vehicle parked in hospital parking lot for day. New damage consists of 3 scratches on drivers door and 3 scores or scratches on the drivers side windshield. Each scratch about a foot long. Attn. Morrison and O'Riley.

<u>November 1:</u> [written by C. Morrison]

On 31 Oct. Com. contacted writer to advise that sus. [suspect] is still contacting her. She has received three more scratches on her vehicle.

On 30th sus. approached her while she was walking home, again asking why they couldn't be friends.

Com. was advised that she should cont. [contact] hospital security to advise them of the incident on hospital parking lot. There is no evidence to identify Scott as being responsible for these incidents.

I asked Com. to prepare a statement relating her relationship with Scott and her feelings about her safety.

Scott has no CNI, no traffic violations and nothing on PIRS.

I have left 2 messages on his ans. machine Oct. 31 and Nov. 01 to which he has not replied. S.U.I.

<u>Nov. 3/4:</u> [written by C. O'Riley]

Velisek to Dit. [detachment] with statement and stated she is very concerned for her safety. Vel. stated that Scott recently located Vel. as she was walking home and followed Vel. wanting to talk. Scott has made no threats however his persistent actions in contacting and following

Vel. has made her very concerned and frightened. All the described damage to Vel. vehicle has not been witnessed thus it is difficult to prove Scott is responsible.

However due to Vel. genuine concern for her safety to Scott contacting / following her charges made under sec. 264.2B cc. will be sought.

<u>Nov. 4</u>:

1001 Scott not home
1530 Scott not home
Attn Cst. Morrison

<u>Nov. 5</u>: [written by telecom operator]

Call rcvd. from Sharon that her ex - boyfriend L.S. had just called her res. from resort. App. [apparently] we are trying to locate him to arrest re restraining order / bar c/1800
cc: Cst. O'Riley
Rang once - Vel went to answer but phone dead. Pushed *69 on phone and found that call originated from Scott's address.

<u>Nov. 6</u>:

Velisek called stating she got a hang up call from public phone at Village Green Mall.

<u>Nov? [no date given]</u>: [written by C. Morrison]

Attempt to contact Scott's lawyer to have Scott warned against any further contact with Velisek.

<u>Nov. 8 @ 1430:</u> [written by C. Morrison]

Morrison spoke to lawyer advising him of the circumstances. Lawyer states he will advise his client to have no contact with Com. If this continues or if Scott refuses to except advise he will contact myself or C. O'Riley.

<u>Nov. 8 @1645:</u> [written by C. Morrison]

Spoke with Com. She is satisfied with action and feels that L.S. is finally coming to grips with this relationship ending. She does not want to proceed with any court action. NFAR

<u>Nov. 17:</u> (written by C. O'Riley)

Turned items over to Scott

Bibliography:

The Gift of Fear - Survival Signals That Protect Us From Violence, Gavin De Becker, Little Brown and Company, 1997, ISBN 0 - 316 - 23502 - 4, Boston, New York, Toronto, London

To Have Or To Harm: True Stories of Stalkers and Their Victims, Linden Gross, Warner, 1994, New York

The Batterer, A Psychological Profile, Donald G. Dutton, Ph.D., BasicBooks, A Division of HarperCollins Publishers, Inc. 1995, New York, ISBN 0 - 465 - 03387 - 3

The Domestic Assault of Women: Psychological and Criminal Justice Perspectives, Revised and Expanded Edition, Donald G. Dutton, Ph.D., UBC Press / Vancouver, 1995, ISBN 0 - 7748 - 0462 - 9

Recommendations For Amendments To "E" Division R.C.M.P. Operational Policies Pertaining To Relationship Violence And The Processing Of Firearms Applications, Josiah Wood, RCMP, 1998

"E" Division Violence in Relationships Policy, OIC Contract Policing, RCMP, 1998

Inquest Into The Death of Larry Allen Scott, Coroner's Inquest, 1996

Inquest Witness Statements, Coroner's Inquest, 1996

RCMP File 95 - 1611, 95 - 13919, 95 - 14540, RCMP, 1995/1996

Criminal Harassment Training Material, Sgt. Doug LePard

Sharon Velisek

***Guidelines For Police and Crown Prosecutors:
Investigating Criminal Harassment***, Dep't. of
Justice, Canada, 1999

About the Author

Since Sharon Velisek's miraculous recovery from her near fatal stalking experience she has appeared in numerous documentaries including "To Have and To Hold," "Without Warning—Menace to Society," "Stalking...It's Not Love," and "The Extreme Crime Quiz Show."

Because Sharon lived to tell her tale, she felt compelled to write about her story of survival to give others the benefit of her personal experience and to dedicate her book to the many women and men who, for one reason or another, never got a chance to tell their own story.

CPSIA information can be obtained at www.ICGtesting.com
Printed in the USA
LVOW100554301111

257031LV00001BA/4/A